The Eagle Strikes

To Marilyn
Enjoy

John P. Kincaid

The Eagle Strikes

John P. Kincaid

Writers Club Press
San Jose New York Lincoln Shanghai

The Eagle Strikes

Writers Club Press
an imprint of iUniverse.com, Inc.

For information address:
iUniverse.com, Inc.
5220 S 16th, Ste. 200
Lincoln, NE 68512
www.iuniverse.com

ISBN: 0-595-18460-X

Printed in the United States of America

This book is dedicated

to my

wife: Ley A. Kincaid

and my

two sons: John C. and James E.

Three of the best

PREFACE

When Carl set his goal of *Universal Freedom for all Mankind,* he expected objection and misunderstanding. He knew government bureaucracies would distort the purpose of his efforts while concealing the tyrannical oppression of their own policies. But dramatic and violent eruptions occurring in public view cannot be suppressed. Such exposure weakens the position of those in power and builds growing distrust within the government's structure. Personnel begin competing among themselves for power and prestige. The end result is chaos.

Yes, distrust and destruction are very similar, and to make his work easier, the United States Government excelled at fostering distrust. People were more readily accepting the premise that corruption in government was a way of life. One big catastrophic event to demonstrate the lack of governmental control could cause the people to openly rebel.

Carl would provide that event, and another step toward a second *Golden Age of Freedom* would be complete.

ACKNOWLEDGEMENTS

I have many people to thank:

Bill Lien, who read my first draft and offered encouragement even though his lovely wife, Elaine, refused the be swayed from her novels of romance.

Hazel Sands, who was the first to understand my sincere request for a detailed edit. She returned the manuscript with pages of notes, but also words of encouragement. I shall always remember her remark: "It makes you think."

Margaret Hahn, a proof reader in Palm Springs, CA, whose talent was obvious and praise was graciously accepted.

Ray Gordon, author and lecturer, who read and critiqued the story. To gain his attention and incisive comments was truly a milestone.

Jean Bangel, Mary Townsend, Molly Brock, and Joyce and Carl Moehring must also be cited for their encouragement, though dear friends are always suspect.

The support of my lovely wife, Ley Ancell Kincaid, and my two sons, John and Jim, have provided a firm base for my efforts in life. Their encouragement was the major thrust to finish my efforts for publication, a process that sometimes made me feel Neil Armstrong's giant step was nothing more than a respectable hurdle.

LIST OF CONTRIBUTORS

Front cover by my son,

Jim E. Kincaid
Graphic artist
Turlock, California

CHAPTER 1

EASTERN TURKEY

"Karl!" The shrill scream of terror filled the thick canopy of trees surrounding the small wood and stone cabin on the mountain side north of Hakkari, Turkey.

Karl Izgur froze in his tracks. That was his mother's scream! But she should have left for work an hour ago. It was almost dark.

Karl rushed up the path, the physique of a mature woodsman belying his eighteen years. He cleared the three stone steps to the small front porch in one long leap and grabbed the protruding window frame to stop himself. Inside, the man in a dark brown uniform with a wide leather belt and oversize holster was unmistakable. A Turkish cop had a choke hold on his mother, and on the far side of the room stood another cop with one leg half out of his shorts!

Karl jumped back and lunged at the heavy wooden door. The latch snapped, the broken tip ricocheting off the far wall. The door caught the table beneath the window, toppling the lamp, its glass base shattering on the heavy plank floor. The acrid smell of coal oil flooded the cabin.

The barrel-chested cop, trying to quiet Karl's mother, saw Karl's wild-eyed expression. The cop's morals may have been in doubt, but he recognized unleashed fury when he saw it. He jerked Karl's mother backward, swung her across the bed, and made a frantic grab for his pistol.

1

Karl's reflexes were as a single motion. He lunged forward, grabbed the leg of a wooden stool by the kitchen table, and charged forward.

Each flashing image: his mother rolling across the bed and slamming against the wall, the large black mustache and frantic eyes of the back-peddling cop, the raised flap and partially drawn pistol, they each burned a searing picture in Karl's brain.

Karl swung the stool over his head and slashed downward.

"You miserable son-of-a—."

The blast of the cop's gun drowned Karl's roar of rage, the completed trigger squeeze a reflex to the cop's face caving into an ugly mass of blood, skin and crushed bone.

The explosive energy in Karl's body had no direction, no thought, no plan. Consideration? Explanation? Not in Karl's mind. Raw bitter rage had been unleashed. No one touched his mother in anger…no cop…no one!

The young cop on the far side of the room, his leg still in midair, had reason to hesitate. To openly object to "let's get us an Armenian woman" on his first day of duty would have been unthinkable under any circumstance, but he had also remembered the subject coming up in training, and it had always ended with some remark like "Those Armenian women know better than to complain about us." At the time, the subject had been a main source of humor. Well, something sure went wrong this time; but no overgrown Armenian was going to bash in his head, even one built like a bull. He stumbled forward and frantically yanked his bayonet from its scabbard.

Karl saw his mother's large butcher knife on the center table at the same time he saw the young cop's movement. He grabbed the knife and lunged.

The young cop made one slashing swing with the bayonet's blade that he had so proudly honed during training. The swing was probably his first, definitely his last use of official physical force.

Karl glimpsed the flash of steel near his face. There must be no second chance. He drove the butcher knife into the young cop's chest and yanked sideways. Blood spurted. The wide eyes in the startled face turned blank. Karl stood rigid as the body slowly fell from the blade and sank to the floor. He turned, rushed back across the room, and drove the blade into the exposed back of the body draped over the chair. Neither act appeased his fury. He released the knife handle and jammed the chair with his right foot. The tumbling body stopped with one arm under the overturned chair, the other extending awkwardly into space.

Karl's face was expressionless. Only the fierce intensity in his eyes betrayed him. One final act must be completed. He walked back across the room to where the young cop lay on the floor beside the table. Slowly, he bent down. Movement was not easy. He pried the bayonet from the still firm grip of the young man's hand.

The next action required one quick stroke.

Karl dropped the flaccid penis on the limp body, stuck the bayonet in the floor between the young cop's twisted legs, and slowly stood up. The innocent expression on the cop's face filled him with disgust. Even in death the damned Turks lied. He rubbed his sweating palms against his trousers. The ordeal was over, the problem solved. There would be no recurrence by these two miserable people. The adrenalin driven power in his muscles began to subside. He sucked in a chest full of air and slowly exhaled. A feeling he could not explain filled his body. It was not fear, not concern. It was more a feeling of release, running counter to the surging bitterness within him.

He turned toward the bed.

No!

A rising cry of anguish stuck in Karl's throat. His mother's stark white stillness left no doubt. She was dead. He stood quietly. He must not lose control. He moved to the bed and gently pulled her torn dress over her breasts, overlapped her hands on her stomach, raised her head and straightened her hair. The moves brought a throbbing sense of loss surging upward. No longer would he be able to watch her raise a hand

and casually toss her long auburn waves back into place. The thought nearly overwhelmed him; but why didn't he cry?

Was the hard-rock stoicism of his mother's Russian lineage holding him in check? Had the idealist drives of his Armenian father driven him to this carnage around him? A confused sense of loss and rage and accomplishment and growing satisfaction fought his physical numbness. The knowledge that he was badly hurt also nudged him but failed to gain recognition. A sense of moving toward some unknown, yet finite destiny seemed to be trying to surface within him.

Arnar Monmoksha, their closest neighbor, came running through the open door. He stopped and gasped for breath as he took in the scene. A little man, he was too old to be running so far. "What in the—?" Then he glanced toward the bed, "Oh, no!"

"They were going to rape her."

Mr. Monmoksha paused. His stomach churned. Death he had seen, even maimed bodies on occasion, but this was hard to believe. He started toward the bed, then stopped. Karl was the one who needed attention.

"Sit on that chair, Karl, so I can look at that cheek. You are bleeding like a stuck pig." He twisted Karl's face to one side. "Looks clean. Could have been worse, I guess, but not by much. Try holding it together while I find something to try and stop that bleeding." He looked around the room, then turned back, "I heard a shot." His glance caught the blood and frayed cloth on Karl's left leg. "Is that it?"

"I guess so." Karl felt as if he were in a trance, watching the scene from a distance.

Mr. Monmoksha bent down and tore the trouser leg open. The wound was a mess! The bullet had slashed through the calf, as if it had ricocheted and tumbled as it tore through the muscle. The result, a gaping wound in the outside leg muscle, but the blood oozed rather than flowed. That was good, or so he thought.

"That is really a mess," Mr. Monmoksha said. He leaned down for a closer look. "Looks like the bullet missed the bone, but why that muscle is working is beyond me." He shook his head. "Miracle of youth, I guess."

Mr. Monmoksha glanced toward the open door. If the police walked in now, they would both be dead: no questions, no discussion, just shot. He shrugged. Dwelling on the inevitable served no purpose; speed was the only thing that could save either of them. "At least, it's not bleeding too much," he said. He really did not know what to expect from such a deep gash. "One thing for sure, we need a bandage. You can't do much moving around without one, and you are sure going to have to travel." He stood up. "Take off your trousers while I find something. And try to keep that cut on your cheek closed. You are going to need every bit of the blood you can keep inside that young body of yours."

Karl had to forget his cheek for a moment. Keeping his trouser leg clear of the gash took both hands. He sat back down. Strange how his body felt so heavy, but holding the cheek did seem to slow the bleeding.

Mr. Monmoksha found a cotton slip in the dresser drawer and tore it into strips. He aligned the jagged edges of the leg wound as best he could, formed a pad with one of the strips, laid it over the open cut and began wrapping, trying to gauge how tight the bandage should be. Not tourniquet tight, that much he knew. It would have to be somewhere in between. Must have missed the veins, he decided, damned miracle. But the boy was going to have problems. Maybe the skin would eventually grow over, provided he could get away and survive, but he would sure have one huge scar. The muscle? Well, there was nothing he could do about that. Maybe the half on the other side would keep the leg working.

"It throbs a little, but mostly just feels numb," Karl said, noticing Mr. Monmoksha's questioning look.

"That won't last long," Mr. Monmoksha answered. "It will start hurting soon enough. You can bet on it." He stood up. "Let's look at that cheek." He made another pad and slipped it into place as he lifted Karl's fingers. "Careful, now. Put a little pressure on it."

Karl flinched.

"Not that much!" Mr. Monmoksha said.

"Sorry," Karl said disgustedly. Why had he flinched? He could not feel anything.

"Me too, Karl, for raising my voice. I guess we are both getting nervous, but we gotta get this done. Try holding the pad while I wrap some of these strips around your head. Gently now. That's it. You keep your head still so nothing moves. I'll work around you."

Mr. Monmoksha's limited medical experience was obvious. Even Karl sensed the absurdity of the old man's handiwork.

"Looks ridiculous, but it ought to stay put," Mr. Monmoksha said, "if you don't wiggle your face too much," he added. "Can you breathe?"

Karl nodded.

Mr. Monmoksha bent down, touched the leg bandage gently and stood back. "Well, that's as good as I can do. You can sure tell I ain't no doctor." His expression lost its brief touch of humor. "Now, let's face your real problem, Karl. Like I said, you gotta get out of here, out of the area and out of the country, and fast. How? I haven't the faintest idea, especially in your condition, but the Turks will tear these mountains apart looking for you. I know you are hurt, hurt bad. Worse yet, in a little while the real pain will set in. But forgetting all that, somehow, someway, you've got to find the strength to travel."

Mr. Monmoksha's expression turned more somber. "I am sorry, Karl. I truly am, but I have to make it look as if I notified the cops as fast as I could, and the longer I wait. Well, you know the damned Turks." He started toward the door then stopped and looked back. "Now remember, after I go, you get out of here. I'll stall as long as I can, but don't you mess around." He paused. "Our lives are filled with moments, Karl. This was one of yours. Bad as it is, it's over. So go. May God be with you."

"Mr. Monmoksha."

Mr. Monmoksha stopped by the door. He looked back.

Karl tried to think how to say it. "Thanks, Sir."

"Glad I could help, son. The least we can do is try." He walked out the open door.

In the ensuing quiet, Karl's plight suddenly hit him full force, but even as the realization crystallized, a feeling of confidence grew within him. Could it be that since the time the radical *Young Turk* regime had murdered his father, for no more reason than writing an article protesting the treatment of Armenians, the man inside him had been waiting. Though only four at the time, he vividly remembered the event. Of one thing he was now certain, he had to get away, so he could come back. The thought gave him strength.

Karl paused only briefly. Every minute counted. He put on a clean shirt and loose fitting shorts, threw another shirt and trousers and sweater and some bread and dried meat into his back pack, and started toward the door, then turned. He almost forgot about the money box. It was under the floor boards, beneath the table.

There was not much. That his mother had worked so long and so hard for so little, flashed in his mind. It was unfair. When this mess was over, he would learn how to make money work for him, but for now, what should a funeral cost? He had no idea. He tucked some of the lire in his mother's dress pocket, and slipped the reminder in his own. The gold coin, the one his mother's Russian grandfather had given her when she married, he put in his shirt pocket, and carefully buttoned the flap.

The large medallion had been a gift from Czarina Catherine. It was one of a kind, struck for the old Cossack to honor his valor in battle, as was the custom then. Karl remembered his mother's words: "It must remain in the family, Karl. It proves who we are." He turned toward the door.

As Karl stepped into the darkness, the chilled night air set every nerve on fire. He had never experienced such pain. The leg held a myriad of sensations, but none that responded. It suddenly was nothing

more than a horrendously heavy throbbing burden. He leaned on the
porch railing. Without support he would soon be immobile. The pain
said to accept the fact, sit down, lie down, but Mr. Monmoksha words
rang clear. He must leave if he wished to live, and he must be quick
about it. He hobbled down the steps, and worked along the outer edge
of the porch, toward the kindling pile. He needed some type of crutch.

*The star-filled sky, the blurred trees, the maze of bushes, they kept
shifting positions as he worked his way along the narrow forest trail. He
knew every tree and bush for miles, but tonight they kept moving. The trees
swayed eerily against the silver-black sky. The bushes and underbrush
fought him: jabbing, poking, slapping him in the face. The tripping was the
worst part.*

*Was the crutch too short? Something was wrong. Keeping his balance
was almost impossible. If only he could have found a fatter limb with a
wider crotch. This one cut his underarm. He could feel the warm blood on
his sweat covered body. If he was so cold, why were his clothes so wet? Or
was it the leg that kept him off balance? It felt like it was on fire, hanging
like a lead weight.*

*He tripped in a small stream that he normally stepped across and fell on
the opposite bank. He sank down. The cool ground felt good. The grassy
slope was soft. He needed the rest. The timing was perfect. But he had to
keep moving. The village was not much further. He scooped up a handful
of water. He couldn't suck! The little he got in his mouth burned. His cheek
started bleeding. A name flashed in his mind: Pernelli, his mother's best
friend. Get up....Why bother?...The pain under his arm hurt worse than
his leg....He needed to keep moving....He grabbed at the ground. The
weeds would not bend.*

Karl tried to roll over. The leg refused to move. It was still dark, but
where were the bushes? He looked up. And where were the trees? There
was no moon, but there still should be some trees outlined against the

stars? Where were the stars? The air smelled musty, heavy. A wave of fear rose within him. A low moan escaped. Something touched his swollen lips. A straw. Must be his moth—. No, she was—. A massive sense of loss flooded over him. He sucked in. Water! Had they caught him? Impossible. He was alive.

The soothing voice could have been an angel's, but Karl knew better. It was Mrs. Pernelli. He moved a hand, felt a blanket beneath him.

"Rest yourself, Karl, but please, try to be quiet. The police are scouring the countryside, searching every house. They've been here twice already. They know I was your mother's friend. You are in the crawl space over my bedroom."

"How—?"

"You walked. Don't ask me how. I heard you on the back porch and managed to get you up here as best I could, but you must be quiet. Try to rest, but whatever happens, be quiet. It will be light again soon, and they will be back, scouring the area."

She climbed down, pushed the armoire back under the attic opening, and put the ladder back in the store room.

Reflected sunlight seeped into the small space. How long had he slept? Karl had no idea. He looked around. He was alone. He tried to roll over. Pain stabbed his leg. He relaxed and tried to wiggle his toes. They worked. He forced himself into a half sitting position. His head was no longer wrapped, but his cheek seemed to be a huge sore lump. He pulled aside the blanket and tried to lift his leg. The pain was excruciating. He fell back. Moments later he was unconscious.

Living in the tiny attic was a nightmare of confusion and suffering for Karl, both mental and physical. The excruciating pain, need for complete silence, and inconvenience of existing in total confinement were testing the limits of his self-control. After regaining his normal consciousness and rational thinking, he knew his present position was untenable. The need to escape this immediate area offset any consideration of his weak physical condition.

"I have to leave, Mrs. Pernelli. Being here is too dangerous. Sooner or later the police will notice something, and we will both be killed. Besides, I would rather be out in the open where I have a chance."

Mrs. Pernelli stood on the small back porch and watched Karl disappear into the darkness, using the same crude crutch as when he arrived. She had made a thick pad to ease the pressure. Hopefully, his leg could support some of his weight. Tears filled her eyes. Once again the place would be empty. Ten years ago it had been her husband, two weeks ago it was Karl's mother, and now the son. The emptiness pressed in on her. An era had ended. Hopefully, Karl's had just begun.

She decided to scrub down the crawl space. The police would be back. They never gave up. Not that she much cared. Like the small amount of food and money she could give Karl, everything seemed so useless, so temporary.

For the first few days Karl moved only at night, no more than a few miles, using the last hour of darkness each night to prepare a camouflaged daytime shelter. Mrs. Pernelli's dried lamb's tongue and bread, wild berries from the bushes he passed, and water from the streams provided his nourishment. After leaving the immediate area and gaining a better degree of mobility, he chanced buying food in small mountain villages, explaining he had hurt himself while hunting, a common explanation for the area.

His destination? Iraq. To the region of the nomadic Kurds, where he hoped to hide until his wounds healed, and where he would be out of Turkey. If he remembered his maps correctly, he should stay on the east side of the valley, move southward.

In his hours of solitude Karl's deep sense of loss over his mother's death gradually numbed into a jumbled mass of emotions, and the strange but satisfied feeling he had noticed that first day continued building within him. He knew he was going to survive. He could feel it, but the bitterness he felt toward the Turks was fast becoming a consuming hatred. Each time he thought of their oppressive actions, he would break out in a deep sweat. That the feeling might be mentally unhealthy bothered him at first, but became less important as the days passed.

Time and youth gradually worked their magic. Karl's physical stamina increased. He would walk along the more remote back roads as the distance increased and accept rides when conditions felt safe. A wagon filled with hay, a truck filled with boxes, or riding atop a donkey's four-legged gyrations was accepted and appreciated. Finally, sensing he was nearing the border, he disappeared into the heavy forest and followed the steep mountain trails of the natives. In the remoteness, such things as borders and government authority should disappear. He was right, but it was not until he lost himself in the city of Rawanduz that he was certain he was in Iraq.

The room in the small inn was a luxury he did not want to leave, but now he knew that being out of Turkey was not enough. If he could cross the border with such ease, so could those sent to find him. After a day in the comfort of a bed, he continued southward.

The sun felt warm in the crowded bazaar of the old section of Sulaimaniya, and the smell of freshly baked bread too strong to ignore. Large chunks of the hot, heavily-crusted loaf rapidly disappeared down Karl's hungry throat. He stood under the tin awning of the small bakery, fascinated with the crowd wandering through the shops and stalls in the sprawling square.

Donkeys stacked high with merchandise, similar to those he had seen on the back roads, were being lead through the crowded area. Peddlers, on foot, with their wares stacked on their back, or draped over their arms, competed with shopkeepers for the attention of the milling crowd. A sense of activity and confusion filled the late morning scene.

Karl watched quietly. Organized panic is what his mother would have called the scene. The thought refreshed him. It was his first sense of accepting his past life since he left their cabin.

One of the things he had noticed previously, was that many roofs in the area were covered with a layer of dirt about two feet thick. Most buildings around him were similarly constructed. He stepped out in the street to check the bakery.

"Keeps out the heat when it's hot, and in when it's cold," a voice beside him said.

Karl turned quickly. The comment, though friendly had caught him off guard.

"Didn't mean to startle you, but I saw you studying the roofs and thought I would explain." The young man's angular face broke into a wide smile. "The so-called experts in other countries still can't get it right. They waste money building houses underground instead of just putting dirt on the roof."

Karl smiled at the man's enthusiasm. He was a sinewy, energetic man, about Karl's age, several inches shorter, more wiry, with an easy friendliness in his manner. Long black hair lay loosely on his shoulders. Next to Karl he appeared small, but only in comparison.

"Are you a builder?" Karl asked. He liked the man's open, friendly attitude. Vitality showed in every movement. A sense of innate trust that he thought he had forgotten kept surfacing.

The young man laughed, made a sweeping arc with his arm, his wide sleeve trailing in the air. "Oh no, for me one day in this crowded place is a day too much. I came down for supplies, nothing more, and will gladly be gone by nightfall." A multicolored, embroidered sash cinched the loose-fitting dark pants around his narrow waist, the pants a stark contrast to the bright yellow shirt that almost flashed in the sunlight. An open leather vest hung on his broad shoulders, the intricate design on the panels matching the colorful waist band. The fur trim around the tops of the soft leather boots suggested warmth.

Karl's dark knit sweater, wool shirt, and heavy brown pants suddenly felt shabby.

"Came down?" Karl asked quizzically.

The young man pointed to the hills behind the city where the distant ground gradually rose into jagged snow-capped mountains. It was the land of the high plateaus where the nomadic tribes lived their harsh, free existence.

"You live up there?" Karl asked. He sensed an openness, a freedom and release from the chase. Was his search ending?

"That I do. Not on top," the young man added with a laugh, "but close." He held out a hand. "I am Azerki, son of Zergenghis Khan."

Karl's mother had been the first to tell him stories of the Kurdish people, people whose fierce determination for independence was legendary. They also had suffered under the Turks and Iraqis, but instead of accepting subjugation peacefully, or migrating as so many of his own people had done, they had consistently fought back. Few people had risen in rebellion more times. Karl remembered asking his mother, "Are they giants?"

An instant friendship formed between the two young men. Maybe it was the stress from his long trek, or his good fortune in correctly judging another man, or his inherent need for a friend his own age that caused Karl to relate some of his recent experience. But for whatever reason, perhaps understood by only the young, Azerki, invited Karl to return to the sanctuary of his nomadic existence, a place Karl soon learned had to be safe. Not even a friend of the Khan's son could remain in the area without the Khan's approval.

When Hulagu, grandson of Genghis Khan, swept through the area, destroying Baghdad in 1258, he put one of his sons in control before returning to the great plains in the East. It was this son, from whom Zergenghis Khan was descended.

As skilled breeders of cattle, horses, sheep, and goats, the Kurds roamed the open mountain ranges freely. Permanent buildings were built in centralized areas to maintain control, but those tending the herds on the tundra spent their time in yurts, large, movable, skin-covered tents.

Karl entered into the tribe's activities with enthusiasm, quickly learning the rudiments of riding from his friend, Azerki. Riding the high mountain valleys and plateaus in search of strays, and learning the techniques used in controlling the huge herds, fascinated him. Plus, the hard physical labor provided a release for his pent-up emotions. To ride at a full gallop across an open plain created a feeling of exhilaration difficult to describe. Though his leg would most likely give him trouble for years, his strength rapidly returned, the soreness soon ignored, then forgotten.

One afternoon while searching for strays, he and Azerki paused on the edge of a bluff overlooking a lush green canyon. Azerki spoke. "You may have injured your leg my friend, but you have the eyes of an eagle." The remark fascinated Karl. The freedom of the eagle was a pleasant thought.

The Kurdahnka tribe accepted Karl's enthusiasm for their way of life as a compliment. He in turn had found people that accepted freedom as an irrefutable fact of their life. Their country may presently be divided among foreign powers, but that was a temporary status to be rectified by time.

The night Zergenghis Khan asked Karl to stand before the tribal council came as a complete surprise to Karl. The tribe's dome shaped yurts surrounded a large shallow pit holding a roaring fire on the up-slope of the broad plateau. In the cold crisp air, the stars danced brightly in the silver-black sky. Azerki stood quietly next to his father, the bright fire highlighting a wide knowing smile on his face.

The Khan spoke solemnly, "We have watched you since you arrived among us, Karl Izgur. We watched you rebuild strength by relying on your own abilities. We watched you accept our customs, support our traditions, and work with us to better the status of our tribe. We appreciate your dedication. Other systems may work better for less fortunate people in other locations of this great world, but a discussion of such details is not why you are before us tonight."

The Khan was enjoying himself, even permitting his eyes to betray his stern look. "Today, your name was placed before the Council of Elders. A resolution was passed, one reserved for few who are not part of our tribe by birthright." He paused again, plainly enjoying the suspense. "The Elders have declared you to be a member of the Kurdahnka tribe."

The possibility of such an honor had never occurred to Karl. Azerki had given no indication. It was a moment before he spoke. The words did not come easily. "I am honored to become a member of the brave and powerful Kurdahnka tribe," he said, trying to speak in sonorous stentorian tones so all could hear, hoping to emulate an authoritarian presence. "Wherever I may go, I shall always remember this moment."

Karl was truly moved. He had a home. Maybe his words were not the best, and were a little theatrical, but he had spoken honestly. From the smiles and approving nods, he decided it was adequate. He felt good.

Karl had often argued with himself about remaining with these people. Here, he was safe. He liked the people, their way of life and their rugged country, but safety and a happy life were no longer primary considerations for him.

At night when he lay awake and let his mind have its freedom, an increasingly burning need surged inside him. An insatiable bitterness and driving need to strike back at those in authority rose within him. He must repay those who had created so much misery and hardship for his parents, and yes, for himself. That such thinking may be wrong no longer entered his mind. How could a handful of men gain control of a government, then use greed and unjust laws in complete disregard of those they controlled? They already had all the authority and power they could reasonably use. He did not understand, but he knew it must be corrected.

"I shall remember you, Azerki, my friend." It was the morning after the tribal farewell party given for Karl, after he told them of his decision to leave. "I go with regret, but go, I must."

"I know." Azerki also looked somber. "I have seen it in your eyes, and in your restlessness. Nor have I forgotten your wounds when we first met. You will be remembered with affection by my people," he paused, "and by me."

They stood quietly, both ill at ease. Karl looked at his friend. Now was as good a chance as he would have.

"I have never told this to anyone else, but I want you to know," he said quietly. "Other than you and my two friends who helped me escape, I trust no one, and as we learned not long ago, one of them is now dead. Whether my feelings are justified, I'm not yet sure. But I do know I must go. Those who were so wrong must be repaid." He paused. "Perhaps it is also foolish that I intend to use a new name, a name you helped me pick, but I know I will feel safer with a new identity."

"Such a change may not be so foolish in this world we live in," Azerki said. "Things I read about make me wonder."

"I shall call myself, Eagleman, Carl Eagleman," Karl said, "and as I use the name I shall remember our times together."

Azerki threw back his head and laughed. His laughter broke the tension, "Perfect! Absolutely perfect!" Then he lowered his voice and smiled, "Eagleman. I like it. When I next hear *The Eagle* is coming I shall prepare a banquet, for I shall know you are returning."

Karl smiled at Azerki's enthusiastic response. "It is true I will be back," he said firmly. "But I may be gone a long time. I have many accounts to settle."

CHAPTER 2

(Time passes)

ISTANBUL, TURKEY

"Ah! So you have finally been so good as to arrive, Mr. Eagleman. Please do come in."

Dr. Von Becheimer had been told to expect a large man, but still he was surprised. His guest stood six foot four, maybe taller, wide shoulders, powerful body, coal-black hair and a neatly groomed full beard; but it was the dark piercing eyes that held the doctor's attention. They penetrated, not belligerently, devoid of emotion yet intense, conveying total confidence. The effect was disconcerting.

The doctor, slightly over five foot eleven, in excellent condition and meticulous in his own grooming, noted the hand-tailored, slate-gray, pin-stripe suit. If this was not *The Eagle*, *The Eagle's* standards for those working for him were exceedingly precise and strict.

Doctor Helmut Von Becheimer was in room number 312 of the Pera Palas Hotel in Istanbul. He had arrived last evening, and had complied with every instruction received before departing Germany, even those he considered unreasonable. After landing on Deutsche Lufthansa AG Airline's late afternoon flight from Munich, he had sat in the front of the shuttle bus to the hotel, had immediately signed in on arrival, and then proceeded directly to the room reserved for him. Though the bar had looked inviting, and his brief glimpse of the dining room on the way to his room had whetted his appetite, he contacted no one, not even room service. It was now almost noon the next day, 11:47 to be exact. He was piqued, and hungry.

"I complied with your instructions, Mr. Eagleman, but I resolve I should confess, some of the restrictions were most unusual, to my method of thinking, unnecessary." He intended the remark to sound stronger than a casual expression, and was confident his English was good enough to carry it off. "And I also must explain for you to hear, I am hungry. Breakfast is my most important meal of the day."

"I regret the inconvenience," Carl answered easily, "but we felt the precautions were necessary." His tone implied he expected no further discussion of the subject. "Would you prefer lunch or a late breakfast?"

"Lunch would be most excellent and very much appreciative," the doctor said. He did not want to irritate the man, but neither did he feel he should comply with such restrictions without expressing a degree of displeasure. Subservience was not a family trait. He felt satisfied. He had made his point, yet remained polite.

Carl picked up the telephone, his expression reflecting no reaction to the doctor's remarks. "Room 314, please." The response was immediate. "Jacques, bring the doctor a lunch." Carl glanced toward the doctor. "Any preference?"

The doctor shrugged. "Anything substantial would be most excellent."

"Your choice, Jacques." He paused. "Yes, a bottle of red would be fine." He replaced the phone in the cradle.

"If the word, red, means wine in that instance, I hope it is not for me. I seldom have the desire for the alcoholic beverage."

"So I was informed. No matter, our men will be happy to take it."

Doctor Becheimer had assumed the adjoining rooms held men from *The Eagle's* organization. Considering the restrictions that had been placed on his movements, expecting anything less would have been foolish. That he was correct was gratifying, but what had Mr. Eagleman meant by 'we felt'. He did not intend for others to be involved. Another thing, had the restrictions been imposed because his presentation was in question? He hoped not. He intended to be forthright and factual, and from the information he received prior to departing Munich this man surely must be *The Eagle,* or a very close associate. So, regardless of the annoyances, the meeting must run smoothly. He needed *The Eagle's* help for the type work he was pursuing. Alternatives were nonexistent.

"I am exceedingly surprised you are so well informed. You must have troubled yourself immeasurably to know the irrelevant details as my drinking preferences," the doctor said. "That being so, I must conclude you have determined by this time, I have done little to be considered spectacular in my life." He intended the remark to be humorous, even a little disparaging, but knew as he spoke, its truth removed his effort at humor.

"Checking does take time," Carl said. "But most men leave some trace of a record. You heard of *The Eagle.*"

The doctor decided not to mention it took him almost a year to find a person who could arrange this meeting, or admit he was not yet certain who stood before him. "Yes. You are again correct, but I am very much flattered by a comparison to *The Eagle.*" The doctor looked into Carl's eyes hoping for some reaction. There was nothing. The man, regardless of whom he may be, was obviously here to consider facts, not flattery and small talk.

Carl walked to the window. On the far side of the manicured entrance gardens Ayaz Pasa Avenue was busy with noontime traffic. He looked down at the entrance gardens. His black deluxe Citroen sat on the exit side of the long circular driveway. With its low slung chassis and its look of speed it was his favorite car. Nearby, two men, one constantly facing the hotel, stood in the shade of a small tree. Carl placed the palm of his left hand on the window and leaned forward, his face visible through the window. He spread his other hand on the glass. The man facing the hotel removed his hat and ran his fingers through his hair. Carl turned back toward the doctor.

"You are correct, Herr Doctor. Your record is filled with voids, a fact that did delay this meeting. The delays may have seemed excessive to you, but the process does take time." He began listing facts.

"You are the son of Standartenfuhrer Jurgen Von Becheimer, Deputy Assistant Director of Chemical Warfare in the German Army during World War II. Your mother was Margot Bachek, daughter of a prominent business man in Munich. Our records indicate he manufactured metal pipe. You were born on the seventh of March, nineteen-sixty-four, in your family home in Munich at one-one-four Burkostrassan. Our report states the house resembled a small French museum, considering the silver, crystal, antiques, and paintings therein."

Doctor Becheimer gave a half smile. "Fortunes of war," he said casually. The many specific details the man was citing without the use of notes astounded him. Hopefully there would be no forgotten incidents of embarrassment

Mr. Eagleman continued. "You were a good student. At least, your grades were good; and you also did well in sports, especially soccer, but it was your father's work that substantiates the basis for our consideration. During his career your father developed a lethal gas that was practically undetectable, a fact still mentioned in science periodicals, though now less and less frequently. Had the gas been used, his name would undoubtedly be known throughout the world. Obviously, that was not to be."

"My father was a fine, hard working, dedicated man," Doctor Becheimer said. "And an outstanding officer, I must emphasize."

Carl nodded, the comment expected. "Since earning your doctorate in biochemistry from the university in Munich, you have been in semi-seclusion. Not because of a personality deficiency, nothing seems to refute that evaluation, but apparently from a genuine interest in your father's research. The two of you reportedly worked well together until his death."

"Yes, extremely well," the relationship apparent in the doctor's expression.

"That you continue to be so dedicated to his principles of research is the reason we agreed to this meeting." Carl paused. "We regret your long wait, but we constantly receive requests of little merit from people. I believe an appropriate English word is, crackpot. Your letter would have been placed in the same category had our preliminary check produced the usual results. But I am told you have made important findings. We shall see."

There were a series of soft knocks followed by the grating sound of a finger nail dragged across the room door panel. Carl stood. "I will get it. That is your lunch."

Doctor Becheimer began laying the ground work for his presentation as soon as Jacques and the waiter left. He was soon so engrossed in his presentation that after twenty minutes he had taken no more than a dozen bites of his more than adequate lunch.

"You mentioned my father's success in producing a gas that was almost undetectable. You are absolutely accurate in your evaluation. My father did do such a thing, and all the work was entirely his own. But, as is true in other cases where the product does not receive major acclamation, the people who realized the true significance of his work were most few in number. Do you know the medical practice, homeopathy?"

Carl nodded.

"I thought you might have the knowledge. It is a recognized practice in the countries of Europe. My father's work, and now also mine at this time is similar to that principle of using chemicals in a solution so dilute that nothing remains to show cause for the effect obtained. By adding powerful chemicals called free radicals to oxidize any waste, and employing a mathematical algorithm based on counteracting inverse ratios, I can obtain no residuals except the result. Another way to express the idea is to say there is no traceable basis for the reaction, the only property remaining is the memory of the original substance."

Doctor Becheimer walked to the dresser and picked up a small glass vial. He came back, placed it before Carl. Four small brightly colored capsules lay in the bottom.

"Each of those capsules has sufficient potency to poison a large lake," he said proudly. "One capsule will kill every thing that lives in or drinks the water, if I choose to make it that powerful. But, if you chemically analyze the water, nothing harmful will be found. Nothing. A few earth metals and several harmless substances might be isolated, but nothing will evidence the lethal potency." The doctor smiled. "Even I find the idea much difficult to accept. And if you are wondering, the only reason the capsules are brightly colored is so we will not be disposed to lose them."

"Obviously there is a phase of your research that needs further work," Carl said. "You are here."

"Control," Doctor Becheimer said. "The easiest way to explain what I mean is to say at the present time, now, the water would be entirely poisoned forever after."

Carl was an expert in using threats as a weapon of persuasion. The doctor was correct. If use of the capsules resulted in an irrevocable action that could not be controlled, much of their effectiveness as a threat would be lost. Ability to control the time element would expand the threat value exponentially, proportional to the accuracy of control. Carl leaned back in his chair. The possibilities were as significant as his associates had indicated. Proving the validity of the findings may have to wait until the work progressed to a larger scale, but there was no doubting the potential.

Doctor Becheimer searched for his next words. "What needs yet to be done—."

"I understand," Carl interrupted. "You are talking about the half life of the substance."

"Your assistant informed me you were much knowledgeable, but still I exceedingly misjudged you."

Carl ignored the remark. "Your explanation is intriguing, apparently related to micro-chemistry. If your records support your statements, you have a powerful product."

"I have the absolute proof, though a full scale test will take special planning to insure proper control," Doctor Becheimer said. He stood and started toward the window.

"Do not go to the window, Doctor," Carl said emphatically. "I was hoping such conversation would not be necessary, but just as you have something that may well prove beneficial, so must we insure you can remain around to use it. As I understand your remarks, you are both offering and requesting. Your product is available, but you are requesting money and time to continue your research, preferably in a place where you can move and work in relative freedom. Is that correct?"

"You are most accurate, Mr. Eagleman. And from what I have read about the United States, there are places there that would be ideal. My research indicates the existence of several self-contained drainage systems in that country. That type system would be perfect, a clean, stationary, stable, test vehicle. With such a place entirely available, and with freedom to work without the interference, I should be able to complete my work in a short time." Then he added, his words both a question and a statement. "And fortunately, I am told I have a good knowledge of the United States language."

"Yes, your fluency is satisfactory." With added study and practice, Carl thought inwardly. Some of the doctor's phrasing was atrocious. "How do you define, a short time?"

"A year, two at the fartherest most. Controlled tests in a laboratory, and tests outside the laboratory sometimes produce results not entirely equal."

Doctor Becheimer noticed a quick unreadable change in Mr. Eagleman's expression. He had been worried about how he would justify the time needed. "Basic research takes time," he added, having found no eminently good answer. "Results are not affected by our concern over the world's real time." He noted what might have been the start of a smile on Mr. Eagleman's face.

"You chose the correct time to be explicitly honest," Carl said. He looked at the doctor, typically German, blonde, light skinned, clean-cut facial features, in good physical condition, and exuding the confidence inbred from his father's background. There was also the typical arrogant attitude and bearing of the old German aristocracy. That trait needed to be corrected if the man was to spend time in the United States as an American citizen. A plan began forming in Carl's mind.

"Since you seem to appreciate the honesty, perhaps I should as well now tell of my single personal request for which I have the very deep feeling," the doctor said.

"Never withhold such remarks. To do so, is not wise."

"So do I feel also, myself," the doctor answered. "After I have resolved the timing element, so we can control the effectiveness of my discovery, I must be sure my product will be used. My father perfected a product that was never properly recognized, though many applications of his research were applicable to peacetime as well as war. He died without the recognition he much deserved. Now that I have carried his work to an even higher level, I wish to be absolutely sure, this time, to insure his work is finally at last recognized. You support me in the ending steps of my research, and I will place myself at your disposal, entirely. My father's name must be recognized."

The telephone rang.

The doctor looked startled. "Who could possibly know...?"

Carl had already picked up the phone.

"Yes?"

There was a knock at the door.

"That must be the waiter, coming for the dishes," the doctor said. "I haven't...."

Carl dropped the phone, leaped forward, and shoved the doctor to the floor behind the bed. "Stay down! Don't move! Regardless!" He jumped on the bed and dove toward the wall next to the door. Using a floor mat roll he aligned himself against the baseboard. From somewhere a Makarov 9mm pistol appeared in his extended arms with both hands clamping the grip, the sight trained at the door, head high.

The door burst open. A thick dark-skinned man in a too small waiter's jacket rushed in. The Skorpion VZ 61 in his hands sliced the far wall with a trail of 7.65mm ammo. The sound of Carl's first shot was lost in the shattering fire, but his accuracy was obvious. The side of the gunman's face tore loose as his gun dropped toward the floor. The second shot caught the man's chest, spun him against the blood stained door. The lifeless body jerked once in delayed reflex then slumped over the gun and rolled forward.

A voice sounded through the door. "Jacques here. Hold your fire." A man ran in, medium height, deeply tanned, brown hair, classic features, and but for the gun in his hand, cosmopolitan, controlled. A blonde man of similar size with Nordic features followed close behind. "The man was alone," Jacques exclaimed. "Our outside men thought they saw someone watching, so I had the kitchen checked. The waiter was knifed. We should switch."

"Agreed."

Carl and Jacques traded guns. Slipping Jacques's gun into his own sheath, Carl hurried over to the doctor, grabbed his arm and pulled him to his feet. "No time for questions. Come with me." He ran into the hall, ducked into Jacques's room, yanked the doctor in behind him, and softly closed the door.

The doctor leaned against the dresser, catching his breath. He started back toward the door. "My capsules!"

Carl's fist caught the left temple. He placed the doctor's body on the bed.

Loud yells and sounds of confusion filled the hallway. Carl stood quietly and waited for the inevitable.

A heavy fist hammered the door. Carl waited quietly.

"This is security. If anyone is in there, open the door, immediately!"

Carl cracked the door and peered out, hesitantly.

The man wore a hotel security uniform. "Please, monsieur. Some questions while we wait for the police."

"Am I glad to see someone in authority," Carl said, opening the door wide and exhaling a relieved sigh.

"Did you see anything?" the man asked.

"Me?" Carl acted as if the question were absurd. "I don't rush out into gunfire. And as you can see, my friend here is even more confused."

The doctor sat on the edge of the bed, holding his head.

Carl turned back to the guard. "Whatever happened? The noise sounded terrible."

"A doctor and his business acquaintance were attacked by some crazed fanatic. Now the doctor is ranting and raving about going home. Normal, I guess, but it's a good thing his friend reacted. That is one crazy gunman that will never try that again. Sorry to bother you. There should be no further trouble." He turned.

While Carl waited for the investigation in the other room to end, he pacified the doctor by explaining how Jacques and his assistant had replaced them by reacting to a preplanned option. The doctor's composure pleased Carl, enforcing his thoughts.

The doctor's idea was good. With the capabilities, limits and means of control for the poison definitely established, most any demand could be made on the United States government. Who would dare oppose him? The poison would be an ideal weapon against bureaucratic oppression. His fight for *Universal Freedom for all Mankind* was about to move one step closer.

Carl turned to the doctor, "When could you be ready to start?" he asked.

Dr. Becheimer stared in disbelief. Could the man really make such an important decision in one meeting, and in the middle of all this confusion, but this whole trip was approaching the unbelievable, so why question that thought? "I am very ready immediately." he said quietly. "I am single and have no obligations."

"That is not a practical solution," Carl answered. "Return home and start making plans to leave for an extended period. Devise some logical reason for a long absence." He paused. "Let it be known you plan to continue your studies elsewhere. Do not rush. We have time. A program must be established. Financing must be arranged, and we must find others to work with you. You will be advised."

Others? Perhaps that was the reason for Mr. Eagleman's previous remark 'we felt'. "I would prefer to work alone," Doctor Becheimer stated firmly.

"I understand your desire for independence," Carl answered with equal emphasis, "and will consider it when possible. But you, in turn, must make your decision now, Doctor. You will work within the parameters I establish, comply with every detail of the final plan, and participate fully in the training program I develop. The research will be under your control, but everything else, every single thing, will be under my absolute control. Decide now. There is to be no second choice. We are both here for the same reason, to fulfill our goals. I believe I have been simple and direct." There was no need to explain to the doctor that he fully understood the poison would require a person of *The Eagle's* expertise, if the doctor was to gain the instant notoriety he desired. The doctor may be vane, but he was not stupid.

Doctor Becheimer looked at Carl, no longer in doubt about a division of authority, or who the man was. The arrangements for this meeting, the detailed precautions, the people in the adjoining room, and the man's control of today's events removed any doubt. As *The Eagle* said, he was being simple and direct. There would be no subtlety or evasion, no variance or confusion in the agreement.

"It will be as you say."

"Good."

Noting the silence in the hallway, Carl picked up the phone. "Are conditions acceptable, Jacques?"

"Exactly as planned," Jacques answered. "Herman makes a good doctor, and his duplicate set of papers were as good as his acting. I will have to go to headquarters to verify the final report, but the doctor is cleared. Who was the man, another of the Jackal's men?"

"Probably. They may have been a foolish outfit, but they were loyal. This should end it. The few that remain should disperse. At least I hope so. I have no desire to eliminate them all. As for this meeting, I will be using Doctor Becheimer, Jacques, but for now he is free to leave. Considering the unexpected activity, I suggest he catch the next flight home. Would you come over and arrange to get him aboard the plane? I must leave immediately. Incidentally, be sure Carlotta is generously compensated for her fast action on the switchboard, and express my regrets for not spending the evening with her." He put down the phone.

Doctor Becheimer looked shocked. "You are saying I may not have been able to leave?"

Carl's expression was noncommittal. "Do not concern yourself with conditions that no longer exist, Doctor. Concentrate on what lies ahead. That is what deserves your consideration." As for himself, he had already decided how to handle the funding.

General Chernykov could again use his expertise to release KGB funds. The Soviets enjoyed supporting disruptive operations against the western block, especially the United States.

CHAPTER 3

MOSCOW

The only record of an alliance between *The Eagle* and the Commanding General of the KGB's First Directorate existed solely in the minds of the two men involved; and one of them was not positive who the alliance included.

General Aleksandr Chernykov stood by his office window and watched the low rolling clouds brush the tops of the pointed spires in nearby red square. Neither the sight of the fast moving cold front, nor the biting wind in Dzerzhinsky square infiltrated his thoughts.

The trace of a smile crossed his face when he finally turned back toward his desk. Being certain *The Eagle's* request for funds would be approved was not overconfidence on his part. It was pragmatic reasoning based on simple logic. Providing funds for guerrillas and counterinsurgents to battle the tyranny of western powers had been government policy since the days of Cheka, forerunner of the KGB. As a military man, he accepted the day could come when even that policy might change, but he would let politicians fumble with that decision.

The General leaned back in his chair, the pleased expression still in place as he permitted himself a brief indulgence in the past. So long ago, yet like yesterday he reflected with a twinge of regret for the energetic days of lost youth. It had been his first assignment outside Rodina, the motherland, as commander of the Counter-Insurgency Training Center in South Yemen, a camp the western countries so vehemently opposed. Especially after he changed it into a facility superior to anything they had even contemplated.

Perhaps a few details of the program had slipped his mind during the intervening years, but none that involved *The Eagle*. Few people knew the man had been both a student and instructor of his. Fewer yet, if any, that the man was the great-grandson of a Cossack Cavalry Officer. That information he held as privileged.

It was during their first meeting that the General learned *The Eagle's* parents were murdered by Turkish police. *The Eagle's* unemotional description of events surrounding his mother's death was what originally convinced the General the young man was a good candidate for his program, and the General's practice of never divulging such information on his trainees had resulted in a most lucrative association for the two. *The Eagle* profited by having his war chest fattened with generous donations from the KGB, and the General enjoyed ever increasing funds in a private numbered account in the Arab Bank in Baghdad. Though neither ever spoke of the account, and all communications were through a most tactful intermediary, the General had few doubts as to its origin. The one time he did decide to confirm his belief, the bank president disappeared. The General understood the signal.

The General's tour as commander of the training camp had occurred during an exciting period. It was a time when Carlos Marighella wrote his *Mini-manual for Urban Guerrillas,* the Jackal spread terror throughout Europe before mysteriously disappearing, Gabriel Krocher fired a Nakarov pistol into a man's stomach before shoving his suffering body down an elevator shaft, and Ernesto Guevara campaigned to launch an attack on what he called the stronghold of capitalism, the United States.

The General leaned forward, poured himself a small glass of vodka, and swallowed it in one satisfying gulp. Ernesto Guevara may have been ahead of his time, but the man sure had himself an objective.

Reflecting on those early days was one of the few times the General permitted himself a modicum of self-indulgence. His feeling of pride was justified. The training program had been studied, grudgingly admired, and copied by most who originally complained so vehemently. By the time he relinquished command, his students were receiving training in photograph, calligraphy, the techniques of arson, assassination, extortion, ambush, disguise, weaponry, and communications, subjects now standard in training camps around the world.

The General accepted the probability that by now the American CIA, British MI 6, French SDECE and other intelligence agencies had infiltrated the program. Just as the CIA probably suspects I have an agent in their headquarters, he thought with a shrug, and just as we sometimes cover for each other with the implicit understanding the favor will someday be returned. Cooperation between opposing forces can sometimes produce benefits for everyone, but that was a thought the average layman would not readily accept. His thoughts returned to his prize student.

The man even looked like a Cossack, six-foot four-and-a-half by actual measurement, wide shoulders, powerful arms, a grip like a steel vise, and the movements of a jungle cat. The injury to his left leg may have created a slight limp, unless he wore his corrective shoe, but the wound did not interfere with his agility. But strength and agility were only two facets of his proficiency. Sometimes it seemed as if every aspect of training was locked somewhere in *The Eagle's* mind. The man had been a brilliant pupil, quick to learn, retentive, aggressive and totally dedicated to self-improvement. A cold violent force lay buried somewhere within him, driving him beyond normal limits; as if motivated by the need for revenge. There was little doubt he would attain his goal.

Two subjects seemed to dominate the young man's interests, finance, and the study of the body's critical nerve centers, especially those insuring quick and quiet termination.

During the intervening years *The Eagle's* financial success had become an accepted fact, and the General accepted the probability the KGB had not been the only benefactor. Kadaffi's unlimited oil money must certainly have been involved to a substantial degree. But as for *The Eagle's* interest in the body's nerve centers, the General preferred to leave that area undisturbed. *The Eagle's* animal instincts, as if the human race was a normal part of the food chain, and his repetitive practice to improve near perfect techniques had caused the General to use him sparingly on assignments where killing was involved. Not because he was ineffective, the outcome was always as expected, but somehow the act seemed to exceed the bounds of fair play. The small element of chance that belongs in the human equation did not exist.

It was almost time for the meeting. The General stood to leave, then stopped to pour himself another vodka. He drank it slowly in a silent toast to a man who had accomplished more than he had set as a goal in life.

The guard saluted and stepped forward with the authority expected of his position. He carefully checked the General's identification card. Though some members considered the check demeaning, none complained today. The chairman was to be in attendance.

They were all there, the other Chief Directorate heads, the seven Department heads, the Chief of Services. The General looked around the room. Yes, Vladamir Zhukov, Chief of Finance was present. That was a friendship he carefully perpetuated.

The men talked congenially, waiting for the notice that the chairman was about to arrive before standing at their assigned places around the huge table. The General relaxed. He would have no problem. These men enjoyed the idea of inserting disruptive measures into the American bureaucratic system as much as he. That there would be no apparent connection to the motherland was understood. For political reasons that assumption was tacit to any such agreement.

The General took a moment to wonder what his bank balance would be after he obtained approval for this latest request from *The Eagle*. He may not know by how much the account would increase, but it would be adequate. In a few more years he would retire, get out of the country. He and his wife would go to a country where they could enjoy his good fortune.

Through the metal bars on the windows he watched a curtain of rain sweep the wide courtyard. Even on rainy days the sun is up there somewhere, he reflected without expression. The turbulent clouds rumbled in response.

Then again, if *The Eagle's* plan to destroy governments was even halfway successful perhaps he should change his Baghdad account to gold bullion. Paper money was only as good as the government printing it, like that Confederate money in America.

With his contained dry humor the General added a more practical thought, "It sure as hell won't go into rubles."

CHAPTER 4

SOUTHERN LYBIA

Carl waited for the team members to take their seats and get as comfortable as possible. The small thermometer on his desk indicated one hundred and twelve degrees. That was uncomfortably hot, even in the low humidity of Libya's sprawling desert, but it was not the heat that concerned him today. It was the paragraph he had just read in a CIA document from his contact in Langley, Virginia. The information renewed his concern on a subject he had already considered, and had found no absolute solution.

In the case of long range operations, lapse of time alone can erode motivation. There is a need for the development of a technique....to create a viable long lasting motivation....impervious to time.

Carl knew that motivation was difficult to instill, and equally difficult to evaluate, even in the short run. Hopefully, the satisfaction of bringing a world power to its knees would provide the extended motivation needed by his team members. He disliked dealing with possibilities, but accepted that time could be a determinant for this most vital part of his plan.

The four one-story buildings Carl was using to prepare his team were nestled between two huge sand dunes. They were arranged in a square, the two longer buildings forming the sides, the smaller single room structures enclosing the ends. One of the longer buildings was used as the barracks and study area, the other, as a combination mess hall, lounge, and general meeting area when visiting instructors made a brief appearance. One end building was the store room, the other, slightly larger, was the "classified area" classroom they were now occupying.

In the small quadrangle formed by the buildings was a flat corrugated tin roof that shaded a generator, a petrol tank, and a water tank. The tanks were used sparingly. It was three miles, over sandy unmarked desert to the nearest hard road, and another twenty-one to the city of Sabhah.

Carl regretted the austere arrangements his team had to endure, but secrecy dictated the decision. Libya was teeming with agents, double agents, and people willing to sell information for most any price. This area, outside Kadaffi's childhood home city, was ideal for his purposes. He had used it before, when creature comforts were a secondary consideration. He walked around his desk, paused momentarily in front of the fan. Maybe he was worrying needlessly, but except for the nationalistic pride that people develop during grave national emergencies he knew of no dependable motivational technique. And in today's world even that seemed less reliable.

During this last six weeks of training the team would be studying specifics of the mission. Though vital information would be confined to absolute necessities, numerous details must be revealed, and specific actions practiced. From this time forward nothing would justify anyone leaving the area prior to successfully completing the training. Departure would be by death only. That was severe, but an even more severe detail was one he would keep to himself. Only four of the five members in the room would depart on the mission. In the event no one failed the final phase, the weakest member, excluding the doctor, would be covertly terminated. Though the requirement was extreme, there was a good side. The uncertainty of what happened to the fifth person would establish an obedient attitude in those remaining. Further, the doctor would be firmly convinced who was in charge. The doctor's inherent reluctance to outside control must be entirely eliminated. In the event the doctor ever proved unworthy, the entire mission must necessarily be canceled, so it was vital he understand his future if he wavered. The CIA article was correct in one respect, motivation is a serious consideration.

Perhaps the impetus he was about to add would help, but even more important, he must insure the requirements were thoroughly understood. Second chances would no longer exist. It was now time.

"I want the five of you to listen carefully. To misunderstand could prove critical. From this moment on you must outwardly, and I emphasize the word, outwardly, change your attitudes." Carl noted the questioning expressions. He had expected the reaction. "But never forget your true inner feelings. Therein lies your strength, even though those feelings may no longer be expressed." He walked over to the window to insure the immediate outside area was clear, then turned. "As the doctor already knows, and the rest of you have probably suspected, this mission calls for your spending an indefinite time period in the United States. That being true, you must begin acting and thinking like Americans. One week from today, any reference to *those* Americans will result in your termination, a most undesirable word." Carl hoped they believed him. They should. "If required, you will be given a United States birthplace with an accompanying history for your new life, and funds will be provided to match the life style you have inherited. But you must always remember one salient fact, any deviation from your assigned mission will result in your immediate death. I guarantee it. One life may not be important, but the outcome of this mission is most important." He stood quietly. Though he did not want to diminish the impact of his comment, a less morbid conclusion might let them leave in a better frame of mind.

"I would like to leave you with one thought that might aid in making the transition. The expression 'obnoxious Americans' is a common expression known around the world. However, the difference between pride and being obnoxious is small, and that difference is invariably evaluated by the observer. The American considers it, pride."

Carl walked back around his desk after the five departed, his limp noticeable without his corrective shoe. The limp would probably be with him for life, but with the improved surgical techniques in existence he intended to have the scar on his cheek removed during his next trip to San Diego. He had seen the work of the doctor who would do the surgery, and the man was good. The lift in his shoe could disguise his limp, but using a beard to cover the scar on his cheek was no longer satisfactory. The dark hair severely limited the disguises he could use. Also, by now the scar must surely be listed as a possibility in numerous intelligence agency files. It was time to once again insure the facts pertaining to *The Eagle* were inaccurate.

Carl leaned back in his chair and let his thoughts drift. The specifics of how he would use the poison in the United States was not yet firm in his mind, but he would use it, either actually or as a threat. He would demonstrate how weak and ineffective and corrupt the United States Government was. To return to another *Golden Age of Freedom* was not an unrealistic endeavor. Politicians constantly used the idea that big centralized government is bad as part of their campaigns. They just did not carry the argument far enough, and never would. Actual implementation was not in their self interest. The greed of those in power must be replaced by a society where the destiny of the individual is controlled by the individual.

When Carl set his goal of *Universal Freedom for all Mankind*, he had expected objection and misunderstanding. He knew government bureaucracies would distort the purpose of his efforts while concealing the tyrannical oppression of their own policies. But dramatic and violent eruptions occurring in public view cannot be suppressed. Such exposure weakens the position of those in power and builds growing distrust within the basic governmental structure. Various branches begin competing for power and prestige. The end result is chaos.

Yes, distrust and destruction are very similar, and to make his work easier, the United States Government excelled at fostering distrust. People were more readily accepting the premise that corruption in government was a way of life. One big, catastrophic event to demonstrate the lack of governmental control could cause the people to openly rebel.

Carl would provide that event, and another step toward a second *Golden Age of Freedom* would be complete.

CHAPTER 5

PITTSBURGH, USA

There was no indication Christopher Braxton would be entwined in *The Eagle's* plan. For him, these last few days may have been hectic, but that was not unusual. As Vice President of the Environmental Management Division of *Knutte, Ancell & Ferrole* he accepted business turmoil as part of the normal business process, and now that the corporate jet had arrived on schedule he looked forward to the usual rest and relaxation on his flight back to the coast.

The enroute stop at Pittsburgh International had taken less than ten minutes. Bart Haddox, the pilot of the regular Tuesday morning shuttle had taxied up to the terminal, Chris had climbed aboard, and they were now taxiing back to runway two-zero in the predawn darkness. Though no new flight plan had been required, the incoming radio call indicated weather conditions may require a change.

"Five-two-niner-four Yankee, this is Pittsburgh Tower. Ground Control requests you contact them on frequency one-two-one point niner for a weather advisory."

Bart depressed his transmission button, "Roger tower, switching to one-two-one point niner."

Having been friends since Vietnam plus four years with the corporation, Bart knew Chris liked to listen to the radio transmissions.

He flicked on the cabin speakers as he changed channels. "Go ahead Ground Control this is five-two-niner-four Yankee."

"Roger, niner-four, be advised the latest weather advisory indicates the previously reported thunderstorm activity over central Ohio is rapidly building in intensity."

"Roger, ground. Stand by."

In the dim glow of the cockpit, Bart glanced over at his copilot. "Pull out the Jetison Low Altitude booklet, Hank. Let's see if we can't fly south and go around the stuff. Those weather guys seem to be getting serious about that storm. Ask Control for a climb en route to Parkersburg, then direct to Cincy. Ask for sixteen thousand. I'd like to stay under the transcontinental traffic if possible. Got something I'd like to squeeze in, if time permits."

Having heard the transmissions over the cabin speaker Christopher Braxton glanced out of his passenger compartment window. The sky looked clear in the dark gray cast of first light from where he sat, but that had nothing to do with central Ohio. But forget the weather, they would be going around it, and hearing Bart's comments on the proposed change in their route opened a pleasant thought. They would be flying over an area he knew very well. A straight line from Parkersburg to Cincinnati would put them near Middleport, Ohio.

Bart looked back at Chris and pressed his intercom button, "Ready for an aerial view of your old home town?"

Chris nodded, then remembered he was in semidarkness. "Sounds great," he yelled over the low whine of the engines. He should have known Bart would remember.

Daylight brushed away the remaining darkness as the jet climbed southward. Chris leaned back, the discomfort of a short night's sleep and long ride to the airport now gone. Flying was a catharsis that invariably brought him to life. Psychiatrists probably have an explanation for the feeling, he thought with a touch of irony. They have one for everything else. But what I'd like to find is one of those guys who can tell me what I'm going to do, or will feel, instead of how they think I feel. That I already know. When I'm on a downer I want to know what to do about it.

He gazed out toward the northwest. In the distance a wall of dark curtain of cumulus clouds lined the horizon. Above the curtain several thunderstorms towered upward like huge pillars of foam. Inside the pillars, jagged bolts of lightning flashed sporadically, filling the towering columns with crimson graphics. The sight sent his thoughts back to the damp closed in feeling of drenching rains in NAM, and the haunting memory of hunching over a mess kit, hungry, frustrated. If he leaned forward to protect his food, the water ran down his neck. If he sat up, the food turned to watery cold goulash.

He had learned to accept most things during his tour, but that was one of the exceptions. Perhaps because it was such a day that he had sat back to back on a tree stump with Little John, a member of his platoon.

Little John had spoken in his slow Kentucky draw. "Sir, there just ain't nothin' no fuckin' good about this whole goddamned muddy mother fuckin' mess." It was a quiet, non-bitter statement. Chris knew no answer was expected, though it was one of Little John's more lengthy and erudite remarks. Little John was big, heavy, quiet, strong as an ox, moved like a cat, and was just as gentle. His usual remarks were limited to, "OK, Lieutenant. If that's what you want, Lieutenant. If you say so, lieutenant." He never complained.

Each time the memory resurfaced, Chris tried to remember he was supposed to forget such things; but there was a tremendous gulf between the way the doctors felt about Little John's death and the way he felt.

The angular features of Chris's face had lost some of their sharpness since his college days. The features were still strong: definite cheek bones, square jaw, black eyebrows, and wide mouth (When he was a kid his grandfather claimed his smile looked like a mule eating briars), but years had added a firm, more reserved and mature look, most noticeably in his eyes. Sometimes the intense determination would not be hidden. It was a reaction born in combat that the psychiatrists saw, but could not touch.

Chris forced himself to sit back and try to relax. He needed to focus his mind on other things. Such thoughts were not good. Reading his newspaper usually helped.

Bart looked back over his shoulder. "Middleport is coming up," he said over the cabin speaker. "I'll drop down and circle once. Sorry we can't park while you look around, but we do have a schedule to keep."

The town looked small and insignificant in the lush green landscape on the horseshoe bend in the Ohio River. A half smile touched Chris's face. The tightness around his eyes softened. Memories of childhood crowded his mind, the smell of supper cooking, arguing with his brother about who would get the last piece of bacon, the paved brick streets, learning to swim in the river, walking to school in the snow. Was he that old? The thoughts kept rushing together until Bart turned back on course and the town disappeared behind them. Bart looked back, smiled. Chris returned the smile. No comments were needed.

The two men across the aisle from Chris were discussing children. Chris opened his newspaper again. He was not against marriage, as he constantly tried to explain to his friend's wives. The arrangement was a necessary part of the social structure, and maybe one day he would be interested, but not now. Things were fine just. as they were. Not only did he and Ruth have a good thing going, she liked the arrangement as well as he did. He dropped the paper in his lap. He was tired of reading.

The last scheduled stop before Los Angeles was to be Phoenix where they were to pick up a Ms. Dahlia Pauley, a recent addition to the accounting office. Supposedly, she was only a little short of being a financial wizard, or should he say wizardess. At any rate, the office gossip among bachelor's rated her acceptable in all respects, and single.

Maybe he could learn why she signed her name, W. Dahlia Pauley. Did she want to present a masculine connotation? That sure didn't seem logical with a name like Dahlia. Strange.

Chris quit fighting his eyes. The warm sun streaming through the window relaxed him. His mind drifted. Even when he discounted the normal excesses of men's descriptions of attractive women, she sounded interesting, but an accountant?

CHAPTER 6

LOS ANGELES, CALIFORNIA

Chris stepped off the elevator. Neither the sixteen floors, nor the rarified air did a thing for his irritation. That damned Porsche had been in his parking spot when he left last week and was there again this morning. It may be his fault he was behind schedule because he overslept, but losing his parking spot had made it necessary to run from the far end of the visitors area. In a business suit, that was not a good start for any day.

He could still make the briefing, turn right at the end of the corridor and another thirty yards or so, but the parking problem was going to require an eyeball to eyeball conversation with someone. He glanced at his wristwatch, 9:26, four more minutes. He increased his pace.

The sliding glass doors to Mr. Kirkpatrick's outer office rolled back quietly. Chris still felt the room was the nicest outer office on the west coast. The thick maroon carpeting, pleated pearl-gray drape across the rear wall, and large green planter to soften the far left corner gave it an ambiance a notch above the others. No staid pictures of founders, CEOs or gaudy quota charts were on display to mar the scene. The room reflected efficiency, expectancy, success.

"Good morning, Monica. Good to see you. I trust you have been keeping our Director of Operations out of trouble?" Chris's voice reflected both jest and recognition of her ability. The office was Monica's absolute domain, and Mr. Kirkpatrick's reliance on her administrative expertise was a known fact. About thirty, a year or so either way, she was a little too short to be statuesque, but the curves compensated. Especially for Chris, he was not attracted to the professional model type.

"Welcome back, Chris," she answered easily, "your timing is a little closer than usual, isn't it?" It was 9:29.

"Some no good S.O.B. took my parking space. Incidentally, could you call Betty and tell her I am here? I didn't have time to stop by and say hello." He turned toward the sofas.

"No, don't sit down, they are waiting for you." Monica's pointed precision in pronouncing each word was noticeable.

"They?" Chris looked puzzled. "I thought this was between Paul and me."

"So we are both in the dark," Monica said wryly. There was no smile.

"Maybe I should run down to my office and say hello, myself."

"I don't believe so," Monica said understanding his attempt at humor. "I will call Betty. You would do better by going inside."

Chris turned toward the door. "Well, no guts no glory." The old military remark helped relieve his tension, but not his deep gut reaction. A thought had flashed across his mind. *If Monica doesn't know, I better be on my toes.*

"Come in Chris." Paul Kirkpatrick was over at his conference table. "We started a little early."

There were three other men present, and Ms. Dahlia Pauley. Ms. Pauley smiled benignly, as if slightly ill at ease. Hanson Izon, the new Chief Executive Officer, he had met once before. *Monica sure as hell called this one right*, he thought. *What could be important enough to bring out the CEO?* The other two men were unfamiliar. Dahlia might as well have been. She had been polite on the flight from Phoenix yesterday, but reserved. *Maybe it was a good thing the conversation did remain on a quasi-intellectual level,* he decided. About the only thing he learned was why she went by her middle name and used an initial for her first. Coming from a family with five brothers could make any girl get a few male traits, and with a first name of Willawanette the decision was totally understandable, but he had found little else to indicate her femininity had been overshadowed. *Take her out of that female business suit with its fluffy bow tie, loosen the tied back blonde hair so it was soft, like she wore it yesterday, and she would be attractive again. But what happened to those coral blue eyes? Yesterday, they were big as saucers.*

Paul Kirkpatrick unfolded as he stood, his angular hands a part of his conversation. Impeccably dressed, to the degree his gold cuff links matched the design of his wrist watch band, he still could not lose the casual look that accompanied his movements. Maybe it was the shock of unruly gray hair on his forehead. His arm moved gracefully to his left. "You have met Mr. Izon, Chris."

"It is good to see you again, sir."

Mr. Izon's eyes were friendly, but he already seemed intent on the next item on his agenda. "Chris." He smiled in recognition, the utterance like a sentence.

Must be a guest appearance, Chris decided. The thought helped a little.

"Dahlia, you met yesterday." Mr. Kirkpatrick's face flashed a trace of uneasiness.

So that's what happened! Now he realized. *Yesterday's meeting was prearrange so she could—.* Suddenly, the whole damned set up was obvious. *Ms. Pauley had been sizing me up, not me ogling her. Talk about a damned patsy!*

"Life really is full of surprises," Chris said, striving to keep his voice from displaying annoyance. He did agree with her mother's decision though. She should be called Dahlia. She sure as hell did not look like a Willawanette, Willie maybe, but it needed to be something feminine.

"And this is Mr. Jay Gilbert," Paul said.

Mr. Gilbert stood and extended his hand. "It is nice to finally meet you, Mr. Braxton."

The man was about Chris's height, maybe an inch or so shorter, five nine, maybe ten, wiry, brick hard, dynamic, with an old-fashioned sandy hair crew cut.

Like a shifty boxer, Chris thought.

Mr. Gilbert's gray-green eyes swept Chris's face, inquisitive, moving, as if searching. His handshake held the firmness of confidence.

Chris liked the man. Whatever was coming would be wide open, no screwing around with knit-picking details. What the facts would be may be a mystery, but Chris felt he was looking at a moving force in the meeting.

"And this is my associate, Phil Joachim," Mr. Gilbert said.

The man had a friendly smile, the quiet type, another solid hand shake. *The force behind the dynamic leader*, Chris wondered? *Could be.* He had never yet seen a flashing light without someone backing the guy up.

The introductions over, Paul Kirkpatrick folded himself back into his chair. "Might as well have a seat, Chris. The sooner we get started, the sooner these unusual circumstances will fall into place for you."

This was not the first time Chris had felt himself on the outside looking in, but that Paul would do it to him was a surprise. Had to be something unusual. He would approach it as always: keep an open mind, listen, respond calmly, *and quit trying to prejudge until I hear the whole story.*

"Mr. Izon and I had a previous briefing with Mr. Gilbert," Paul said, turning more formal. "It was during that meeting the decision was made to set up today's meeting." He paused. "Mr. Gilbert and his two associates are with the CIA. So, with that rather startling information, I will let him continue the meeting."

Chris shifted in his chair. *This is really going to be a good one.*

Mr. Gilbert leaned forward, his left forearm on the table, his thumb rubbing the tips of his fingers, slowly, steadily. "Just a few words for Mr. Braxton's benefit, before we get too involved." His diction was clear, clean, crisp, somewhere between an English and Bostonian accent, unusual, hard to place. He looked toward Chris.

"As Mr. Kirkpatrick just said, Mr. Braxton, the highlights of this meeting were previously discussed, a necessity you will soon understand. However, to reestablish the basis, I will update the data as of eight this morning, and start my briefing by reviewing a few chemically related disasters familiar to most of us." He paused as if organizing his thoughts.

"I will not go into the details of Union Carbide's poisonous gas leak in Bhopal, India, or the scare immediately thereafter at their plant near yours in Charleston. Suffice it to say, the resultant deaths of the hundreds of people around Bhopal did attract world attention; and the scare in Charleston, though no serious damage resulted, also received wide coverage at the time.

"Later, the pollution of the Rhine River also received world wide attention. Also, you can tuck this away in your memory Mr. Braxton, included in almost every report were the poisonous effects of heavy metals, mercury, and selenium, and the effect of such substances on the water, a fact I wish to stress.

"And to keep the world's balance of power intact, I guess I might as well throw in the Soviet's difficulty with their atomic energy plant at Chernobol. At least it emphasizes a point. We are not the only country with one foot stuck in a bucket of, shall I say, contamination."

Mr. Gilbert seemed to spring from his chair, seemingly more at ease while moving, and again reminding Chris of a boxer starting his warm up. He opened the top manila folder on the stack before him, picked up the papers inside and nodded to his assistant as he turned toward the wall screen. A slide classifying the briefing as Top Secret flashed on the screen.

Mr. Gilbert looked directly at Chris. "Have you heard of the Kesterson Reservoir?" he asked.

Chris nodded. *Whatever this concerns, I am obviously it, but water pollution? Hell, what else is new?*

"I pre-guessed your answer, so I'll review only a few issues," Mr. Gilbert said, motioning toward the screen. "Both Kesterson, up near Los Banos, and Carson Sink, over in Nevada, have had similar problems."

Two large photographs had flashed on the screen. Below each of the aerial pictures were statistics, size of the areas, names, elevations, seepage rates, etc..

Mr. Gilbert pointed to the left photo. "The Kesterson problem, draining water into an area without adequate run off, is the direct result of an unfinished government project in California. I am happy to report that corrective action is now underway, but what is being done to correct that problem is not our concern today." He moved to the right photo. "Over here near Stillwater, Nevada, there is a similar situation. The rivers drain into a big marsh area called the Carson Sink. A few years ago, both the Carson and Humboldt rivers pretty well flooded the area. The water has now receded considerably, but again that is not our concern. With an unusually heavy rainy season the process will undoubtedly repeat itself. Our concern is, each of these areas is having identical problems, problems currently being related to water pollution, with Kesterson's presently being the more acute."

He moved back to the left photo. "The twelve or so huge ponds here at Kesterson, are a nesting place for millions of waterfowl as they migrate up and down the coast. Being one of only eight shore-bird reserves in the Western Hemisphere, it is an important nesting area and migratory stop. Strange as it may sound, the water in both places has suddenly become so polluted that millions of fish and thousands upon thousands of migratory birds are dying."

The maps disappeared. Mr. Gilbert turned toward his chair. His voice settled. "People are frantically working on the problem. Very intelligent people. People associated with some exceptionally skilled groups are working to isolate substances or compounds. References to selenium, mercury, and heavy metals frequently appear in reports, but at this stage all substances mentioned are listed as probable causes, or more accurately, contributing causes. To be honest, no one knows with any degree of certainty just what is taking place." He paused.

"However, and now comes the reason for my being here. Suppose, just suppose, the increase in pollution is not from a natural build up of destructive chemicals, the logical course to research, and the one being researched." He paused again, obviously for effect. "Suppose the contamination is the result of some person, or group of people, polluting the water with some insidious and lethal product, a product undetectable by normal procedures."

Mr. Gilbert stood quietly.

"Holy shit," Chris muttered slowly. He had intended his reaction to be a thought, realizing too late it had been uttered.

Jay Gilbert smiled, as did the others. "I will accept that. Often, a short speech can be most effective."

"Sorry," Chris said, upset with his comment, "but your last remark was really an attention getter."

There seemed to be less tension in the room. Chris purposely did not glance toward Dahlia Pauley.

Mr. Izon stood. The rest automatically did the same. "I am no longer needed here," he said with a smile. He looked at Chris. "Paul and I have discussed Mr. Gilbert's proposal, Chris. Listen, but do not feel pressured. We have no set opinion. If you don't approve of the concept, or the proposal, turn it down, but Paul and I thought it valid enough for you to listen."

Chris smiled. "I will certainly do that, sir. It would be difficult to ignore." *And that's a fair enough offer, if the rules don't change after he leaves.*

Mr. Gilbert looked toward Mr. Izon as the CEO left the room, "Thank you, sir. We appreciate your cooperation."

Paul Kirkpatrick sat back down, "Well, I guess we might as well continue."

Jay Gilbert walked over to Chris. "Tell you what, Captain. If you'll accept, Chris, I'll settle for, Jay. I worked up to Battalion Sergeant Major in NAM, but damned if I could ever get a bar, guess the monsoons washed away my recommendation."

How did he get my military record, Chris thought? *But the CIA? Why not?* He smiled. "I will listen to your story, but you know as well as I, there are few military men who would rank a Captain above a Sergeant Major, regardless of how the manual lists them."

"So be it," Paul Kirkpatrick added with a laugh. "I am happy to report I was old enough to miss that one."

A map of the San Francisco area appeared on the screen. "First, let's discuss the water situation, here in the west coast region," Jay began.

As Jay reviewed problems, such as, deciding how much water in the Sacramento basin should be diverted into the California Aqueduct and then sent to the southern part of the state, Chris realized he had sometimes toyed with the thought of what would happen if our water, food, or energy supplies were interrupted. But, seldom had he dwelled on the idea. For someone to poison the basic water supply would be as bad as using poisonous gas. There would be no winners. *It is like blowing up the world*, Chris thought. *Who wins?*

A map of the United States appeared on the screen. "Now let's check the rest of country," Jay said. Shaded areas indicated drainage patterns surrounding the major rivers across the country. Jay waited for everyone to orient themselves. "If you look at the Red River and the Arkansas and Missouri and Ohio feeding into the Mississippi, then check the Colorado and Snake Rivers, you can easily see there is not much left, except the east coast. Imagine what would happen if someone were to pollute them at their source, one, several, or all of them. The effect would be catastrophic."

Mr. Gilbert walked back to his chair and sat down. "For today I will just say we have enough information to believe our premise of what is happening at Kesterson and Carson is realistic and reasonable. To best pursue that premise, we need a man with certain qualities. He should have a good knowledge of chemistry, be familiar with our environment, have acceptable personal characteristics, and naturally would be willing to accept the assignment. Our records indicate you fulfill the known requirements, Chris. Your willingness is another matter.

"I have only a few more remarks," Jay continued. "Then you can get back to work. We know you have been gone for a week, but we would appreciate your thinking about the idea overnight, and meet with us again tomorrow morning. If you do accept, and I hope you will, I'll fill you in on the specifics. But there is one thing I want to be sure you understand and consider carefully."

That, you can depend on, Chris thought, somewhat sardonically.

"There will be no permanent damage done, but the records in your company will be temporarily modified to reflect some possible, ill-advised, financial decisions on your part."

Here come the changes!

"That was the main reason for Mr. Izon's appearance," Jay continued. "He insisted he be present for the initial part of the briefing, and that Mr. Kirkpatrick hear the entire discussion. The purpose of the deceit is to establish justification for what might appear to be unusual actions by you, or Ms. Pauley. Right now we have no idea what those actions might be, but it does give us an operational advantage. And regardless of how this turns out, if for some reason the press gets the story, Ms. Pauley will insist the investigation was an egregious error on someone's part. A completed audit will immediately be published finding everything in perfect order. Mr. Izon would accept nothing less."

"Let me interject something here," Paul Kirkpatrick said. "I am not certain the premise you people developed has any validity, but I want you to know one thing for an absolute fact." He looked directly at Jay Gilbert. "The first time any of you indicate you are deviating from this agreement, a carefully prepared statement will place the blame exactly where it belongs. No one in this company will be left with his balls nailed to a stump while your agency marches off into the sunset on another wild goose chase."

That tilts things back a little more toward even, but he left out something, Chris thought as he noticed everyone except Dahlia shift in their chair. "I appreciate your consideration, Paul," he said smiling, then turning toward Jay, "and I will consider your offer Jay, but." He paused.

"Yes?"

"If something does go wrong, don't use a rusty nail."

Dahlia Pauley also smiled.

CHAPTER 7

Chris unlocked the hallway door. Betty's welcoming remarks would have to wait. He needed a few more minutes.

He hung his suit coat on the rack in the corner, walked over to his desk, and immediately felt a twinge of guilt. The clean desk before him was a testimonial to Betty's expertise in the wheat-versus-chaff game, and if this CIA proposal materialized into a meaningful operation he would need a lot of that type help.

Chris swung his chair toward the window and leaned back, his fingers wrapped behind his head. The aircraft in the traffic pattern at LAX (Los Angeles International Airport) seemed to be moving in slow motion, some hanging motionless, others sliding slowly down the long final approach before dropping behind the low hill this side of the airport. The repetitive precision was mesmerizing.

What the devil would he do if he became involved in the CIA's project, and for some reason could not let go? Had Paul or Mr. Izon thought about that? They probably had, but it could not have been for very long. The planning for the meeting he just attended had to have happened during the last few days, and Monica's lack of knowledge indicated the staff was not involved. But if so, how had the CIA worked Dahlia Pauley into the picture so quickly? Loose ends were hanging all over the place; except for the prime candidate for having his balls nailed to a stump.

The assignment did present a challenge though. An aura of excitement surround the whole idea. The scenario, at least the part he had heard so far, was a damned good one, a poison, or whatever it was that could not be detected, or maybe did not exist, being worked on by unknown people, perhaps. That type situation could work into a real challenge. Another thing, Izon's remark about him using his own judgment had been a boost in self-esteem, but one night was not a hell of a lot of time to think it over. Then again, what was there to consider? The CIA held all the cards. He chuckled silently. Maybe they could label the project, Christopher's Caper, but how or why did they pick him? He leaned across his desk and pressed the intercom button. Maybe the confusion would all fall into place tomorrow.

"Yes?"

"Good morning young lady, your wandering boy has returned."

The gentle laugh was relaxing. "Welcome back, Master. I thought I heard your door. I will be right in."

Betty opened the door. "Must have been a long briefing. You almost missed lunch."

"Monica call?" He couldn't decide whether he has was pleased, or chagrined that she didn't become effusive over his absence.

"Yes, she explained why you were running late. Apology accepted."

"Good. I've got to get that damned parking problem solved. Hopefully, it's a man. It will be easier to explain myself in clear terms." As usual Betty looked neat and fresh, perhaps a little heavy, but her clothes fit exactly as they should, no wrinkles, no frills, good taste, and color coordinated. Even the plastic rims on the bottom half of her glasses complimented her auburn hair, and served to put her face in balance. She had been with him nearly a year now, and her personal standards had never varied. Her secretarial ability was commensurate. He would have to be careful. Jay's stress on secrecy had been clearly stated.

"It was quite a morning," he added, nodding toward his 'In' box. "Anything there that is monumental?"

"Not really."

"Okay, then let's put it all on hold for a few minutes." An idea had flashed in his mind. If this project gelled and began occupying a major portion of his time, he would need flexibility. The vacation he had been talking about for months could be the perfect ruse. "Do you think this office could fall into neutral for awhile? I am getting in a mood for a few days off, just plain old relaxing."

Betty smiled, not quite coquettish, perhaps coy. She would have been glad to help him relax. To lean over his shoulder and accidentally brush against him while she helped him sort papers was electric, at least she hoped he thought it was accidental. "I should think you could easily manage a few days," she said. "It's been a long time since you've had a full-fledged vacation."

"Think I'll try. If it falls through a crack, then to hell with it; but at least I tried." Maybe now was as good a time as any to plant another idea, the first part had gone so smoothly. "I just found out I might be picking up a new project. If it comes about, maybe I can work out something in conjunction with it. Then again, maybe I better wait. Well, we'll see."

"Must have been some meeting." Betty slipped her last paper under the small pile, a questioning look on her face. "Monica didn't say much, but she did sound, well, different. Anything I should know?"

"No. Not yet anyway. Everything is still tentative, and may not amount to much even if it does materialize. You know how those things go, everybody talks, an idea rises to the top, the bubble bursts, the cycle repeats. This meeting broke up before the bubble popped."

"Well, you deserve some free time. Just go. Lock the door and go." She laughed that pleasant laugh, "Let the bubble pop. But before you leave, Randy Blake wants you to call, at your convenience, and Mr. Davis called from Sacramento. Claimed he is having difficulty getting anyone to listen to his side of the story on that environmental impact report." She took a breath. "The Charleston plant still can't find why consumption and production figures don't seem to balance, but that certainly is nothing new; and finally," she paused. "Hey, this is an excellent idea. Larry called just before you came in. Said he is flying down to Baja for a couple of days of good fishing. That's the way he described it, and he wants to know if you are interested? You really should go, you know, and since you want some time off anyway—."

Chris laughed. "It's amazing how you jam all that in, while my guard is down. As for Larry, that would be fun wouldn't it?" He motioned to the papers on his desk. "I'll settle everything after lunch. Then we will see what happens."

Betty turned to leave. "Very well. I tagged several of the items I thought you might want to discuss before you sign them. The rest are pretty much routine."

Chris watched her leave. Nice. Very nice. She had a feminine softness that called for a man, but he was aware of the boss-versus-secretary problem. With Betty, it might be worth it. He picked up the phone.

"Hello?"

"Ruth? Glad I caught you at your desk."

"Well, welcome home Chris." She sounded pleased to hear him. "When did you get back? I thought you might call last night."

"I planned to, but we were delayed in Dallas, and I was just too damned tired. Mind if I come by tonight?"

"Not at all. Around six? I'll fix something."

"Excellent. I hadn't planned on such a treat, but it couldn't come at a better time. Know what your planning? I'll pick up the wine."

Chris went to the restaurant on the mezzanine. After lunch, he returned, completed the paper work, called Randy Blake out in Ontario, and then finally located Paul Davis in Sacramento. The shortages in the Charleston plant had been around forever. That problem could wait.

Betty gave him a quizzical look when he told her he would be absent the next morning, and she did not conceal her surprise at his leaving early. Not that he blamed her, but he needed time to think, and his office was not the place to make decisions involving the CIA.

Arriving back in his condo, he slipped off his shoes, opened his shirt collar and poured himself a glass of Chablis to accompany the paper he had not had time to read this morning. After finishing both, he picked up his phone.

"Hello?"

"Hi Larry, figured you'd be home by now." Larry Bertelli was his closest male friend in Los Angeles. "How's life been treating my fine friendly fornicator?"

"Welcome home you old S.O.B., I called Betty on the chance you might be back, so don't unpack." He paused, then laughed. "Damnation, I'll be a poet before I know it. Everything is set for a weekend of chasing marlin. Should be a ball. We will have two plane loads. Jack Harlon is taking his. No women, just damn fine fishing. I saved you a seat."

"Betty told me about it. Sounds terrific, but I can't make it." Chris gave his reasons. Mainly, there were just too many things needing to be done. He knew Larry would not buy it, but also knew there would be no drawn out objections. They respected each other's privacy.

"Well, okay," Larry said, clearly disappointed, "but it sounds like the same old line of shit to me. I still think you should tell that old fart, Paul, to take his job and shove it. Hell, you could work for me."

Chris laughed. "And what would I do, serve subpoenas?"

Larry was a partner in the law firm of *Bertelli O'Grady & Swartz*, specializing in corporate law. Serving subpoenas would not be too challenging.

A laugh came back. "You could damn well do it. I've seen you in action, old buddy, and you are fast on your feet. Especially when about to be caught screwing some guy's wife."

Chris laughed again. "Balls! You know I don't do that. That is, as you lawyers are always so careful to stipulate, intentionally."

"Yeah, but it makes a damned good story. Sure you can't come, fishing, that is? I have already called ahead, and been assured there will be plenty of beer, all iced down and waiting, and *Old faithful* is primed and ready." Larry's twin Beech was old, but he kept it in top condition.

Chris held the phone briefly before laying it back in the cradle. God, but it was good to have a friend like Larry. He and Larry had met just after he moved here. Life was so much easier when Larry was around. Everything seemed to revert to some care free existence when they were together, as if they were two disinterested spectators. Chris never checked, but maybe they both had a lot of forgetting to do. It was a good relaxed feeling.

He glanced at his watch, time to get dressed. He still had to pick up a bottle of wine, and Ruth liked to have him arrive on time.

*   *   *

Jay Gilbert drove into the underground parking area. He eased into the red zone painted on the floor before a wide metal door, came to a stop and waited. Three cameras, one on the wall above the door, and one on each of the concrete posts on either side of the zone moved to scan the area, then all three returned to focus on the car. Jay adjusted his tie, being sure to use both hands. The door rolled up, closing after he drove through. The parking enclosure could easily hold ten cars. He parked beside a dark blue stretch limousine, and walked to the metal door in the far wall. A large round button filled the hole where the knob was usually located. He pushed it, then looked up into the camera. The door rolled back. Across the small room was an elevator. The door opened as he approached. He entered and pushed DOWN.

The local CIA office was not elaborately furnished, but was functional. The communications room, behind the main lounge was jammed with electronic equipment, and the wall opposite the duty desk was filled with electronic gizmos, TV screens, and panels with unmarked levers. The agent on duty waited until Jay was beside his desk.

"Thought this might be your first stop. Want the Chief?"

"If you can get through, Hank."

"Already checked, the line is clear. I'll activate the scrambler. Use the green phone on the table by the back wall. Coffee?"

"Now that's what I call a mind reader. I could use some, but I'll get it." He poured half a cup. As he picked up the phone, Hank closed the console switch.

In the basement communications center in Langley, Virginia, a small red light began blinking below the letters, LA-1. The agent on duty recorded the time, and noted the steady yellow light. It indicated that the line was open, but the chief was not in his office. The equipment automatically searched twenty locations outside the complex. He watched as the bank of green lights to his left quickly flickered then shut off, except for the one under the number twenty. He smiled. The Chief does love those crabs. He broke into the circuit. "That you, Hank?"

"Yeah, I have Jay Gilbert here, Jim."

"The Chief is out on the bay. I am making a line check for you, Hank. Only take a second."

Once the line was found clear, Jim activated the scrambler. A matching slave unit on the Chief's boat automatically responded. Each day a different seed number resulted in a series of constantly changing frequencies used to carry the transmissions. The four digit number was chosen at random by one of the three agents assigned to monitor the system. Jay's comments, when he was briefed on the system was, "It'll be secure until some high school nerd starts working on it."

"You are cleared Mr. Gilbert."

"Evening Chief, just checking in."

"Should be here Jay. Fine evening. The crabs are grabbing the meat as if they are as hungry as I am." He leaned back in his chair, his huge hand making the cordless phone look like a toy. The darkening skyline accentuated his mass of flowing gray hair, softening the strong features of his lined face, the drawn look in his deep-set eyes lost in the lengthening shadows of approaching darkness.

Jay knew where his boss was, maybe not which cove, but close. He was in one of the small coves on Chesapeake bay that the two of them so often visited, dangling raw meat tied on the end of a string in the shallow water. The crabs absolutely refused to let go until forced, and on a good day they could easily bring in enough for four people, when supplemented with an adequate supply of cold beer. It was one of their favorite outings.

"Save a few, Bill. Didn't realize you were so busy. I will make it short. I think we have the man we need, John Christopher Braxton. Goes by, Chris. There's no doubt about his intelligence. That is good in itself, but he also has some plain old smarts."

"Glad to hear there are still a few around. If you approve, he must be the right man. Anything I can do?"

"Not really. I think our most convincing argument is already in place."

"Dahlia?"

"You are a perceptive man, Chief. Your suggestion to get her in place early is really paying off."

"Always was a sucker for compliments, but a blind man could see this one coming. Does he accept the premise?"

"We are meeting in the morning to firm it up, but I think he will go along. In fact, I've started putting things in place." Jay looked at the bank of twenty-four clocks displaying the different time zones of the world. "If you don't hear from me by four tomorrow afternoon, your time, consider it done. Either way, I will drop by your office the next morning."

CHAPTER 8

Ruth Callahan's tenth floor condominium was a block off Wilshire Boulevard. She paused by the large picture window and watched the thin strip of ocean on the horizon turn to shimmering silver. The sky above it had reached the deep red and purple phase of what she called her evening color show. The climax should arrive about the same time Chris arrived. That was good. Sunsets relaxed him. As so often happened, her thoughts drifted back to her first meeting with Chris, in Vietnam. It had been a simple yet traumatic event.

When Chief Nurse Major Ruth Callahan heard the hospital speakers announce the incoming helicopter with three wounded aboard, she proceeded directly to the emergency room. Colonel Kaplan, Da Nang Hospital Commander and Chief of Surgery, was already present.

First Lieutenant John Christopher Braxton was one of the wounded. Two Corpsmen carried him in on a stretcher.

Ruth looked down. Chris looked up.

She was in love. Like a silly little school girl, Major Ruth Callahan stood there in her starched white uniform, helpless against the overpowering sensation.

"Well now, that's the kind of face I had hoped to see," Chris had said with a forced smile before he turned serious. "And don't you dare let them fly me out of here." The remark sounded as if he had been saving energy to make that single statement.

A surge of joy shot through Ruth. If this foolish man wished to remain in Da Nang, she would see to it. Setting his broken leg would normally be done here, so if no serious internal injuries existed from his shrapnel wounds, there would be no medical need to evacuate him to Japan. Colonel Kaplan was a fine surgeon and a nice commander, but had never professed to being an administrator. She would use that fact to her advantage.

Though no ravishing goddess and currently nine pounds under her desired weight, Ruth's full facial features, short auburn hair and pleasant Irish personality were charmingly acceptable. She felt her shoulders were too broad and her brown eyes too large, but those were personal opinions. No one else seemed to notice.

Ruth smiled as she looked back on the event. That was the first time she had fully appreciated the advantages of being a Chief Nurse. She had placed Chris in a room near the emergency ward where she could check his progress without seeming to be ever present. Men would have called it stacking the odds, but she had thought it was a rather practical solution to an ongoing situation.

More than a week passed before Ruth felt she could safely question Chris's reason for wanting to remain in South Vietnam. The two were having what she hoped was becoming one of their mutually enjoyable evening chats.

"You really want to know?"

Ruth nodded.

"Secret?"

"Cross my heart."

"Selfish. Plain old selfish."

"Selfish!" Ruth mimicked surprise. "You would have a hard time selling that to anyone, especially here. Maybe nuts, but if there is something in this part of the world to be selfish about, I am not aware of it."

"Well, maybe selfish is the wrong word," Chris said, "but I did it for my own advantage. Whether that is selfish or not I am not sure, but I'm sure not staying because I like the life. Present company excepted of course." He chuckled, then winced slightly as he shifted his weight to ease the pressure on the leg cast. Two of the shrapnel wounds in his back were also still more than slightly tender. "I want to go home," he continued, "be returned to inactive status, and get back to civilian life as badly as anyone, but when I do get out of this hot muggy mud hole, I sure don't want to return. I want everything to be clear cut, no partial tour with the possibility of returning, no nothing, just an absolute final get-the-hell-out-of-here end."

"Does muddy mother-fucking mess ring any bells," Ruth asked with an expressionless face.

Chris roared in laughter, pain be damned. "Where did you hear that?" His eyes watered.

"For the first day or two you rambled," Ruth said. Maybe she should not have touched such a tender nerve. "Little John must have been some man."

"That he was. Guess I'll have to start locking my door," he added with a forced laugh. He brushed his cheek, hoping to catch the moisture before it became a stupid-assed tear. Then again, Little John wouldn't have complained. The thought was too much. He raised his pajama sleeve and wiped his eyes.

For the short time they were together in Vietnam, Ruth had been deliriously happy. With Chris's arrival, life turned into a beautiful experience for her; but to have him show up in Los Angeles, had been a dream come true.

They had gotten together immediately. It was like old times. Chris still seemed to need and appreciate her friendship, and there was no doubt about her need for him. Physically and mentally they meshed. Sex, good food, dancing, a drive in the mountains, an evening of conversation, or a shared TV show always made her day complete. She knew the arrangement could not remain static forever. The possibility of a younger, more attractive women was always a worry. She was four years, five months, and three days older than Chris, but until that day arrived—. She stood slowly and walked into the dining area.

She had chosen the robe with the rolled collar and wide sleeve cuffs. The higher collar gave her neck a better proportion, made her feel like her hips better matched her shoulders. And Chris liked the slippers with the high heels and gold lamé straps. She did too. They made her feel petite, feminine. Girls have that right.

She looked at the table. It was ready. She had chosen wine glasses for a Burgundy. She knew he would bring a red. Having been gone for a week, it might even be a good Bordeaux, not a vin ordinaire, but something special, perhaps a Rothschild. He had done such things before

A few cocktails, some conversation, she smiled, or whatever, and dinner would be ready. She had planned it so nothing would be critical. She checked the time, turned on his favorite tape.

The door bell rang.

If it had not?

She laughed aloud.

The clock would have been wrong.

CHAPTER 9

Chris felt good. The morning was beautiful. The sky was a deep crystal clear blue, like Los Angeles natives always claim was common a few years ago. Sparkling sunbeams danced along the pulsating arcs of water spewing from the fountain in front of his condominium. The splashing water even muffled the drone of traffic out on Wilshire. Yes, the whole world was beautiful.

Chris grinned and nodded good morning to four stewardesses stepping off the airport bus. Why they never looked tired after working all night had always been a mystery to him. There had to be a machine somewhere that spewed out the cute little things on demand, immediately repairing any that became rumpled or frayed. He hoped their night was as good as his, but he knew better.

With a night like last night, this day would be magnificent. What he and Ruth had was magic, absolute magic. The way he felt, he could solve Jay Gilbert's problem before the end of the week. The thought brought him back to normal.

Dahlia Pauley should pick him up any minute. Jay Gilbert had suggested she drive, saying she would know of any last minute changes for the planned meeting. He had not objected. Driving in Los Angeles was no big thrill.

A cream colored Mercedes-Benz SL, with its top stowed, swung into the long circular drive. A blonde was at the wheel with driving gloves, scarf, flying blond hair, dark glasses, and wide smile all in evidence. The sight reminded Chris of a TV commercial. She braked to a stop.

"Need a lift?"

Dahlia's wide smile left little doubt she was enjoying herself. Her teeth sparkled in the bright sunlight. And those coral blue eyes were once again as big as they had been two days ago.

"When you go, you go in style, don't you?" Chris opened the door, sat down and looked around. "This yours?" he asked, amazed. The CIA may have a secret budget, but this was ridiculous.

"On my salary?" Dahlia laughed. Her eyes danced. "Don't be foolish. I couldn't afford the bumpers. Mr. Gilbert agreed to a day of fun in the sun before I had to return to earth. Tomorrow it will all be back to normal."

That made a little more sense, Chris decided, his mind refusing to discard the advantages of a secret budget. "Well, I will gladly help you enjoy your last day." He leaned back in the contoured seat and let the soft leather massage his spine as he looked around. "This is really some piece of machinery," he said.

"Would you believe 227 horsepower at 4750 RPM, and a 5.6 liter V-8 engine clocked at 138 miles per hour? With a compression ratio of 9:1 and a rear axle ratio of 2.47:1 it will do up to fifty-five before you've had time to get your foot off the brake." Her joke pleased her.

Chris paused, holding the end of his seat belt in his hand, "Christ Almighty, you're not a mechanic, too, are you?"

"No, just read the specifications while checking the manual for all the buttons, bells and switches." She felt good, energetic. "I must admit though, the specifications on acceleration are my own." Her inflection and sideways smile indicated more was to follow. "The book says it takes a few seconds to get up to speed."

"I give up." Chris shook his head in mock frustration, squirmed back in his seat and settled himself. "Just be gentle with this delicate body of mine. Anything over ninety-five makes it extremely nervous."

The way Dahlia added throttle to slide into the heavy morning traffic convinced Chris she had done more than read the basic book on driving. As for her recitation of car specifications, that outburst belonged to a quiet, studious, librarian type, but she sure did not fit that description today. She was attractive, very attractive, even when he considered his relaxed outlook on life after last night.

Dahlia felt his eyes on her. She had not purposely tried to impress him, though she liked the idea. The car's capabilities were impressive. Then she remembered her brother's advice about "pretty little girls, too smart for their britches". She found the thought tantalizing, and cinched her seat belt a little tighter. The pressure felt, nice.

They drove west, then south on the San Diego Freeway. From there she followed Chris's recommendation to miss the traffic congestion on Century Boulevard by taking Sepulveda Avenue to the 96th Street exit, then entering the complex next to Terminal One.

Chris raised his voice to compensate for traffic noise, and pointed to his right. "Take that ramp to the upper level. It is less crowded. We can park easier up there, then catch the shuttle to Terminal Seven."

"Every time I enter this place I feel like I missed a chance, by not buying up all the tile companies in California," Chris exclaimed. His voice sounded hollow in the passenger tunnel. The floor, walls, and ceiling were all solid tile. He held Dahlia by the arm. "Hang close, wouldn't want to loose you in this mob."

"Is it like this every day?"

"Mornings and evenings. Gets more reasonable in the afternoon." The clicking heels, mixture of languages, and knowledge that most people would soon be somewhere else, added a degree of excitement to the transient atmosphere.

The concourse was jammed with people bustling toward departure gates. A woman's hollow voice echoed an endless list of arrivals, departures, phone messages and location of facilities.

"The conference rooms are down this way," Chris said taking Dahlia's arm again. "Which room did Jay reserve?"

"We will have to check. He stayed here in the hotel, I think it is called the Skytel, but he said he had decided to wait until this morning to set up the meeting. Said he didn't want to reserve a room too far in advance. Seemed silly to me."

That figures, Chris thought somewhat sarcastically. The whole idea of Dahlia driving was to eliminate that process.

Chris tried the doorknob. It was locked.

Jay opened the door. "Thought I would keep it locked," he said with a smile. "You never know who might wander in." He stood back. "Come in. I just arrived a few minutes ago, myself. Phil came in earlier."

The room was small but contained the basics. It had a good size table, ten chairs, briefing easel, a pull down screen, and two small tables, one with a typewriter. But for Chris, the best thing was the smell of fresh brewed coffee, over on the other small table.

Jay noticed the look. "Better have a cup. Phil ordered it extra, so we might as well enjoy it."

"Don't mind if I do," Chris said. "Being exposed to all that fresh air and sunshine on the way over here made me thirsty."

Dahlia sat down across from Jay and Phil.

"A big glass of orange juice would be better for you," she said, glancing over her shoulder.

Must be the mother instinct in them, Chris decided. He took his cup to the table and sat down next to her. Jay leaned back in his chair. "Well, Chris, I guess we are at the point where it is your call. We need your decision before we can get into specifics. If you have general type questions, I'll give them my best shot, but I don't want to bore you if you're not interested; and I am sure you understand our reluctance to go much deeper into classified information, unless there is a need to know."

Chris waited a moment. "You know, this entire presentation has something macabre about it. It is difficult to accept how anyone would do what you are suggesting. If people were smart enough to develop such a sophisticated product, and do it under such unusual circumstances, you would think they would have the intelligence to see the horror in it all. Maybe there have been no human lives taken yet, and maybe we are just lucky in that regard, or maybe in some weird way we might even consider it thoughtful consideration on their part, but damned if I can understand how anyone could implement such an idea. It would have to be some stupid terrorists, at least, you would think so. No normal organization, even one of our weirder type governments would plan a mass poisoning to the degree you are inferring. Terror is one thing, but what you are talking about is killing thousands of people. Carried to the extreme, millions. My mind doesn't work right when I start thinking in those terms."

"I accept your logic, Chris," Jay said, "even understand your reaction. Mine ran a close parallel when I first started picking up reports on all this. But the type reactions you are talking about are based on the premise that people react in a predictable fashion. That is not necessarily true. Remember, Hitler could be very charismatic, but I doubt you would find many people who would consider him stupid, many other adjectives perhaps, but not stupid. And today's terrorists with their warped minds have pulled off some sophisticated and spectacular projects. It is difficult to predict what people will do, be they governments, groups, or individuals. Yes, intelligence is a factor in the mix somewhere, but trying to figure out what people will do still needs a lot of research. One thing is certain though, if our premise is true, there is a good possibility a great many people could soon be dead."

Chris felt a sense of the unreal. Calmly discussing killings, Hitler's atrocities, terrorists, and genocide created a feeling of detachment from reality. "Actually, if your premise is true, I would say the possibility of many deaths is not only possible, it is highly probable."

He stopped in frustration. Hell, why kid himself. He was committed.

"I can't really think of any logical reason why I shouldn't help," he said resignedly. "I am sure I have as good a research facility at my disposal as anyone, and with my background, am probably as well qualified as the many others you undoubtedly considered. Besides, the concept does present a challenge." He shifted his weight. "Consider me a volunteer." He felt better with that decision behind him.

"Excellent," Jay said, "but I should warn you. There will be more than research involved. In fact, I am not certain there will be much pure research on your part. We hope your expertise will enable us to substantiate whether or not such a program is actually in existence, and if so, how to destroy it, or them. It would be nice to know how they plan to do it, and if we do learn something, fine; but that is a secondary issue."

Chris nodded. "Makes sense, I guess, but couldn't eliminating people be the last consideration?"

"It will be, but those type solutions go with the type business we are in," Jay said. "And though the idea may sound gruesome, there is a hidden advantage; the time frame to bring the misfits to justice is shortened."

"If you have the right misfit."

"I can't fault the statement, but it is a topic we could debate for days." Jay pulled some papers out of an envelope. "Let's start getting down to details. There are plans we need to set in motion, alternatives to consider, and most certainly some clear cut emergency procedures for your safety. I am being perfectly honest when I say we do not expect violence, but not planning for such a contingency would truly be stupid."

Jay opened a folder. He shoved aside the top five or six pages. "Your knowledge makes some of this useless," he said with a slight smile, "but let me cover a few points to help you better appreciate the possibilities involved. He picked up a paper that looked as if some of the larger print was French.

"When the reports first began to filter in, we thought some of our normally reliable sources were again padding their pockets by selling false information, a practice we are forced to accept if we want to keep our contacts. But then more concrete facts started appearing.

"The French SDECE broke down a man who claimed he was released from a project in Libya that was targeted for somewhere in the United States, in his opinion. He claimed he was released before he knew the specifics, but if the man was in the program and then disqualified, something special is definitely in the works. He was educated, an expert in explosives, fluent in English, and should have been considered qualified for most normal projects. The SDECE suggested his occasional irrational behavior could have disqualified him, but we will never know. He was killed while trying to escape through a basement window in the building where he was temporarily detained. Clearly the man was also an expert at picking locks, if he actually was trying to escape. Several people felt the news release about an escape was a ruse, and he was murdered, but nothing further developed." Jay put the paper aside and glanced at the next sheet. "About the same time, both British MI 6 and German BND received indications *The Eagle* was developing some type of long range plan. When we heard that, we began checking in earnest. One thing was certain, if *The Eagle* was involved we better start giving the idea consideration. Perhaps the name means something to you."

Chris shrugged. If it did he could not associate it with anything or anybody, but he did notice the change in Jay's eyes. *The Eagle* was obviously effective at his work.

"To be brief," Jay said. "Compiling everything we have available leads us to believe a terrorist team is here in the United States, working as I have described. We are covering alternative possibilities, but the hypothesis I am tossing your direction fits best. A small group of extremely intelligent but ruthless people, intent on using or developing some horrendous product. If it works, it will undoubtedly be a masterful weapon. If a mistake occurs in the process? Well, the results could be disastrous. We have too much evidence to assume otherwise. We just can't pinpoint it, either who or what or why or how many. But if it is what we have pieced together, and an undetectable substance is actually developed, Armageddon could be near."

Jay paused, his expression even more firm, "Hopefully, with your help we can eliminate the problem, Chris. But let me make one very important point at the outset, no outsider must know the real purpose of your work. You can be sure the people we are looking for are intelligent, and expertly trained to pursue any tactic necessary to attain their goal. Remember when you mentioned we may not be considerate? They do not even take the time to consider. They kill and walk away. At the risk of overemphasizing the point, I am trying to convince you that revealing any of this information to even your closest friends, could cost you your life." He smiled benignly. "Though the problem may then no longer be a concern of yours, it could ruin our chances of solving the case."

Chris returned a half hearted chuckle. "You made your point."

"I was not striving for false dramatics," Jay said. "It really is a serious problem that if handled properly could be nothing more than a check into the current problem at Kesterson and Carson Sink. If you do discover something, tell Dahlia. Hopefully we will be able to handle it from there." He closed that folder and picked up another. "Let's discuss a few other items."

As Jay's explanation unfolded, Chris learned he was to become involved in the research at the request of the Metropolitan Water District, that the CIA and his boss agreed the Ontario research facilities could be used for any laboratory work required, and a visit to the Kesterson and Carson areas was planned.

"You still have your portable computer, don't you?" Jay asked. "It is IBM compatible, if I remember correctly."

Chris laughed. "You mean you are not sure? You haven't missed on anything yet. Yes, it is compatible, and has been very reliable, so far."

"Good, I will explain an emergency system we have previously used with success. People used their modems to notify us of trouble, even when their transmissions were being monitored. You might say it's as simple as ABC."

"I have heard that type generalization used before," Chris said dryly.

"Well, you do have to remember something," Jay said. "There are three things you must remember, the telephone number needed to connect to your company's main frame, and that, you already know, the number twenty, and the letters ABC. Here is how it works.

"You log on your company's main frame, start typing your message within twenty seconds after lock-on, and within the first twenty letters of your text, use the letters a b and c, in that order. Punctuation and spaces will be ignored. That's it. Just be sure in the first twenty letters, the letters, a b and c, are entered in order. For instance, typing 'tab c' would qualify, or 'the lab check shows so and so', or any similar type comment that comes to mind

"We will program your company's main frame to automatically forward a copy to our office, and when our Duty Officer receives the info he will immediately dispatch help."

"I can handle that."

"I am certain you can," Jay said. "One other point, we will assume that type message infers you need help, regardless of its contents. Any helpful information you can include will be appreciated, but that will be at your discretion. When our people arrive, they will assume positive action is required until they are certain you are not under duress."

Chris looked at Jay. "I am impressed, but couldn't you get a lot of false alarms?"

"Some messages may accidentally match the pattern, even meet the twenty second time frame, but the message will not be transferred unless it is yours. You are the one who should be careful unless you relish being visited by strangers who will be obstinate about leaving until you positively prove you are not in danger. That type of unexpected visit can sometimes prove embarrassing. Just wait more than twenty seconds after lock on if you do not have time to check your wording."

Chris shook his head. "You people are something else. What the hell is coming next?"

"Are you a turtle?" Dahlia asked, straight faced.

Chris laughed. "You bet your sweet ass. I might miss some things, but don't ask an old G.I. that question unless you're ready for the answer that goes with it."

"I guess Tom was right," Dahlia said.

"Who is Tom?"

"Her brother," Jay answered. "They were very close."

Chris shook his head in disbelief. "Does everyone around here know everything about everybody, except me?"

"Probably not everything," Jay said with a smile.

CHAPTER 10

"Come in, Chris." Paul Kirkpatrick stood by his office window overlooking the city.

"Well, I agreed to go along with their idea," Chris said, "but I have the feeling you thought I would."

Paul laughed. "I may have had the feeling, but I would not have put money on it until a few minutes ago. Here, I want you to see something." He walked over to his desk and picked up a paper. "Check this out. You, my friend, are in a fast moving crowd. Monica brought it in awhile ago."

"Oh?" Chris started to scan it, but quickly found himself carefully weighing each word. The article referred to a recently approved Andreeson account, an unusually lucrative contract in which he had played a major role. The possibility of irregularities while getting approval of the Environmental Impact Report was being restudied. Further, an audit to check into several unusually large cost overruns in a second contract with the same company was seriously being considered. That second contract had been under his direct supervision.

Chris looked at Paul. "The way this letter is written, even I would have doubts about me." He laughed, haltingly. "Didn't know so much could happen during a business lunch. We ate in *The California Place*, the restaurant beneath those big crisscrossed arches. Not too bad. Has a nice view."

"Never been in it," Paul said, "but it does look interesting, hanging up there in space. Often wondered how they put in the toilets." He nodded toward the paper. "Jay Gilbert had to have had this ready for release before you went there to eat. That was rather nervy, but fast and efficient."

"I guess so, but damned if I know when he released it. We were together most of the time. Maybe they decided I would agree and set it up before hand. As you said, pretty nervy, but if that is what they did, it worked."

Chris briefed Paul on the meeting, including his planned trip to the Kesterson and Carson Sink sites, and his tentative schedule for a series of briefings before departing. "Most of the agencies are near by, so the briefings should not interfere too much with my normal functions." He decided to save the idea of combining his trip north with a few days of vacation until a better time.

"There will be no problem with your new assistant handling the office while you are gone, will there?" Paul asked.

"Shouldn't be. He is doing fine, has a solid background. I am not certain I mentioned it, but he was the manager of West-Pac's plant in Rialto, the one that burned down last fall. Maybe you remember. It was a spectacular display of what can happen with chemicals. The media loved it. Anyway, West-Pac wanted to transfer him, but he preferred to remain in the immediate area, and was not interested in a temporary assignment while they rebuilt the place. Said too much could go wrong in the process. I was lucky to get him. He is quiet, but a quick learner; but if anything major does comes up, I would appreciate your having Betty call me. I'll stay in close touch."

"Sounds satisfactory."

Chris glanced at the wall clock as he stopped by Betty's desk. "Didn't realize it was so late. Must have taken longer with Paul than I thought."

"No problem, everything is under control," Betty said, a strange look on her face. "Mostly routine, Mr. Blanchard took care of a few things that had answers pending, but nothing major."

"Good. Come in for a minute." He walked in his office and picked up the small stack of papers on his desk. As usual, Betty was right. Then seeing a copy of the letter Paul had shown him, he feigned surprise. "What's this?" He paused while pretending to read. "They've got to be kidding. An audit of our files on the Andreeson Insecticide account?"

"Probably nothing," Betty answered. "It came in some time ago." Should she tell him about the rumors flying through the building? He would find out soon enough.

Chris read the letter again. He had to admire Jay Gilbert. The man was efficient, but he could have waited a day. Maybe he wanted the audit to act as a distraction, Chris decided as he reconsidered the situation. If so, it certainly worked on Betty. That had to be the reason for her peculiar expression when he first came in.

"Well, we will see. Damned if it makes any sense to me." He dropped the letter on his desk and picked up a note she had made of a phone call from a Mrs. Strater, in Charleston, West Virginia.

"Do we know a Mrs. Strater?"

"Not to my knowledge. The woman sounded as if she was not too certain about what she wanted. She said not to worry. Said she had a paper, and would like to talk with you sometime when you were not too busy. Sounded elderly and very sweet. Maybe she is a friend of your parents. Didn't you say your grandparents lived in one of those valleys up behind Charleston? I tried to find out more, but she, very sweetly and very nicely, let me know she would call you again. It was strange, but she was nice enough." Then Betty added as an after-thought, "She sounded almost secretive."

Chris looked at the note. "Strater? Isn't there a grocery chain by that name? Well, we will find out when she calls back, if I am here. Apparently I am the only one she will talk to, and it looks as if I am going to be in and out for a few days."

"Gone? Good. You're going fishing, or as they say in my family, fishun. I am glad you finally came to your senses. This place could drive you nuts if you—."

Chris had started laughing. "Just a damned minute. I am neither going fishing nor fishun. I'll tell you about it later, but I am going to try and work in a vacation with the trip I will soon be taking. Hopefully, I will have the chance to take in Reno, maybe even get to Vegas for a few days. But first I have to attend some briefings. I need to find out what the devil I am trying to do."

"I see." How these men could get so many things going at once was beyond her, but let them play, the secretaries would hold the place together. "You said yesterday you might get a new job. Ready to put out a news release?"

Chris smiled. "Hardly rates that. The corporation was asked to help try and figure out the cause of the water pollution at Kesterson and Carson Sink. I have been chosen to coordinate our effort."

"The Carson what? Sounds like a plumbing problem."

"Not quite, but don't let it concern you. It is just another of those assignments that could keep me busy, off and on, for the next few weeks. There sure isn't anything unusual about that. I will brief Alex. He can handle the routine work if I am not available. I cleared that part with Mr. Kirkpatrick, an easy task since he was the one who volunteered my services. At any rate, he knows what is going on."

Betty looked at him, happy someone did. She said nothing.

"Oh yes, I told Larry I couldn't go with him. I told him, I was too busy." He gave Betty a mock stern stare. "If you ever let him know I knew this trip was coming up, and went to Vegas to watch gorgeous chorus girls frolic instead of going to watch whales mate off the coast of Baja, I'll," he paused, "well, I'll think of something.

"Very well," Betty smiled demurely. She smiled again as she slowly closed the office door.

For some reason Chris remembered other times he had seen that same expression. There was something in it he did not understand. He glanced again at the note. Strater? The name seemed so familiar. Statlor brothers? He would get it. Sometimes some things seemed so insurmountable. He smiled. Then again some things seemed mountable when they were not.

He sat down and started cleaning off his desk. What he was going to look for on his trip up north was a mystery, how he would know it when he saw it was another mystery, and what he was going to do with whatever it was he didn't know he had, after he had it, required a little more thought.

CHAPTER 11

Air conditioning, cruise control and stereo may help, but there was no way of taking the monotony out of traveling on Interstate 5. Chris watched the cement ribbon narrow in the distance. Larry came close when he said, "They designed it with a fucking ruler, because they didn't have to worry about hitting a damned thing."

Chris tried not to think of the fun he had missed on Larry's fishing trip. Like watching a beer can fly as Larry yelled "got the sonofabitch" over the whine of his reel. Larry had a knack for savoring life's fleeting pleasures as if they were erupting bubbles of pure fun. At times he felt a twinge of resentment at his own lack of ability to do the same, but Larry's exuberance was genuine fun to experience, even if from the outside looking in. Regardless of what really happened though, Larry's story would be another wild one. And why not? If the number of fish actually caught was the determinate, the last man to go out would probably have been Jesus. A road sign flashed by: Three Rocks 4 miles. He was getting close.

Los Banos had a clean agricultural community look: trees, picket fences, a railroad crossing in the center of town, more pickups than cars, and a restful open feeling. He drove through the main section to give it a quick check, stopped for gas, then turned back.

The motel surpassed his expectations. The small pool looked inviting, and not a soul was in it. He could almost hear it calling him.

After exercising in place to work out the kinks, he pulled himself up over the edge and turned one of the lounge chairs toward the sun.

The reaction of the young man in the service station had caught him by surprise. When he mentioned the Kesterson project, the attendant's response seemed almost a reflex. "Which side are you on?" the fellow had blurted out with a laugh, the expression lacking humor. There was no doubt the cleanup was a topic of contention in this nearby community. That the differences might interfere with an open discussion in his meeting tomorrow flashed in his mind.

The thought sent him back to his room where he called to confirm the time, and pin down the location. The map indicated the headquarters was only ten or so miles up route 165, but there was no use in taking a chance.

As Chris had hoped, differences of opinion had been a needless consideration, at least, among those working on the problem. The briefing by Mrs. Hasting's team indicated their concern was finding a solution, not self-promotion or interagency bickering. They had established two goals: to properly treat the condition, and to find a cause so they could forestall a repetition.

Chris appreciated Mrs. Hasting's comment, "We are more than happy to have another corporation of your stature aiding us in our research." Her statement was so sincere and seemingly heartfelt that it was hard to think some of these people could be involved in a clandestine activity of the magnitude he was investigating, but Jay Gilbert's caution returned. "It is impossible to pick out a well trained subversive by looks, and just as difficult by observing their actions. What is even worse, most of them complete their assignment before their intent is obvious." It was a scary thought.

After the formal briefing broke up, Clanton Darnel, the chief biologists acted as his guide. Clanton's story was enlightening. "At first we had no problem with channeling the water into the ponds," he said as they started their tour around the area, "and had the project been completed as planned, there probably would be no problem now. The overall idea was a good one, but the government shut down the project after the first eighty miles of the drainage canal into San Francisco Bay was completed. Tomorrow everything may change again, but except for a few small streams in the mountains west of us, the system is fairly well closed for now. Of course, all the drainage can't be shut off, but the level in the ponds is receding."

Chris interrupted. "Are both soil and water samples being taken as the level drops."

"Oh yes, most of our previous work was concerned with the water, since that's where we thought the problem originated, but now an increasing number of soil readings are being taken. Many think the problem is a build-up of selenium in the soil. Can you imagine what would happen if we decide we have to get rid of the soil?" He laughed. "Burying dirt. Doesn't that sound like a government project?"

Chris smiled. "I guess it could eventually come to that. Incidentally, do you drive around the entire area when you make your checks?"

"Just about every square foot of it at sometime or other."

"I have no special reason for asking," Chris said. "It just flashed in my mind, but how about those streams you mentioned, the ones emptying into the drainage ponds?"

"Nothing much to them. Most are dry most of the year. They used to stock one of the larger ones a few years ago, but no more. Never amounted to much anyway. The water was so warm the trout acted as if they wanted to be caught. Fishing was about as exciting as washing your feet with your socks on." He laughed. "I heard that reference made to another activity once. Anyway, there were a couple of cabins built up along the stream bed, but not much else was ever done. Funny how people rush in and do things before they are even sure what's happening."

Chris drove back to his hotel. Nothing strange or unusual was occurring that he could see. They all seemed to know their job, and were qualified to do it. He had not expected any dramatic revelations, though the possibility of one surfacing did add an element of excitement. The only unexpected problem he had encountered was how to ask questions without seeming to pry into unrelated matters, like asking about the streams flowing into the area. But secrecy must have its limits, he thought. Why shouldn't he ask? As long as he used a degree of intelligence? Those small streams could be dumping all sorts of crap into the basin.

It was late afternoon when he checked out. He rechecked his map on the route through Sacramento. Shouldn't be a problem. He took the on ramp to Highway 5, settled for the speed limit, and let his thoughts drift.

By now, Randy Blake should be receiving written reports from the numerous other agencies studying this same contamination problem. Betty had submitted Randy's address for any information the agencies felt would be beneficial, and Randy had undoubtedly set up a team to analyze the information as it was received. If Randy was anything, he was efficient and dependable, to the point of being overly attentive at times. It was a characteristic Chris found annoying. On several occasions he had noticed Randy staring at him with a look he did not appreciate. If it were anyone but Randy, he would already have classified him as gay. How he would resolve the problem, he had no idea. He chuckled as he thought of what Little John might have done. That type direct action would not be too well accepted in current society.

He had intended to drive to Reno before stopping, but on entering the freeway system in the south end of Sacramento the thought of another few hours on the road seemed undesirable. He was not in a driving mood. Besides, Reno's gaming tables would still be there tomorrow. The Red Lion motel sign appearing above some trees convinced him.

*　　　　　　　*　　　　　　　*

Chris took one last look across MGM's huge casino in Reno and turned toward the bank of revolving doors to leave. He had arrived yesterday, performed with his usual level of expertise on the dice tables, deposited his allotted funds in the one armed bandits, seen a show dedicated to the integration of boobs, butts, feathers and sequins, and had slept well. He was ready to leave, and his feeling about gambling was still intact. There obviously was something about the system he did not understand. Next stop Stillwater. That briefing was set for one-thirty.

A lonesome way-out-in-nowhere feeling came over Chris as he pulled into a parking slot by the cement block building. Several cars were in evidence, but the vast expanse of openness around the compound made him feel small, insignificant.

Would this end up like Kesterson? Another of Jay Gilbert's ruminations came to mind, "Nothing beats having direct contact with the people involved. Vague distinctions, sometimes lost in written reports, often suddenly appear and become obvious."

Soon after the briefing started Chris had to admit Jay was right. No one had briefed him on how rapidly the change had occurred, especially here at Stillwater. In less than a year, the deaths of birds and fish had reached an unprecedented level. There was nothing to explain the shear devastation. Dr. Gardener was straight forward.

"As of now we don't know why it is happening. It is baffling. We are stumped. Selenium? That seems to be garnering the center of attention in most reports. Mercury? We found the element present in dead tissue, but not to a toxic level, at least, not as we know it. But some fish died so fast they had smaller fish hanging out of their mouths." He noted Chris's brief look of wonderment. "I am not exaggerating, nor are those type occurrences isolated incidents."

"Unbelievable," Chris said incredulously.

"I am not trying to take away Kesterson's claim of having the greater problem," Dr. Gardener added, "but lately, we have been running a close second. As you probably noted when in Kesterson, Kathy Hasting is not the flippant type, but she stresses she will happily trade her claim to first place with the first one qualified."

Chris smiled. "Yes, we had a pleasant visit. I can well imagine she would appreciate being relieved of such a distinction, even if she did obtain it through no fault of her own. But if you do inherit the honor, it would be nice if it were from her problems improving, rather than yours deteriorating."

Dr. Gardener looked pleased. "It's a pleasure to hear someone take a positive approach. Lord, knows it does not happen too often with environmental problems. Sometimes I think the Indians on the Fallon reservation have advantages in their isolation."

Chris looked quizzical. "Doesn't the Carson River run though their reservation?"

"Under and through. It resurfaces in the northern end of their area. Why do you ask?"

"Had no reason," Chris said, "just noticed from the map it seems to start from nowhere and go nowhere."

"A good description," Dr. Gardener said, smiling. "Geologist claim it starts in Carson Lake, south of here. I assume it does. Those fellows are accurate more often than not." He glanced at his watch. "I am sorry I have to leave, but I did expect you yesterday, and previously agreed to a conference in San Francisco this evening."

"It's my apology," Chris said hurriedly. "And I do appreciate your working me in. Had I gone straight to Reno instead of stopping in Sacramento, I would have been here, plus would probably have lost less money."

Dr. Gardener laughed. "We will see you get all the information you need. At least, all we are capable of furnishing. Ralph Demerick, our chief biologist, will show you around. He is familiar with all phases of the program."

"This is a much larger area than Kesterson, isn't it?" Chris said. He and Ralph Demerick had driven into Fallon, and were now following route 95 northward, on the west side of the project.

"Not only larger, it also has fewer options to consider, since there is no way to control the water flow. As you can see, out there in the flats the water is receding, but not because of any control on our part."

Chris looked at his map. "Does the underground river resurface just north of the landing strip on that Indian reservation?" He pointed off to his right, then added, "Strange how those things happen."

"Never thought much about it, but I guess it does. Of course, that type thing varies with rainfall, what little we have, but the strip is not used much. Can't even recall the last time I noticed a plane over there. Of course, with the Air Base so close I probably wouldn't notice it anyway."

"Navy aren't they?"

"Mostly."

"Wonder where they dock the aircraft carriers?" Chris asked with a silly grin

"Next to the dry dock they use for sandblasting dried out barnacles," Ralph said without pause.

"Touché." Chris decided to stick to business.

It was late afternoon when Chris finished his visit and drove back toward Fallon. A small plane was circling the airstrip on the Indian reservation. Must be a small military plane on a sight seeing excursion, he decided. The plane's markings were blurred against the setting sun. He pulled into a service station.

As he filled the tank, he looked around. Why should he stay here? A restlessness was building in him, the miles of wide open nothingness were depressing. He would be too late for the shows in Vegas, but gambling was better than sitting in a void. Then again, maybe he would stop off in Tonapah. See if he could figure out why the chaplain from the nearby air base had gone AWOL during World War II.

CHAPTER 12

Randy Blake, manager of *Knutte, Ancell & Ferrole's* Ontario plant, stood by his office window, contemplating an exotic cocktail of some type. Any type, as long as it was in a long stemmed glass and he was in a plush bar listening peacefully to a small combo providing soft dance music. An organ or piano with guitar and vibraphone would be nice, especially if soft mallets were used on the vibes, or maybe a piano drums and bull fiddle. That may not be as mellow, but would be acceptable. The Dragon's Nest came to his mind. He often stopped there when he felt like being a little up scale. Then again, what made the difference where he went, if all he did was sit by himself and watch others enjoy themselves?

In the back of his mind Randy knew what he really should do. Go home. But he also knew he would not, and tomorrow he would hate himself because of it.

From his patent leather Italian oxfords to the wrinkle free collar on his pastel pink shirt, Randy radiated pristine impeccability. The french cuffs on his shirt, turned up two folds, now that regular office hours were over, revealed the light auburn hair of his forearms. In the reflection in the window he could see that his tan beltless trousers were smoothly molded around his waist, the creases sharp and straight as though he had yet to sit.

Window reflections can lie though, he mused as he gazed at his image. He was getting soft. He could feel it. The pressure on the waist band of his trousers was a sure sign. He must get back to a regular workout. He absolutely simply must, three times a week, minimum, no more excuses. There was nothing worse than a flabby, unkempt body.

But weight was not Randy's main concern this evening. That familiar need was starting to creep through him again. The sense of disparity between desire and how he wished to be was starting to surge upward inside him. His rational mind denied it, but he knew what was coming. The restlessness would grow, increasing more rapidly with each passing hour until it took control, forcing him to relieve the desire, but never the need. The urge would permeate his mind and body until once again he would act. Frustration had already started to show in his expression, in his eyes.

The city of Ontario rested quietly at the foot of Mount Baldy. The mountain, a towering white helmeted sentinel, dwarfed everything in the area. He watched the sun begin its magic act. Hues of red, magenta, bright orange and pale yellow bounced off the towering mountain, the varied colors working their way slowly up its side, their movements imperceptible, yet changing from surface to ridge to jagged cut, then spreading across the snowy peak in a brilliant fluorescent display before fading into the pre-night sky. Somewhere in the heavens those beautiful colors had to be saved. They were too gorgeous to be wasted. What a shame so few people have the time to stop and enjoy such fragile beauty and massive strength, he thought as he lowered his gaze to the stream of freeway traffic below. All lanes on both sides of the sweeping San Bernardino freeway were filling with a stream of homeward bound workers and their swing shift replacements. The white headlights and red tail lights were starting to meld into the usual night time ribbons of light.

Randy quietly watched the exchange. In another hour, the rush would dissolve into other but equally crowded activities, teenagers cruising, happy couples searching for an exciting evening of entertainment, and older couples searching for restaurants. Couples, he thought in frustration, why did he have to be, different?

He walked back to his desk. Whether in the mood or not, he simply must prepare a letter from the data his team had been tabulating, and the way he was feeling he better start now. The feelings within the depths of his inner self were all too familiar, but the letter could not wait. Chris was always so appreciative of his effort, and so thoughtful and considerate about expressing his gratitude for a job well done.

Randy reflected on his current information. His team had been tabulating details and data into what should eventually prove to be relevant and related categories. The choices reflected their expertise, but one thing had rapidly become obvious, government agencies had no monopoly on redundant and useless verbiage. The reports of some of the universities rambled as endlessly as their supposedly less scholarly counterparts.

One point he had emphasized to the team. Though he and Chris accepted the idea that anyone can have a WAG, a wild-assed guess, the team must not opt for that solution. If it became necessary to play the guessing game, he and Chris would make the judgment calls. The team members must stick to facts.

Randy pushed the recorder button. "Ashley, I would appreciate your sending the following brief to Mr. Braxton as one of your first actions in the morning. He is currently out of the city, but not being aware of his schedule I want to insure the brief is on his desk when he returns. Start transcribing now.

"Subject: Initial comments on Kesterson and Carson Sink.

"To: Mr. J. Christopher Braxton:

"Since you offered our services on this project, I have received numerous reports and studies from varied sources: federal and state government offices, the University of California, private and public colleges and universities, and even reports from our competitors. Most of them place this problem in the monumental category. It makes me wonder if perhaps it might not be similar to the dinosaur experience.

"There is one significant note the team did note. Computers are starting to be used to simulate underground water flow, and track the path of pollutants in our soil. Preliminary checks indicate our guesses may be as good as some of the computer findings to date, but we should be patient on this. Time will undoubtedly bring improvement, perhaps becoming exceedingly effective. It is an area deserving follow up.

"One of the better computerized efforts is in Florida. They have interconnected networks that are monitoring water quality in more than eighteen hundred wells. I was surprised when I read of the extensive program." He released the button and listened to what he had dictated, then rewound the tape to record over the last sentence. "The results from such an extensive program should be meaningful. We must follow up on that study.

"In addition to the above, others have said they are also developing computer programs in the hope a synergistic approach to processing new data will isolate some specific item. Your knowledge of computer programming should be extremely helpful in this regard, especially since several agencies inferred the current computer software is less than adequate.

"I am sure you have been briefed on selenium. Practically every report emphasizes its importance, but we must remember there were other trace elements found, i.e. boron, chromium, iron, lead, lithium, molybdenum, vanadium, and zinc. Interestingly enough, new findings suggest they all can accumulate in people to a much higher level than they can in water itself.

"Although selenium is a necessary nutrient for our bodies, and in small amounts may protect against some types of cancer or even heart attacks, more recent findings show only three times the desired safe amount may be toxic. Also, additional small increases may be enough to create deformed embryos, still births, or even limit procreation. To make matters worse, it appears selenium may be more toxic, and may concentrate in our bodies more easily than previously thought.

"I guess I too am emphasizing selenium, though I did not intend to. I suppose it is the preponderance of suggestions in the reports being received.

"Now, since our company is deeply involved in isocyanates, as are most other companies in our profession, I will touch on them briefly.

"Both of us know, methyl isocyanate, the gas that escaped in Bhopal, India, is one of our most dangerous chemicals. In a closed container it is a liquid. Exposed to air it quickly turns into a colorless, odorless, reactive gas. At high levels it causes muscle constriction and blockage of the nasal and bronchial passages. It can even lead to a reaction comparable to a severe asthma attack, the reaction that caused most of the deaths in Bhopal.

"God, but it sounds so casual when we talk about death this way.

"Anyway, industrial uses include the carbamate derivatives used in insect killers, and as we are both aware as a compound in the different plastics.

"I seriously doubt I have said anything earth shaking, but as we have agreed previously we will express our thoughts, and let the other review them unedited so as not to lose the pearls.

"Another thing, two universities have issued reports showing isocyanates entering our system have an affinity for only a few specific proteins. If so, it could be good news for a change. Maybe we can detect their presence with blood tests, and possibly reverse the destructive process. But as of now, there are just too many unknown factors.

"Finally, and I say this because I know how we both feel about the unknown, I can not find one comment concerning the interaction of any of the trace elements with isocyanates. So, if it is true that trace metals build up much faster in humans than previously thought, and if isocyanates can build up until becoming lethal, perhaps the interaction of the two, should be considered.

"The moon is now full. Mt. Baldy stands tall, gray, and lonely in the white glare. How can the sky be so black in so much light? Must be martini time. Buenos noches."

Once again he rewound the tape to record over his last remark. "So much for now. I have been compiling a complete data file on the material received so far. A technical summary should be in acceptable form soon. Give me a call when you are ready.

"End of report. Use your usual expertise in editing my poor phrasing, Ashley. Thank you."

Randy shut off the recorder, turned off the office lights and walked back over to the window. The cool white moonlight covered the flushed look in his face. How much longer would he have the churning and frustration in his body? Women never sufficed. Yes, it was a temporary improvement, the same with a good sports car, a good opera, even whiskey, but never would he be fulfilled. He was not stupid. He knew his problem, and he resented his classmate in college who helped him learn the truth, but how would he act if the man were here tonight. Though he had so far managed to resolve his problem by going with women, things were getting worse instead of better. Women were so soft and messy.

If he did not get help soon, he may ruin all he had worked for, even hurt a friend. He would never forgive himself if because of his indiscretion, he did something to ruin the relationship with his dear friend, Christopher.

If only Chris would give some indication, one way or the other, not knowing was becoming unbearable.

CHAPTER 13

Betty felt good. There were so many advantages to coming in early. She stood behind Chris's desk, sorting correspondence and reflecting on how the business world reacted to nine o'clock, as if a spring were tripped. She checked the time. She still had thirty-five minutes of peace and quiet before bedlam started.

An aura of expectation hung over the office. She smiled to herself. Was it because Chris was due back? Probably, but the fact that most such days turned out to be less than spectacular, or earth shaking, as Randy Blake called it in his letter, was to be expected. Still, something could happen. To her, anticipation was one of the better spices of life.

From the itinerary, as she understood it from his last call, Chris, as she called him in her thoughts, should have been back yesterday. Probably having too good a time. She shrugged. Why should he rush back? She sure wouldn't if she were in a position to get away with it.

She put Mr. Blake's letter aside. It would go on top when she finished sorting. It arrived yesterday morning, and she knew Chris would be interested in it. That pollution problem must be more serious than the news media was treating it.

She was glad Mr. Blake was out in Ontario. There was no way she could relax around that type man. Women knew who they were. Could it be because they were always so squeaky clean? God, they better be.

The sound of a key in the hall door caught her attention. She glanced up.

"Good morning, Betty." Chris looked relaxed and refreshed.

"Well, think of the devil. Welcome home. I was just finishing up your desk. Have a good trip?"

"Very good, but it is nice to be back." He meant it. "Vegas is fun, but it is so damned unreal." He dropped his briefcase in his chair. "Ended up paying for another floor of the MGM in Reno, and Caesar's Palace in Vegas is far richer by my having passed through their doors, but it was fun." He hung up his suit coat and came back to his desk. "Really did not plan to be gone so long, but everything was so nice." His sense of guilt about an actual lack of enthusiasm bothered him. Had he not fussed so much about getting away he would not have stayed the extra day.

"Well, it is good to have you back. You are a little early though, aren't you?"

"Got back at a reasonable hour, and had a good night's sleep. Got up early. Kind of missed the place."

Betty laughed. "I'll bet."

"No, really. Sitting around by yourself is not much fun. Even in Vegas." Somehow, admitting the truth, helped.

"Ha, again. Let me know where the volunteers sign up. I love the place. Of course I get as much fun out of using the nickel slots as most people do using the dollar ones. Maybe that is why I can come home happy."

Chris laughed. "Perhaps we can arrange something some time. Get Mr. Izon to have our next annual meeting over there, and I will recommend you for secretary."

"You've got yourself a deal."

He glanced at the papers on his desk. "How did things go?"

Betty tossed her last paper in the box labeled 'Whenever' and stepped aside. "Fine. No major problems. Marty Davis called, and said he appreciated your call the other morning when you were passing through Sacramento. He liked your thoughts on that environmental report. He must be having one devil of a time getting it accepted. Incidentally, he came back yesterday. Said he intended to leave again soon, may even have left last night. Seemed frustrated. Said he would call you when you returned. Also, Mr. Blake sent a report on the pollution problem you are checking into." She pointed. "That's it, there on the right. It's straight, to the point."

Chris glanced up.

"All in all, things have been quiet," Betty said, her face expressionless. "Mr. Kirkpatrick was less demanding, and of course Mr. Blanchard was available if I needed him. He is most efficient."

"Feel free to accept his judgment in routine things, but he is new. I would feel better if you held the more important decisions for me, or referred them to Mr. Kirkpatrick if time is a factor." He paused. "As you know, in the pecking order around here, Paul is the head pecker." He had to try out Larry's latest joke.

Betty winced. God, that was old. "Try that when your boss is a woman," she said pleasantly. "The length of effectiveness is shortened, but no problem. I think I can handle the situation."

"I'm sure you can," he said, showing mock disappointment in her ignoring his humor. Her answer sounded strange, just like a woman. Then he realized what she had said. He felt foolish

"You talk as if you may be leaving again soon," Betty said

"No, not necessarily, but this new project does seem to have a lot of loose ends."

"Maybe I should not say anything," Betty said, her voice hesitant, "but for the last few days, while you have been gone, Ms. Dahlia Pauley, the Ms. had a sarcastic inflection to it, has been doing a lot of nosing around. Nobody seems to know just what she is searching for, but she apparently is determined to find it, whatever 'it' is. Frankly, I find her aggravating."

"Well, we must remember. She is like the rest of us, has to do as she is told." He felt good that Betty was supporting him in the face of that damning letter. "Must have been a flaw in that Andreeson contract somewhere, or in the accounting. Maybe we had a duplication of environmental study costs. Anyway, if there is some mix up, I am certain it can be resolved." Chris looked at Betty. In normal circumstances he, too, would be upset about such news. Perhaps he was acting too nonchalant. "At least, I sure hope so," he added.

"I am sure everything will be all right," Betty said, happy he was not too perturbed. It could all blow over. "But since you are back, let's hope that our Ms. Pauley will slow down a little, and let us have a few routine days. Yesterday she mentioned going to Charleston. Perhaps she thinks their problem is part of the whole mix up." Betty looked thoughtful. "Maybe she should go. If she is so darned efficient, she can resolve that shortage problem while she is there."

Chris decided to ignore the sound of jealousy, and tried to sound casual. "I better check with her. I may not be in a position to ask too many questions, but if you don't ask you sure don't get answers, and it would be advantageous to pinpoint my situation without creating too much confusion." The remark even started making sense to him. "If the problem in Charleston, and the Andreeson account are tied together, maybe we can get it all straightened out in a hurry."

"You do have a point," Betty admitted, not too happy with his sudden interest in arranging a meeting. Then again, she did start it all.

"Incidentally, speaking of Charleston, do you still have your notes on that woman who wanted to talk to me?" Chris asked. "You know, the one you said might be a friend of my parents, Stanton, Stater, or whatever."

"Yes, in fact, she called again while you were gone. This time I got her telephone number." Betty paused. "Of course, it may be too late. It is almost eleven back there, and she sounded like an active type, you know, garden club meetings and all that. I'll go place a call."

Chris sorted through his correspondence while he waited. He really appreciated Betty attaching brief notes on various requests to remind him of the position he had taken in similar cases, or attaching incisive comments on some of the more difficult proposals. Perhaps Monica had more experience, but he doubted her insight was significantly better than Betty's.

Betty's voice came through the intercom, "I have Mrs. Strater on the phone, sir. I explained you had been away, and just returned this morning."

Chris picked up his phone. "Good Morning, Mrs. Strater. This is Christopher Braxton. Miss Koch informed me you have been trying to contact me. I am sorry I missed your previous calls. How can I help you?"

"I am so happy you called, Mr. Braxton. My, but you have a nice secretary. She has such a pleasant voice." The gentle voice removed any rush from the morning schedule.

"Well, thank you Mrs. Strater. I will let her know what you said. She will appreciate your thoughtfulness."

Mrs. Strater's voice turned serious. "You know Mr. Braxton, I still wonder if I might not be acting like a foolish old lady, but I am not going to let something Jack did go unnoticed if I think it deserves attention." She paused. "Last month I called Jack's old friend Jason Blair, and he stopped by to see me a week or so ago. He is retired now, but he said you used to work for him, and I should talk to you."

She was coming on fast, but he was keeping up, except for whoever Jack was. "Jason Blair?" Chris said. "Yes, I used to work for Mr. Blair in his research department in Pittsburgh before I went off to Vietnam. Yes, I remember him very well. In fact, he was instrumental in getting me assigned to the environmental program out here in Los Angles when I returned from Vietnam. Are he and your husband old classmates?"

"Were," Mrs. Strater said, "my husband died in an accident."

"I am sorry." Of course, now he knew why the name was so familiar. Things started falling into place. Jack Strater, Chief chemist at the Charleston plant, was killed in an explosion before *Knutte* acquired the company. The man had practically been an institution in himself, supposedly researching a nonporous plastic, and from all reports the type of man who could pull it off, though nothing was ever found in the records.

"Yes, I remember hearing of your husband," Chris said. "I knew him by reputation only, but with the reputation he had among his peers he must have been quite an individual."

Mrs. Strater laughed pleasantly. "An individual? Yes. Intelligent? Yes. Brilliant? Perhaps. Unorganized? Absolutely. Even his dog used to look at him with a puzzled expression."

Chris laughed. "Well, I have to admit, I do remember hearing he did some of his best work in some rather unorthodox ways, but your comments are intriguing. Why did Jason Blair give you my name?"

"I am not sure. Like I said, he and his wife stopped by in their motor home. They do a lot of traveling now that he is retired and they were on their way to Washington state and," she paused. "I'm sorry, I remember how Jack used to complain about my rambling. Anyway, Jason said he would help straighten up things if I needed help and since the kids didn't want any of Jack's tools I asked if he could use any of them. About half an hour later he came in and he looked excited, saying he had some papers Jack had left in his tool box. Jack liked that tool box. I gave it to him years ago. He always kept it on the shelf, right beside his car. Kept his favorite pair of pliers and his screwdriver in it along with his garden seeds and flower seeds and—. Anyway, Jason said I should put the papers in an envelope and call you. He tried to act calm, but I have known him too long to be fooled. I saw that look in Jack's eyes only a few times and believe me it had nothing to do with, well, you know. I use to try to cause him to look that way because of something I did, but you men." There was a lengthy pause.

"Mrs. Strater?"

"Yes? Oh yes. Well, Jason just said I should call and tell you. He said you would be interested in the papers since you are a wine aficionado. I had to look that word up. Then he said something sounding like 'enophile'. Is there such a word? I looked for that one too, but can't find it in my dictionary. Of course I've had my book for years and."

Mrs. Strater was still talking, but Chris's thoughts flew out of gear. Holy shit. Did Jack Strater actually find the answer for a non-porous plastic, then put all his notes in a tool box in his garage? No wonder nothing was ever found. The man must have really been weird. Had

Strater found an unbreakable bottle, suitable for storing wines, at one-tenth the weight of glass? That may be a wino's dream, but could definitely be some corporation's fortune. And that was just the start. How about a non-breathing, safe, inert, unbreakable storage container for hot chemicals? Maybe plastic weapons. Think what a group of terrorists could do with a gun like that? The list was endless. A replacement for glass? Hell. It could be a complete revolution!

Mrs. Strater was still talking. Chris interrupted, "I am sorry Mrs. Strater, but the phone faded for a short time. You were asking if I am a wine aficionado, an enophile?"

"It must be this thunderstorm we are having," Mrs. Strater said loudly. "It is raining cats and dogs, but we need it. Last rain we had was about two weeks ago. Anyway, Jason said you should see the papers, so I called—." A crash of thunder filled the phone. Chris's receiver went dead.

"Goddamnit." He hit the intercom button. "Betty!"

"Yes sir."

"Get that woman back on the phone!"

"Yes Sir!"

"Please," Chris added.

"That's the magic word, sir."

Chris walked to the window, looked out, seeing nothing. If Jason Blair was excited about what he saw, something needed to be done and fast. Funny how a man's name brings back memories. Without Jason Blair's help and encouragement he would probably still be working in that research department back in Pittsburgh, a fact he would never forget, but that was then. Today he had a more pressing problem, and now that his mind was focused, his memory of Jack Strater's accident came flooding back. The man had been in his garage on a Sunday morning when an explosion killed him instantly. It had been a terrible loss to the company. Strater was responsible for getting the jump on the liquor and soft drink plastic bottle craze, and that led directly to *Knutte* taking over the outfit.

From the sound of this latest information, the man obviously had been as unusual as everyone said, but now was not the time to get lost in rumors. He turned as Betty entered.

"Yes?"

"Some of the lines are down. I can get Charleston, but the operator says they are having trouble in different parts of the city. Mrs. Strater's phone sounded as if it was ringing, but she didn't answer." Betty looked at Chris. When he was tense, it was like looking at a animal, standing naked, waiting to spring. She caught her breath.

"Are you okay?" Chris moved toward her.

"What? Oh yes. I just had a catch in my throat. I am fine." She saw him relax. Damn! How dumb can a woman be? Get a terrific entry, then blow it. She deserved her stupid art classes.

"Good. You had me worried for a second. Perhaps you had better try calling the plant, if you are sure you're okay. See if you can get Walt Couser. He can be trusted."

"Trusted?"

Damn!. If a man could really kick himself, he would be flying through his own office window right now. "I meant someone I know, so I can discuss a private matter."

"Mrs. Strater must have been a friend of the family." Betty had the look of someone recognizing intrigue when they saw it, but not quick enough to hide the fact.

"Something like that."

"I will see if I can reach Mr. Couser." She left the office.

Chris sat and waited, his thoughts wandering. Why hadn't Jason Blair had Mrs. Strater call someone in Charleston? They would have been happy to run out to her house, and get whatever it was. As he remembered the story, Jack Strater may have used highly unusual methods of operation, but he was respected and well liked, and no one ever questioned his capabilities. Since the stories about his wine bottle still persisted was it possible there was a reason for the odd set of circumstances, or was he getting paranoid about all this cloak and dagger business?

Betty's voice came through the intercom. "I have them on the line. They are paging Mr. Couser. He was out in the service yard."

Chris picked up his phone and waited. Hopefully Mrs. Strater was not telling too many people about those papers.

"Walt Couser, here."

"Walt, this is Chris Braxton. Nothing important really. I am out here in L.A. and had some free time, so thought I would touch base. See if we had any mutual problems we might resolve before they turned into major events."

CHAPTER 14

"Hello?" Ethel Strater waited expectantly, then spoke a little louder into the telephone. "Hello?"

She removed the telephone from her ear and turned it from side to side as if looking might fix it. Perhaps she should tap it against the back of the chair, she thought, remembering. Jack would have said, "If it don't work, whack the damn thing." She smiled. Jack would have kicked Hoover Dam if it had quit working while they were there. She put the receiver back to her ear.

"Hello?"

She waited a moment then placed the phone back in the cradle. At least the phones don't go out as often as they did when we first moved here, she thought resignedly. Don't feel nearly as solid, but they do seem to work better. Maybe there is a place for plastic in this crazy world. Jack always seemed to think so.

A jagged bolt of lightning lit up the room as its sound crashed around the house. From years of experience in this same wood shingled house, Ethel knew the storm was directly overhead. Once she had suggested they move, but Jack claimed if it was good enough to raise the kids in, it was good enough to stay in. She walked over to the window and pulled back the lace curtain. Good, a patch of sky showed through the dark swirling clouds to the west.

Ethel looked around the room. Strange how a place can be so empty after so much love, joy, and just plain fun of living go into it. Even the sound of the storm did not penetrate the hollow feeling. The cool damp emptiness had nothing to do with weather.

While she had been talking to Mr. Braxton on the phone the place had been alive and warm. The house had that old sense of impending activity, so natural when Jack was alive. Perhaps it is inevitable for one in every couple to end up this way, she philosophized, but it sure as the dickens did not lessen the pain. What she missed most was the unexpected. Jack was a real kick in the behind. He may have been different, but he was never dull.

Mr. Braxton had sounded so nice. It was a shame the phone went dead, then again, it did give her something to look forward to. Now she had an excuse to call back. She slipped on her boots, buttoned her raincoat, snugged the belt around her waist, picked up her umbrella, and walked out the front door. The drumming rain on her umbrella drowned the sound of her telephone as she concentrated on the front porch steps.

Ethel was an attractive woman, softly rounded, sixty-seven, with white short hair neatly combed to frame the gentle features of her face. As she trudged up the hill, holding the umbrella against the rain, she thought of the phone call. Wait till she told the girls. Now they would believe her. Last time they acted as if she were making up the story. Even Patrick Riley sounded kind of funny when she called and told him about making her first call. Well, now he (Should she refer to him as Christopher?) had actually called her. Let's see now, how could she dress up the story? Just a little, mind you, her face held the trace of a whimsical smile. Little old ladies did not tell fibs. What was that word again, aficionado? Maybe she and Jack were a little strange, but that was not a word they had ever needed.

She was turning into Molly Brock's entrance gate when she stopped. She had forgotten the salad, and hers was the only one. "I'll swan," she exclaimed aloud. Well, there was only one thing to do. She turned. "I guess Jack was right," she mumbled. "Give me two things to do, and I will forget one of them."

Liz Hoskinson arrived as Ethel started walking away. "You are headed the wrong way, Ethel."

"Tell Molly I will be right back," Ethel called over her shoulder, "I forgot the salad. Only be a few minutes. It's all made, just have to get it out of the refrigerator." She hurried along the sidewalk.

"All right, but take your time, dear. Don't slip and fall."

Ethel was glad she had worn the rubber boots. She really should put rubber mats on those front steps. The girls were right. Everyone was getting a little wobbly. She hung the open umbrella on the arm of the swing, unlocked the front door, and walked in.

From the entrance hall, Ethel saw the papers scattered over the living room floor. How did—? She hurried through the double doors. A window must have broken. There was a soft rustle behind her. A blinding red light flashed through her eyes. She felt herself falling forward. A searing pain stabbed her brain, then nothing.

The man dressed in a gas company uniform stepped out onto the back porch of Ethel's house. He turned as if finishing a conversation with someone inside, then walked to the edge of the porch, took the time to frown at the rain, hunched his shoulders, hurried along the walk to the rear gate, and hurried down the alley.

CHAPTER 15

"Where you planning to go with the Land Cruiser, Clanton, go mountain climbing?" The morning briefing at Kesterson headquarters was about to start. Sean O'Connor made the remark. The other four men laughed. Mrs. Hasting gave her usual quiet smile.

Clanton Darnel also smiled. He did feel a little foolish. "Well, kinda. Thought I would drive up along that stream over on the west side, the one with the cabins."

Sean looked surprised, and not particularly pleased. "Why up there? That part of the project hasn't been used in years. I thought, Fish and Game, quit stocking it over a year ago, even before I ever got here. At least, that's what I thought."

"You're right about that, Sean, but the area came up in a discussion when Christopher Braxton was here, and I thought I would check it out. Don't worry, I won't put any scratches on your vehicle."

Sean looked resigned. "That fellow from L.A., huh? Well, if that's where you gotta go, you oughta have four wheel drive, that's for sure."

Clanton drove out of the parking compound and turned south. Last week he had started at Five Points and checked the south end of the area. Today he would start at Mendota, near the bend in the San Joaquin River and work north. Sean's questioning did not bother him. The man was an excellent mechanic and actually had complained less than expected, considering his own late request for the Land Cruiser. Four wheel drive could easily prove to be a necessity on this trip. Probably hadn't been anybody around those cabins in months.

Since Chris Braxton's visit, Clanton had been thinking about the inspections he had been making and was not too pleased with some of his thoughts. More and more he was doing little more than noting the water level was receding, as normal, taking his normal soil and water samples which he checked and always found normal, then was sending his normal reports to the normal agencies with the normal endorsements. Having fallen into that routine, he readily accepted the normal findings published in the normal reports reenforcing the normal belief that selenium is the causative agent for the major part of their problem."

Maybe it was the interest Christopher Braxton had displayed that had rekindled his desire to find something new. Regardless, it was a welcome change to meet someone with opinions not set in concrete, even though they probably should be. Clanton shrugged. So what if it is a waste of time? Cynthia and the boys were up in Sacramento shopping for school clothes. The timing was perfect.

$$*\qquad\qquad *\qquad\qquad *$$

Sean O'Connor was steamed. "I get everything set so I can make a name for myself, and some nosey sonofabitch starts backtracking and double checking," he ranted to himself. "Now Darnel is starting to act like some fucking big shot. If he gets too goddamned nosey, I'll have to take him out. That sneaky Braxton guy ought to have his balls stuck in a vise."

Sean's job included all phases of maintenance supervision, automotive, building, landscape, and general repair, a job requiring a wide range of capabilities. He was qualified. His knowledge was as sharp and wide spread as his temper.

Other than black hair, there was little about Sean's appearance to suggest his Irish lineage. He was medium height, on the thin side and had plain facial features that would dissolve into any crowd. If the occasion demanded, he could talk as if he left the "Old Sod" this morning, but the same was true of Paris, London, Rome, or Brooklyn. Language was as much a specialty for him as explosives. He tossed his suitcase in the back of the Jeep Cherokee as he passed it, then continued towards the headquarters building. *The Eagle's* caution to "never let the intensity of your feelings get the upper hand" popped in his mind. Hell, he knew what he was doing and it was a crisis he could handle.

"Yes ma'am, I'll probably be gone most of the day. I have to be a goin' up towards Sacramento to get a transmission part for the big truck, that's for certain. So I might as well be gettin' everything I need while there." Just a tad of brogue, it always seemed to soften the old bitch. "But I still wish Mr. Darnel had not taken the Land Rover, though it will be okay."

"Oh, what do you mean?" Mrs. Hasting asked. There was something disquieting about Sean, nothing she could pin-point, but something resembling a hidden sulkiness he worked to contain. She had no complaints on his work, that was superior. Sometimes it even seemed a little too perfect. People with his temperament were not usually so conscientious. "You would not let him take an unsafe vehicle, surely?"

"Oh, no. Of course not, ma'am. It was just a day overdue for an inspection. He'll be all right, and he'll be needin' it for where he'll be a goin' today."

Sean was happy. He had planted the seed. These people would never know where the hell he was going. Even if they did check, he could furnish sales slips, parts, and mileage records to establish any story he needed.

*   *   *

A short distance before coming to the stream where he planned to turn off, Clanton Darnel pulled into a small grove of trees. He finished his lunch, returned the thermos to his lunch box and leaned back against one of the tree trunks. A gentle breeze brushed his face. If he was lucky, he could stay in this area when he retired. Maybe even come back to this very spot and take the nap he didn't have time for today. He reluctantly stood up, took a leisurely stretch and started up the Land Cruiser.

The dirt road followed the edge of the stream bed, except where trees or undergrowth caused it to leave the bank for a short distance. Over on the far side of Interstate 5 he could see the ground gently rise as it neared the mountains. Again, he began feeling a little foolish at what probably would be a waste of time, but he would go as far as the cabins, if only to see how they held up in this mild climate. Back east, they would fall apart in no time.

The backwater pools in the wandering stream surprised him. Many had doubled in size during the rainy season. Rushing water had cut deep into the soft dirt on the outer edges of the bends. After passing several, he decided to stop and take samples as he went along. Not that contamination can flow upstream, he thought with a grin, but he would keep an open mind.

The first cabin was a mess. Most of the roof had collapsed, the door hung loosely on one hinge and some of the side boards were missing. Probably taken by people looking for easy fire wood, he decided. He drove past without stopping. The second cabin should be in better shape. It was farther upstream, farther off the beaten path.

The ground rose as he entered the foot hills, the trees and underbrush more concentrated. Nature was obviously reclaiming the land faster in this area. His short detours became more numerous. His resolve was again about to dissipate when the cabin appeared in a grove of trees around the next bend.

He pulled into a small clearing behind the cabin. A few tire tracks were still visible in the heavy grass, but nothing that looked recent.

The front door stood open

"Hello, anyone here?" There was no answer. He had expected none

A heavy wooden table and two chairs sat in the center of the room. On the back wall, a wooden shelf held a few cans of food. There was no other furniture, not even a bed. That someone had been inside was obvious, but whoever it was must have driven down from the high side and had much the same reaction he was getting and left. The place was not a top notch vacation spot. He decided to make a quick check of the area and leave.

The path to the stream led through a band of heavy brush and trees. Pushing back the overhanging branches, he stepped into a small clearing. Two of the three wide boards on the table top had been pulled loose and the small fire pit had been purposely destroyed. Even here, vandals were doing their work, he thought grimly. The sight was disgusting. But there was a good side to the scene. The tree covered seclusion reminded him of the Peekskill Mountains where his dad had taken him when he was young. He did not remember catching many fish but he sure remembered the trips.

He walked over to the stream. The memory of screaming loudly as he jumped into his childhood stream hit him as if it were yesterday. Underneath an overhanging bush he noticed a submerged bottle in a shallow spot. The glass glistened in a shaft of sunlight. Maybe it was the urge to at least feel the water. He picked up the small bottle and dropped it in a plastic bag. Probably some type of insect repellent, he decided, but at least he had something tangible to show for his effort.

Not more than a hundred feet upstream Sean O'Connor wore a camouflage jacket, faded green fatigue trousers, and sat perfectly still between two trees in a thicket of bushes. He had chosen his concealment well, observing every move Clanton Darnel made, yet undetectable himself. Like an animal in hiding, he sat absolutely motionless.

It was not until Clanton picked up the bottle and put it in his satchel that Sean moved. He moved fast, quietly, and with precision. Circling to his right until the cabin hid him, he dashed to Clanton's car, no indecision in his movements. Quickly, he unbuttoned the wide breast pocket of his jacket and removed a round flat object about four inches in diameter. It had an adhesive backing covered with a plastic film that, when removed, would activate the adhesive. No normal force would break the seal once it was pressed against an object.

On the top side of the device was a small digital timer. Next to the dial were two small knobs, one for the timer, the other to activate the detonator for the plastic explosive when the timer returned to zero. He set the timer.

Glancing toward the cabin to be certain he was still alone, he took a similar device from his right breast pocket, set the timer and slid under the car. He pulled off the plastic covers, pressed a disk against each gas tank, twisted both actuator knobs and quickly disappeared into the trees.

Clanton Darnel walked back to the cabin, sat on the door stoop and looked around. The old frontiersman really didn't have much of a life, he thought idly. Some even started families in cabins not much larger than this. He chuckled to himself. There obviously were advantages to progress. He looked at his watch. The day was still moving at its regular rate. He should do the same.

The return trip was much easier. His tire tracks eliminated the jockeying back and forth that was necessary on the way up. At the first of the backwash pools that he had skipped on the trip up, he parked. He would take one last sample.

Clanton had walked about thirty feet toward the stream when the Land Rover exploded in a huge ball of fire. The force of the explosion knocked Clanton more than six feet into a patch of scrub brush along the stream's bank.

Clanton did not move.

The pillar of black smoke could be seen for miles, clearly visible from the freeway. A trucker, traveling south, saw the smoke. No one burned a field this time of year. Even so, that was not a field burning, that he knew. He had driven this highway too many times. The smoke was black, had to be oil of some type. He picked up his CB microphone, called the highway patrol. Somebody had a problem, a major one.

CHAPTER 16

Dahlia Pauley stood behind the kitchen bar in the apartment she was renting, the telephone conveniently located on the counter top. "Yes…Yes, I'll tell him. He is here now, if you…Oh?…Very well, if I don't hear from you I will check." She hung up the phone and picked up the two cups of coffee she was pouring when it rang. "That was Jay Gilbert," she said, walking around the sofa.

"From your conversation I thought it might be."

Chris had set up this evening meeting with Dahlia on the pretext she might find something important for a trip he felt would prove damned little. He had also suggested his background on the shortages at Charleston might aid her in solving that particular problem when she visited the plant. Another reason, one he did not bring up to Dahlia, was his gnawing worry about Mrs. Strater not answering his telephone calls. It did not make sense. He had called several times since the thunderstorm broke off their conversation. Dahlia's pending visit would be the perfect way to get that paper, regardless of what was in it. An additional reason? Since he and Dahlia first met, she had been constantly on his mind. It was a feeling he needed to resolve.

"And what did Jay have to offer this late in the evening?" Chris asked. He had not arrived until after dinner, agreeing with Dahlia that they should maintain a low profile. She felt an open display of friendship in the face of that damnable audit would not appear reasonable. He usually did not let such things interfere with his personal life, but with rumors in the company already at an excessive level, her thoughts did make sense.

Chris leaned forward and sipped his coffee. A good wine would have been better, a little alcohol might work wonders on that wall of reserve she seemed determined to maintain.

"A man at Kesterson was injured," Dahlia said. "It apparently happened this afternoon, when the car he was driving blew up. Jay said it could be fatal."

A note of disbelief entered Chris's voice. "Blew up?"

"That is what Jay said, and he sounded rather upset. Do you remember a Clanton Darnel?"

"Sure, very well. In fact, he is the one who took me around the area after our meeting that morning. Nice man. Had a wife and two kids. But how the devil—? Cars don't just blow up. I imagine Jay did think it strange." Chris frowned in thought. "And how did he find out so fast? I thought he was back East."

"Who knows? He is constantly on the move." She too, seemed to be pondering. "But I don't think that is why he was upset."

"That is the second time you have used that word," Chris said, "and looking at me rather strangely when you say it. Are you trying to tell me something? Not having heard Jay's remarks, I must have missed some inference in yours." He set his cup on the table. It was not worth drinking anyway, lukewarm and weak. "If so, let's get it out." He smiled. "If you've got something on that chest of yours, let's get it off, to use the vernacular." He was pleased with his manipulation of subjects.

Dahlia smiled absently, seemingly occupied with more serious thoughts.

"At one point Jay did sound as if he may be concerned about something you might have said, or done. I told him you were here, you probably heard that part, but he said there was no need to interrupt any further. Said he would have a complete report by morning, and if anything really important turned up he would call. However, he did mention that he had told you he did not want you taking direct action, and if you did see something significant, you were to just tell me." She paused, her expression questioning. "You didn't...do anything, did you?" She was trying to be diplomatic, but how else could she say it? It would have been better if Jay Gilbert had not called. Who needed business at this time of the night? Most evenings of conversation in a relaxed atmosphere normally presented numerous possibilities, and she felt restless. Chris should ask for a drink.

To Chris, Dahlia's last question was a block buster. So that is why the one-sided conversation had sounded so damned puzzling. Well, if every bad turn in this escapade was going to be his fault, they could take the entire plan and stuff it.

"Let's back up a minute." he said, an edge was developing in his voice, his eyes showing his irritation. "What do you two take me for?" He stood up, walked across the room, turned back. "Of course I didn't do anything, except talk. You can't talk without saying something, but our specifics were damned few. I am as sorry as anyone that Clanton Darnel was injured. Probably more so than your Mr. Gilbert. In fact, I doubt Jay even heard of him until this happened, but damned if I am going to feel responsible. I have been in enough screwed up messes where I was directly involved without taking the blame for some mickey mouse charade the CIA wants to pursue."

Dahlia sat back, surprised at Chris's reaction. "You must have misinterpreted something I said. There were no accusations. Jay was just concerned."

"I believe you used the word, upset. At first, I thought it was just a woman's way of expressing herself, but twice? Jay has seen as much of this type thing as I have, probably a lot more, and you don't get uptight over one incident, especially when you don't even know the man. Unless you think somebody," he paused, withholding the first expression to cross his mind, "made a mistake."

Chris regained his composure and walked back to the sofa, chagrined. To lose his temper when he had heard only half the conversation was not using mature judgement.

But now, Dahlia's face had assumed a more fixed look, her smile had faded with his comment about women's use of words. The look she had learned while defending herself against five older brothers was now set firmly into place. "You must admit," she said quietly, "he has a right to worry. He did organize this project, you know, and to use that expression you had in mind, if it gets fucked up, he is the one who ends up sucking hind teat." She stopped and tried to smile decorously, realizing she had done the same as Chris, lost her temper. "That last expression was from an old farm girl." Damn, now the evening was really screwed up.

Chris had to smile. "I know. Don't forget, I am also from a small town." He was unable to resist a glance downward, wondering which could be considered hind. They both looked fantastic.

"Jay simply requested you think about your talk with Mr. Darnel," Dahlia added, hoping to get things settled down. "He sounded like he also felt there was nothing accidental about the whole thing. In fact, he said much the same as you, about cars not just blowing up." She could see Chris was not especially pleased with the explanation but he did seem more at ease. This was the first time she had noticed his solid arms. And he had strong hands, farmer's hands, good, strong, man's hands.

"You are right," Chris said. "I guess I did overreact, but let me assure you, Clanton Darnel and I met, talked casually, talked business, and I left. I'll think about it, but neither of us made any noteworthy comments. When I left, I felt as if the trip had been mostly a waste of time, and I'd be willing to bet he did not feel he had accomplished a lot, either."

Having made his point, Chris felt better, but there was one more topic he had to discuss: those papers in Mrs. Strater's possession. Being irritated with Jay was one thing, ensuring Dahlia understood the importance of contacting Mrs. Strater was another distinct consideration.

The conversation became more relaxed as he gave his run down on Jack Strater, but the friendly banter of two people enjoying a casual evening had been lost. Worse yet, Chris had the faint suspicion the problem rested with himself, yet the way she had quickly sided with Jay in that phone conversation made that damned wall of reserve of her's look like a fortress.

The door shut harder than he had intended, though it made little difference. Nothing about the evening seemed to have gone right. The more he thought about it, the more irate he became. Not with Dahlia, even when she was angry there was something soft and feminine about her, but with Jay.

If Jay felt I did something wrong, Chris fumed, why the hell didn't he talk to me, not relay it through her. He continued walking. Dahlia may have left out something, but from what he heard from the one-sided phone conversation he was the fall guy

Chris failed to notice the dampness in the night, or the wind whipping across his face. Temper and libido were fighting his normal dependable logic. Everyone may have a right to an opinion, but damn it, Jay was wrong, at least wrong in the way he handled tonight. And it sure screwed up the evening. Chris stopped momentarily as he was about to leave the project. He looked back at the walkway leading through the court. God, but she had a soft sexy body, and that perfume was something else. Forget it. Go home. Take a good shower. Sleep it off. He turned and started briskly down the lonesome looking, dirty gray colored, crummy looking, damned sidewalk.

His car was parked around the corner, and he had considered himself lucky to find a place that close. When he first arrived, he had circled the block twice before seeing a long antiquated car working its way out of a tight parking space. He had stopped and waited patiently; but by the time he was able to park, traffic was jammed up for a block, and tempers were flaring. The whole night was screwed up. Crowded damned city. Parking should be a primary consideration in a large complex, but builders don't give a damn. Build it, sell it, take the money and run. They got theirs. Screw everybody else. He glanced at his wristwatch. It was after midnight, a miserable, sticky, clammy night. Normal people were home in bed; where he would be in about half an hour, by himself.

Jagged bolts of lightning split the sky into flickering sectors of eerie white. Crashes of thunder slammed against the surrounding buildings, the overlapping, repetitive sounds finally catching his attention. Stupid ass! He knew exactly what was coming. The world paused while the echoing sound of thunder rolled into dead silence. There were no warning drops, only the momentary void of time holding its breath, then the sky broke loose.

It was a downpour, a damned monsoon. In NAM, he could have thrown on his poncho. But here? Civilian life was for the stupid-assed bird brains. He turned back in a dead run.

If he could have run twice as fast he would have been half as wet, he reasoned as he slammed into the wall of the narrow alcove at Dahlia's front door. He tried to squeeze under the narrow overhang. The difference between here and the back porch of his parent's house flashed in his mind. As a kid, he used to hunch up on the swing and watch the rain. If the wind blew the rain in on him, he would slide off the swing, go inside the warm kitchen and watch his mother cook. The flash of memory was warming, but just as quickly left him more miserable and uncomfortable

This was so damned stupid, he fumed. The driving rain was soaking the bottom half of his trousers, and his seventy-five dollar deerskin oxfords felt like warm slush. He flipped around, his chest against the wall. He leaned across the front door and jabbed at the door bell. There must be some excuse for his having run back instead of going on to his car. Screw it. He raised his fist to bang for attention when the door opened.

"My God." Dahlia laughed as she peered through the narrow opening. Chris did not appreciate the laugh.

Dahlia unhooked the safety chain. "Come in. You're an absolute mess".

Chris slipped inside and quickly shut the door. "It's a damned downpour." He stamped his feet disgustedly. Dahlia had yet to fasten her robe. Noting his glance, she flared the sheer material to wrap it neatly around her flat stomach. Chris's eyes caught a flash of the dark softness below and the firm underneath side of her breasts. Her eyes had lost the firm resolve he had witnessed earlier.

"I heard it all start. That was some clap of thunder. Your car must be a long way off," Dahlia tied the belt in a neat bow, her nipples pressing provocatively through the soft cloth. "Let's see if we can find a way to get you out of those wet clothes," she added softly. "Maybe you better mix yourself a drink."

Chris was vaguely trying to remember why he was so deeply committed to whatever his point of view had been in their discussion earlier. Viewing Dahlia in the soft, shear robe had created a reaction in a personal location. Hopefully it did not show, but she sure was proving he was correct in his first evaluation of her. This tiger was in complete control. He walked into the small kitchen, looked in the cabinet over the sink, found two glasses.

In the middle of the night as he lay back exhausted, he almost laughed aloud. He had ignored Bart's philosophy about what to do when the unexpected presents itself: "Grab your left nut and hang on, save something of value."

He looked at Dahlia's nude body. She even slept gracefully, somehow gently, on her back, her firm breasts moving with her deep full steady breathing. Tired as he was, he could not help remembering the nights in NAM when he had longed for such a view. For tonight though, he had completely ignored Bart's advise. He had used up everything. He slipped both hands under his head and watched, trying to preserve the view. That she was not leaving for Charleston for more than a week had been a surprise, but an excellent plan from his point of view. Her original suggestion that they meet in seclusion was even a better idea. What could be more perfect? A smile crossed his face, but within seconds he had joined her in her relaxation.

"Ready for breakfast?" Dahlia was sitting on the edge of the bed, a thin blouse hanging loosely over her shoulders.

Chris still lay on his back, uncovered; but somebody had been busy. He glanced down. His morning erection had a yellow ribbon with a big bow tied around it. "What the hell?" The erection collapsed as he rolled over and grabbed Dahlia.

"Aw," Dahlia exclaimed with a pout. "It was so pretty!"

Chris roared with laughter. "Where did you get that idea?" The ribbon no longer supported a mighty weapon.

"I overheard my brother, Tom, telling about going to a party that way. He went as a present."

Chris was still smiling. "It must have been one hell of a party."

"It was his girl friend's birthday. Two other couples were there, and the girls didn't act like they thought it was funny." Dahlia rolled over, straddled his stomach and sat back. "I thought the idea was hilarious. I couldn't wait to try it, but I needed a helper". She smiled, looking down at him. Her eyes softened. "It was fun, exciting. Wow!"

"Glad I could be of help," he said, gently circling her nipples with his index fingers. The warmth of her body pressed against his stomach. Her moistness jumbled his thoughts concerning the time and carefulness involved in her task with the ribbon. His erection returned. A throbbing hollowness rose inside him. "Come down here," he said in mock sternness, "I've got a present for you."

CHAPTER 17

The Boeing 707, carrying *The Eagle* had departed Stockholm in the small hours of the night and followed a standard departure to the heavily traveled Great Circle Route over the northern tip of Ireland, Iceland, and Newfoundland. Final destination for the nonstop flight was Los Angeles, California

The flight covered ten time zones.

Knowing most difficulties with Jet Lag came from ignoring the clock time change, Carl Eagleman preferred to accept the problem as a physical limitation, and had planned accordingly. He had used the extended hours of darkness for sleep.

Now, in the dimly lit interior of the passenger cabin, he awakened quietly, leaned close to the window and in the soft gray light of dawn watched the northeastern coastline of Newfoundland move slowly into view. The sight of tiny lines of white caps moving quietly against the rocky shore reminded him of standing on Sweden's rugged shore with similar waves crashing before him. The remembrance sent a frosty chill up his spine.

But the thought was fleeting, he had more serious and pressing considerations. Foremost was Sean O'Connor's error in eliminating a harmless engineer at the Kesterson complex in California. That had been a serious mistake. He, personally, had emphasized to Sean that such blatant action in such an open society would attract wide public attention. A more subtle solution would have better served the team's objective. That Sean's performance had otherwise been flawless, altered nothing. Mistakes that could effect the outcome of the team's mission could not be ignored

Carl left his seat and walked back along the semi-dark aisle, side-stepping the extended legs and dangling arms of passengers still asleep. In the men's room he splashed cold water on his face, enjoying the expected fresh surge of energy. Without doubt, cool water was one of the world's most overlooked luxuries. He leaned forward toward the small mirror and pulled his chin to one side to check. Not even a blemish. True, the muscles were still tight, but as Doctor Eschadero, had explained, "Return of control will be gradual, Mr. Albernito (Carl had used Mexican credentials during the operation in San Diego), the body needs time to adjust when removing old scars." The doctor had been correct. The process seemed inordinately slow, but feeling was coming back. Only the occasional itching bothered him.

Returning to his seat, Carl opened his briefcase. The paper he was preparing on Castro's interference in the tactical operation of the camp in Cuba needed final review before he released it. In his opinion, Castro was a nuisance, but Carl wanted to insure his findings were supported by facts. Libya and Iraq had already agreed the camp should be closed, but the Russians were still suggesting Castro be humored. The divergence was the cause for his report, and he knew that too adamant a stand would reduce its effectiveness. He needed to convince the Russians an existing facility in North Korean could easily accept the increased workload with minimum disruption, and at a considerable savings in funds. He had the facts, but the wording must be such that the Russians could act as if they had instigated the idea. It was a ruse he had used successfully more than once.

As a representative of Sweden's largest furniture company *La Royale Serene Ltd.*, Carl deemed his appearance at the World Trade Show a necessity. Though the company was one of his properties, the shares spread between two holding companies their subsidiaries and a closely held syndicate, he preferred a public position where his involvement would remain unnoticed. As for the Trade Show, Olga Largenson would handle the details with her usual expertise.

The stewardess began working her way down the aisle with a coffee and juice cart. He slipped the sheaf of papers back in his brief case. No use starting then being interrupted

While waiting, Carl let his thoughts drift back to when he first left his Kurdish friends in the mountains of Iraq. So long ago, he reflected, amused at the simplicity of life as he saw it then.

Wandering around the city of Tehran had been as exciting as it was frustrating in his search for vengeance. After almost three months he was referred to an aged man who reportedly controlled the illicit commerce of the city with an iron hand.

"You must not be so anxious, young man," the old man said. "I have listened to reports of your comments, and of your impatient search, but life demands we take sufficient time to enjoy it. Drink your coffee slowly. Perhaps, the world has reason to call your type *The Young Radicals*. Why must you be so irate?"

"You were misinformed, sir. I am not irate," Carl said firmly. "Also, I am not a Young Radical."

"Oh?"

"I am going to avenge my parents's deaths, and kill those men that killed the man who saved my life. With all due respect, sir, that is not being irate. It is a fact."

"I see. And just what else do you intend to do?"

"I sense you mock me. Please do not. All I know, now, is that those who are in authority are so corrupt they should be removed. We should not have to evade the laws of a country in order to exist. What can I do? I do not know, yet, but I will learn."

The old man's eyes read Carl's intensity. He saw a young man with a mission that may well turn into a rampage unless given a semblance of controlled behavior. He also read traits that could prove invaluable to his own needs. "There are ways, young man. Let us continue our discussion."

Within weeks Carl was enrolled in a training program in South Yemen commanded by an officer in the Russian Army, Major Aleksandr Chernykov.

After completing the extensive course, Carl was asked to remain as an instructor. He gladly accepted. He felt he missed some important details the first time through the course.

When Major Chernykov completed his assignment and was returned to Moscow, he suggested Carl move forward also. During the years that followed, their mutual respect had grown into the solid relationship that existed today.

Carl hoped his friend enjoyed the numbered account in Baghdad. Russian pay was so blatantly insufficient for the nicer things in life, and he readily agreed that Russian support had been a vital part of his career.

Ransom, kidnaping, bank robbery, and hi-jacking had provided him with funds in the early days, but it was Kadaffi, the KGB, and Iraq that had enabled him to eventually establish his financial independence, Kadaffi being even more generous than the Russians. Helping the Bulgarians get their operation *Kintex* operating efficiently had also proved a profitable decision.

Had people been in a position to judge, Carl had one trait that would have been considered acceptable in any society. He had a driving thirst for knowledge, and worked diligently to improve it. During the early years, he even gave up lucrative financial opportunities to complete academic courses he considered necessary to his education. His many alias's and changes of academic institutions, precluded any formal degrees, but his innate intelligence, manifest enthusiasm, and obvious knowledge when interviewed by professors, plus an expertise in forging academic records, enabled him to attend most courses of his choice.

The end result was an education honed to the specifics of his desires: Business, Finance, Technology, and International Relations.

Thinking of his early days reminded Carl of the CIA's first report on *The New Terrorist Movement*. The CIA report had clearly told of how groups in the new movement were banding together to establish training camps, sanctuaries, safe houses, and safe passage routes between countries, even providing support services for arms, supplies, forged documents and cash laundering. Though the report was extremely accurate, most intelligence agencies seemed to consider the movement a fad, another experiment by irrational and unbalanced fanatics. Carl smiled inwardly, resistance to change is such a dependable trait. He used the knowledge often in his planning.

The thought of plans brought Carl back to his current project, a matter of increasing concern. Doctor Becheimer was still having difficulty. The doctor claimed the problem of selenium in the stagnate water was skewing his data, but a completion date for the tests was fast becoming a necessity. Carl reconsidered one of his prior decisions. Perhaps the degree of accuracy they were trying to establish was not necessary. Then again, difficulties should not be used to refute facts.

Another factor entwined in the overall events troubled Carl. That chemist in Charleston, who was supposedly on the verge of a major discovery, had been killed in an accident similar to the hypothetical situation he himself had presented during the team's training. And now the man's wife had been injured after reportedly finding a study that might relate to her husband's research. Was it chance that Jack Strater worked for the same firm as *Eagle 1* and *Eagle 2*? Maybe, but when similarities appear in manmade events, they often indicate a manmade tie in.

As for Sean O'Connor, O'Connor completely bungled that job, and he had been sent to replace the man eliminated last year for making remarks that could have alerted Jay Gilbert. Fortunately, the latest report indicated the injured man was in a coma and may never recover, but that had no bearing on O'Connor's actions. No, *Eagle* 4 must be removed.

"Coffee, sir?"

"Apple juice, please."

"A croissant, perhaps?" The stewardess spoke softly. Many were still slept.

"Just the juice, please. I will wait for breakfast."

The plane started its long, gradual descent. Carl closed his brief case. Another thirty minutes and he would be in the terminal. Unless Olga had some unexpected information concerning the operation in Mexico, he would quickly fulfill his obligations at the Anaheim Convention Center and leave. He would take a taxi to the corner of Sunset and Normandy. From there, a short walk would put him in Hollywood's Little Armenia, an area becoming more like the homeland each year. He must pay his respects to Sarah Pernelli.

To insure the Turkish police never discovered she was the one who gave him refuge during his escape from Turkey, he had moved her to the safety of the United States and provided for her. Never had she questioned his personal activities. Once when the local Armenian paper printed an article on *The Eagle*, she had looked at him strangely, but said nothing. Hopefully, she would continue to remain quiet. He honestly wanted her to lead a full comfortable life, and die naturally of old age.

The seat belt sign flashed on. The approach was being made from the west. He looked down at the Pacific, so peaceful from two thousand feet.

For him, actions had to be taken that were vital to his plan. There would be no peace.

CHAPTER 18

Chris walked toward the door, a broad smile on his face. This was going to be good. "Come in, Alex."

Chris had just learned the information Alexander forwarded to Marty Davis resulted in the corporation gaining final approval on their environmental impact study. For more than nine weeks it seemed that political driven committee in Sacramento changed the requirements for approval every damned time they met. Even unflappable Paul Kirkpatrick was getting annoyed. But Marty now had the approval, and in writing. The projected plant should be in production by next spring, giving *Knutte* a major advantage in the pesticide market, with a 59 per cent reduction in production costs alone.

Chris held out his hand. "Congratulations are definitely in order, Alex. We were beginning to wonder if it could be done." He motioned toward the chair. "Have a seat. God, but we had a time getting approval on those plans. Don't know how many times we provided the additional material that confounded committee wanted, then had to stand back and watch it all fall through a crack. Even Mr. Izon called about half an hour ago, offering congratulations. I explained it was your last minute input that did it. You did yourself proud, my friend. I'll tell you, it is sure a relief to get that project out of the way."

"I was glad I could help," Alexander said in the reserved manner Chris had come to expect. Alex seldom expressed emotion, either enthusiasm or dejection. "I was in Miss Koch's office when she was talking to Mr. Davis on the phone. I suggested I might have the information he needed. That I was correct is gratifying."

"Well, you certainly hit this one on the button," Chris exclaimed. Alex was always tense, but so what? If that was what it took to produce results, so be it. "Marty said every item he could possibly need, even material to cover the usual last minute requests they always threw in, was in the package. In fact, Marty was actually laughing when he called. He got a big kick out of explaining how he rattled off answers and tossed material on their desk until they finally relinquished. Sometimes I think that representative from the Bay Area had a personal vendetta stuck in his craw, but it is a dead issue now, except to save as a reference for the next time, naturally."

Alexander showed what Chris accepted as a smile. He was a tall, thin, young man with blonde wavy hair that was long but professionally groomed, blue-gray eyes, and a well shaped, almost feminine face. His hands were long and slender, unusually strong, as if he kept himself in top physical shape, but not to the point of striving for muscle bulk.

Chris had been impressed from his very first interview with Alexander. The man had an excellent background, was well traveled, educated in France, had outstanding references and flawless credentials, and had the type drive and attention to detail Chris liked.

"Are you able to get much flying in nowadays?" The trace of a smile on Alexander's face had reminded Chris of the phrase 'a little sugar goes a long way', and he thought if he brought up a side issue he might get Alex to loosen up.

"I don't get to fly as much as I would like," Alexander said, "but I am able to maintain proficiency. I fly every other weekend or so."

"Do you fly out of LAX?"

"Well, no. I keep my plane over on Torrance Municipal. They have all the facilities I need, and the rental fees are much less. Also the area is less crowded. But I usually go out of the local area anyway, so that part doesn't matter much."

Chris laughed. "I would think so. Even a non-flyer like me can see the sky around here must be unsafe for pleasure flying; and of course, the papers are constantly referring to the problem. Do you have preferences, or do you use the throw-a-dart-at-the-chart method, like Bart Haddox claims he does on occasion?"

"Well, as a matter of fact, I do have a preference," Alexander said. He did appear more relaxed. "I have a cabin that I lease, up in the San Luis Reservoir area."

"That's near Kesterson, isn't it? Near Los Banos, the town I recently visited."

Alexander hesitated. "Yes. Yes, it is." He seemed to withdraw into his shell again. "About ten or so miles to the east. In fact, I use the airport near Kesterson when I need an alternate. It has a published instrument approach, but I always try for Santa Nella. It is closer to my cabin, and the runway is four instead of three thousand, which actually makes little difference in my case, I guess."

Alexander nodded curtly to Betty as he left Chris's office. He was not happy. The next time he would keep things on a business level. His flying was his concern. He took the stairwell to the floor below and entered his office.

"Damn!" He was totally disgusted. He took pride in controlling his conversations, nudging issues with finesse or firmness when necessary, and producing the results he wanted, not being led into a goddamned subject that was nobody else's business. The age old technique of avoiding a question with a question, or the myriad other techniques he could have used had been ignored. He had flat screwed up.

"Son of a bitch!" He leaned back in his chair. The headache was returning. After going through all the troubles he had experienced to get to this point, he could not afford a mistake, not now. He must remain calm, firm, be like his mother.

*　　　　　*　　　　　*

Alexander had grown up as the only son of Theresa Blanchard of the Blanchard textile family from Massachusetts, who, after her husband's unexpected death, dropped her husband's name, entered politics, and immediately became as influential in politics as her business acumen had made her in the business world. Within a year she had wrangled an appointment as the American Consul to the city of Bordeaux, France. The new assignment fit her plans perfectly.

Alexander was not being nicely accepted by his peers in the private school he was attending here, in the United States. She knew why. The other children were jealous of his exceptional ability. Going to France for an extended stay was the perfect solution.

In France, Theresa reveled in the prestige, social responsibilities, and challenge of her new assignment. And when she was happy, Alexander was happy. He adored his mother. She could do no wrong. She was beautiful. She was perfect.

The years passed quickly.

After high school, Alexander attended the University of Paris, majoring in both law and business. But during the summer of the year he graduated, a calamitous event dramatically changed his life.

In the huge central square of Bordeaux, dissident forces were demonstrating against the government's policies in North Africa. The unusually large crowd was parading, and loudly proclaiming its differing political view, though reacting peacefully. The leaders were satisfied they had orchestrated the demonstration to gain maximum television coverage.

Madame le Consul Blanchard had just left her office. She was being driven by her chauffeur along a nearby side street. "It is a beautiful morning, Bernard, *tres magnifique, n'est-ce pas*? Let's stop and watch the demonstration for a moment, and enjoy the warmth of the sun."

"*Oui Madame Blanchard, si vous desirez, mais je pense que c'est tres dangereux.*" Then he added in his heavy French accent, "Please, be careful, madam. What you do, is not good." He pulled over and parked.

"I will be safe, Bernard. I will stand just outside the car, only a few minutes, it is such a nice day."

As she stood by the open door, there was a minor disturbance on the far side of the square. Left wing dissidents, milling along the curb, began a counter demonstration. The rumble of their taunts and jeers were at first barely audible, but the sounds rapidly swelled. A few rocks were thrown. Clubs suddenly appeared. A small group of parading marchers ran into the watching crowd to chase the jeering offenders. Within seconds a riot erupted. Someone fired three quick gun shots. The man had intended to fire harmlessly into the air, but in that moment of senseless madness, one of the wildly directed shots crossed the square. The bullet hit Theresa Blanchard in the left side of her upper back as she tried to duck into the safety of her car. The driver, seeing her slump forward, ran around the car, laid her limp body on the back seat, and sped toward the embassy. She was dead when he skidded to a stop in the courtyard.

"Come in, Alexander." Carlton Blaisdale, American Ambassador to France, had flown down from Paris, his smooth baritone voice projecting its usual sonorous tones as he stood behind the huge desk. He understood the art of using a voice as an instrument, and the mellifluous tones flowing from his rotund body bespoke his confidence in controlling the situation.

He watched Alexander enter through the stately doors of the embassy's main office, astonished at how the young man had suddenly changed. He had always thought of the boy as a teenager, energetic, always quite proper, mother's boy, most certainly never one to create procedural problems for his smooth running diplomatic program. But the boy was now a man, and from the look on his face, a man who had heard the afternoon news. Getting Alexander to accept the official government position might be more difficult than planned. In fact, considerable finesse and persuasion may be necessary.

Alexander had met the two other men on many occasions. They were Vice Consul Tom Langdon, and the French Prefect of Bordeaux, Monsieur Quash. They stood by the double doors leading out to the narrow balcony overlooking the entrance court.

"The news broadcasts are in error, Mr. Ambassador," Alexander exclaimed. "I am at a loss as to what could cause such a terrible mistake, but I assume you will see the news is corrected." His mother's death was being described as a massive heart attack. The sudden attack took her life instantly, eliminating any possible resuscitative techniques.

"That is the reason for this untimely meeting Alexander," the Ambassador answered smoothly. "We realize that explanations are in order, and the three of us hope to convince you of their importance, since the decisions were made at the highest levels of both governments. We hope you will accept the rationale of the decisions, even though the conflict with actual events may at first appear inappropriate."

"Decisions? Explanations?" Alexander said in disbelief. "I am talking about obvious, flagrant, unreasonable lies. Statements so far from the truth there is no possible way an explanation could apply. Somebody shot my mother, some crazy damn fanatic, and he is still running around loose. Who is doing anything about it? Apparently no one! Get the bastard!" Alexander looked at Monsieur Quash, and switched to French. "Don't just stand there. Find the man. Punish him!"

"*Je regrette monsieur, mais il y a une raison–.*" Monsieur Quash looked pensively at Ambassador Blaisdale, lifting his arms in despair, requesting support.

Alexander turned back toward the Ambassador. "A reason? What is this?" he asked incredulously.

"Please, Alexander, let me explain. I know it is difficult to understand," the Ambassador interrupted, "and worse yet, may be no less difficult to accept, even after you hear what we have to say, but please, hear me out. Shall we sit down?"

"I will stand," Alexander said flatly.

The next five minutes were a nightmare for Alexander. He listened to the story of the telephonic conference, supposedly including both presidents, and of the decision that political relations would be further jeopardized if added publicity indicated there was inadequate security for State Department Personnel.

The ambassador went on to explain how both governments were currently being subjected to criticism, to the point where public opinion suggested a deepening rift was developing between the two countries. Responsible government officials knew there was no validity to the allegations, but the condition did warrant recognition.

So it was decided, at the highest levels (The Ambassador kept reiterating the phrase) that the circumstances of his mother's death would be slightly altered. She would be returned home with the dignity and honor befitting a woman who had served her country in a truly outstanding manner. Her death would be attributed to a heart attack, a demoralizing blow to both nations. She would be buried with full military honors, and her name would be included on the plaque in the State Department honoring those individuals who had so faithfully served their country.

"That is undoubtedly the most ridiculous line of nonsense I have ever heard," Alexander said vehemently. "I refuse to accept your explanation, your reasoning, your philosophy, your news release, or any other damned thing you have in mind. You men know exactly what happened, and I will see to it that the entire world soon knows." He turned and strode toward the huge double doors. He pushed down on one of the ornate handles. The door was locked.

"Please, Alexander, hear me out. Try to accept my explanation without too much rancor. Your mother would have accepted what we are suggesting. The man who fired the shot is in custody and will be punished. The certificate of death, indicating a heart attack, has been signed and certified by both governments, and though I hesitate to be so pointedly honest, if you demand an open casket no physical violence will be evident. The memory of the true greatness of your mother will best be served by all of us accepting her passing with dignity and compassion. The glowing tributes she so richly deserves, will better serve her memory than any attempt to mar her outstanding dedication to her country."

Alexander slumped into a nearby chair. He was speechless, furious, his eyes filled with loathing.

Ambassador Blaisdale walked over, certain he knew how to handle the boy. The young man needed reassurance, interspersed with a modicum of sympathy. The hand of an old and trusted friend would be welcomed. He rested his hand on Alexander's shoulder.

"Get your filthy stinking hand off of me!" Alexander yelled. He jumped up and threw the Ambassador's arm from his shoulder. "Don't you ever touch me or come near me again. If I ever see you or any of these other bastards," he waved toward the two men in the room, "come near my mother or me, here, at the funeral, or any other place, I will personally inform the world of the true sonofabitches you actually are. You people and your weak-kneed governments are a damned embarrassment to society."

*   *   *

The recurring memory of that last meeting still plagued Alexander. Even tiny details, the gold watch chain strung across the gray vest covering the ambassador's fat paunch, the hair piece the ambassador used to camouflage his bald pate, the breast pocket handkerchief ridiculously arranged after being used to wipe a perspiring face, all were clear and vivid. Every microscopic detail of that entire episode held its permanent place in his mind.

He had hoped the fire he set at West-Pac's chemical plant in Rialto would appease his bitterness and frustration, perhaps lessen the traumatic tension headaches. The headaches remained, but two good things had happened. The huge conflagration did give him a sense of accomplishment, and it had been a clever way to arrange for a change in jobs as *The Eagle* had recommended.

The Eagle had suggested a change in work place might lessen his exposure as the one overtly active team member in their mission. He placed the capsules in the stream when *Eagle 2*, back in Charleston, determined it was time for another test run. That his solution had been a good one was obvious, even *The Eagle* thought the fire had been a fortuitous accident.

Looking back at the episode, Alexander was still satisfied. His answers to reporters, inspectors, and corporate executives had helped him leave the company with excellent recommendations. It was one of the few things he could think about that helped ease the throbbing in his head.

Now, if only *The Eagle* can pull off his plan, Alexander thought. Then those politicians in Washington will find out how stupid and self-centered they really are.

CHAPTER 19

Randy Blake sat at his desk, trying to concentrate on the paper before him with little success. Though no firm data on the Kesterson report had surfaced as yet, the team was doing a good job of bringing the details into focus. Several relationships were in evidence.

Chris should be satisfied. He would not be happy, but at least, satisfied. Sudden revelations seldom occur in any study of this magnitude. If answers were easy, they would have surfaced long ago, and they may have. To assume the problem could be anything other than a build up of selenium was difficult, but he kept reminding the team to keep an open mind. That they seemed to be doing so, was a tribute to their professionalism.

Randy tossed the paper in the "Hold" basket. Maybe it would make more sense later. He picked up the top folder in the "In" basket and sat back. It turned out to be the latest Personnel Roster. "Has to be true," he mumbled to himself, "everything works its way to the top, at least once." When was the last time he had read a personnel report? Of course, no one else reads them either, he thought with a shrug, except the person who prepares them and the guy interested in seeing his name in print.

He flipped through the pages.

On a page entitled, Charleston, was a picture of Jack Strater. Now, that is what I really call belated recognition, he reflected with a grimace. Why the devil did they bury the picture in a personnel report? If anyone deserved recognition, Jack Strater was certainly a top candidate. The man's feisty reputation was still alive among those who believed in freedom of research. Suddenly Randy's eyes widened. Who was that fellow standing beside him? Had to be Pat. No. It couldn't be!

Randy looked at the caption: Jack Strater. No mention of the second man seemed to be available. He checked closer. There it was, in the accompanying text: Patrick Riley, basic research.

Randy sat quietly. Well how about that? The picture was old. Had to be. How long had it been since Jack Strater—? Oh well, better late than never. He looked at the picture again. Pat was obviously as quiet and reclusive as he had been in college. At least, this was the first time he had seen Pat's name in any type of correspondence.

I wonder if Pat knows I am out here in California, Randy thought, reversing his train of thought. Probably does, he decided. Being a manager does give a person some notoriety, if only in the corporation, then again, maybe not. He almost chuckled aloud. Pat never used to read anything unless it was needed to solve an immediate classroom requirement. Maybe Pat didn't know.

Randy sat quietly, feeling somewhat chagrined. That he and Pat had not gotten together again after that first night was probably more his fault than Pat's, but at the time, the entire ordeal had been a shock, at least, for himself. He also remembered that for Pat to ignore the affair as if it had never happened had been upsetting, even if it was virtually a crime back then. Of course, he still had to be careful. He stood up and walked to the window.

Maybe he should arrange a trip back to Charleston, maybe run into Pat again, as if by accident.

CHAPTER 20

"We will know it when we are hemmed in by water," Jason Blair said. He and his wife were in their motor home, driving west on highway 90 in Montana.

In the bright morning sunlight the miles of wheat fields spread around them like a golden carpet.

"Then what?" Mary asked.

"How about a ferry ride to Vancouver? They say it's one of the prettiest cities anywhere."

"I would like to see Victoria," Mary said. "My baby sister says it's like a little London."

"Yes, I remember that. The map shows the ferries going to both places."

"Why don't we?"

Jason nodded. "Sounds good to me."

Jason and his wife had been traveling on highway 90 since leaving Cleveland, and Jason intended to remain on it until they arrived in Seattle. From there, it was anybody's guess, but they both agreed they might as well see it all while they were out this way. They probably would not be back. They seldom followed the same route twice.

After Jason and his wife left Ethel Strater's house, they had gone to Cleveland to visit Mary's relatives. From there they headed straight west, using 90 as a base route. The trip had been near perfect. The van performed as well as could be expected, Mary visited everyone and every place on her list, the weather was cooperating, and the AAA had proven flawless in their choice of recommended camp grounds.

The openness of this rich farm country was an enjoyable experience. Jason looked out across the acres and acres of rolling wheat fields. So much different than the mountains back in Ethel's area in Charleston, he reflected and i was nice that the girls in Ethel's bridge group took care of each other. He felt good about taking the time to stop and visit with her. True friendships should be continued.

"Now don't you go off on one of your daydreams," Mary exclaimed. "Pay attention to what you're doing. You have to be careful when you drive something this big." She was in the right front seat, a good three feet from her husband. The upholstered motor box between them made her feel as if she needed to raise her voice to be heard. To her, the thirty-one foot vehicle was as long as a football field, and just about as wide.

"Yes, dear," Jason said. He did have a tendency to let his thoughts wander, but driving was not supposed to be a traumatic function. There was no reason to constantly anticipate a crash. That was not what defensive driving meant.

"Now don't be sarcastic," Mary said.

"No dear." Why would she think that? After the breakfast she had made, how could he be sarcastic? He wondered if Ethel ever contacted Christopher.

From what he could piece together, from glancing through Jack's papers, Jack had pretty much had his formula tied down before his accident. The notes seemed to indicate a nonporous inert plastic that was tough as nails, but maybe he had read too much into Jack's scribbles. Deciphering complicated formulas without cross references was difficult enough without taking Jack's annoying habit of de-emphasizing every brilliant thought he ever had. It sure looked good though.

He smiled as he thought of how the first conversation between Ethel and Christopher must have sounded, if she ever called him, or more specifically, how it must have sounded to Christopher.

"What's so funny?" Mary asked, seeing the smile on his face.

"I was just thinking of how Ethel Strater talks."

Mary laughed. "She sure can talk a blue streak, can't she?"

"I was wondering whether she ever called Christopher. She may have called someone in the Charleston plant, instead."

"I am more than positive that she called your Mr. Braxton," Mary said without hesitating. "You were being very secretive and excited about whatever it was you saw."

"Well now, I will have to disagree with you on that. Sure, I was impressed with Jack's notes, and I thought Christopher should check them, but I was not being secretive or excited."

"Ha. Maybe not to someone who doesn't know you, honey, but to Ethel and me, you were about as subtle as one of those eighteen wheeled trucks that scare the daylight out of me. Even Ethel said you were the same as Jack in that regard. It is in your face, the way your eyes kind of dance, not your voice." She looked inquisitive. "What was it all about, anyway? You had me wondering too. I wasn't going to say anything, but you're the one who brought it up."

"It is a new type plastic Jack was working on, but I would just as soon not say any more until Christopher can check it out. May turn out to be nothing." He should have known she would suspect something. Maybe he was being too cautious in suggesting Ethel contact Christopher, but ever since that CIA agent asked about using Christopher for some type of classified work, he was not certain what to do. Why would they not use someone closer to Washington? It was good they placed so much faith in Christopher, but it made him wonder about the many other qualified men. Why the devil should they go all the way to California?

He had no idea whether or not the CIA contacted Christopher, but if they did, and then Ethel called him, he probably realized the request was unusual and protected the information. Christopher was pretty sharp. If the CIA had not called, Christopher may well think Ethel was just a little strange, a thought not too far off the mark, and ask her to call the Charleston plant. Probably would not make much difference though, either way.

Jason leaned back, placed his hands on the top of the steering wheel and stretched his fingers. The next rest stop was still thirty some miles ahead.

He had always felt there was something unusual about Jack's death. Jack followed routines. To assume Jack made a mistake and caused that explosion by some act of his own may be a natural assumption for someone who didn't know Jack, but it was not a correct assumption.

Jack was too methodical.

CHAPTER 21

Chris parked around the corner, off La Cienega Boulevard. It had been over a month since he and Larry had enjoyed an evening together. They always seemed to be too busy with meetings, deadlines, business trips, that kind of stuff. There seemingly was no end to it. An evening of casual conversation and generous libations would be fun, like it used to be, almost nightly. There was not much money then, but that situation had not changed. Every time he compared his desires with his income he was always a little short. The cool refrigerated air engulfed him when he opened one of the stained glass entrance doors.

"Hello stranger, you also look like you're in a good mood." Gus Delveckio stood in the foyer, overseeing the start of the evening activities. "I was beginning to think you had moved until Larry walked in a little while ago."

"Evening, Gus. You are right. It has been too long. Larry in the bar?"

"Where else? Said he was going to meet the evening head on."

Chris laughed. "It was a foolish question, wasn't it? Sounds like it may be awhile before we eat."

"I should only need about ten minutes after you decide, based on the way the evening is starting. If it stays this slow, I'll be in to join you. I need a refresher course from a couple of experts. My backhand is in the disaster zone again."

"You're on," Chris said with a laugh, "and you know we won't let our lack of knowledge interfere with our advice."

Larry was sitting at the bar, on the same stool he had occupied the afternoon Chris first met him. Consistency was one of Larry's strong points.

Chris glanced around the room. Most of the red leather bar stools were still empty, but those around the piano were crowded. The lineup reminded him of a flock of noisy birds on a barbed wire fence. The chairs around the tiny cocktail tables were also adequately filled. Maybe the dining room was slow, but the bar business did not look too shabby.

Larry, a slender Italian with curly black hair, dark eyes, and Roman nose on a craggy face, was eyeing the women with the Latin confidence he so often proved justified. To him, all women were beautiful, and worthy of his attention and affection. He was a true romantic. Chris shook his head. Yes, Larry was consistent, in romance as well as business.

Larry held up a long-stemmed martini glass in salute as he caught sight of Chris working his way through the tables. Larry's smile radiated pleasure. A girl watching at a nearby table smiled in reflex action, her eyes appreciative. Her date turned to check out the cause.

"I was afraid we were going to forget how to do this," Larry exclaimed as Chris drew close.

"If you don't quit working such horrible hours, we just might," Chris said with a laugh, sliding onto the next stool.

"Me? My fine wayward friend, you are the one who is charging off into the hinterlands. I practically had to threaten Betty, before she confessed where you have been hiding out. Vegas? Now that is what I call a horrendous work schedule." He clamped his hand on Chris's shoulder. "But it's good to see you, old buddy. How the hell have you been? Incidentally, Betty said that when I told you she told me where you had been, to tell you she told me not to tell you she told me when you ask me who told me. Something like that."

"Sounds like her. Have to admit things have been hectic, but you are right, it is good to get together again. This place is a stimulant in itself, like a security blanket." The bartender approached. Chris smiled, "Evening, Tommy."

"It's been awhile, Mr. Braxton, the usual?"

"Please."

"I was betting on it." Tommy placed a fluted champagne glass on the bar and skillfully filled it to the brim. "The Frigid Digit. May its short life prove beneficial." He stepped back, still holding the bottle prominently. He smiled wryly, announcing in mock sonorous tones, "Chilled, as always, to the demanding specifications of one of the world's three best unknown tennis players."

"You are a fine man, Tomas." Chris lifted the glass in appreciation of the recognition and smacked his lips. "Ah yes, here's to the House-of-Gus Chablis, a terrific vintage."

"Larry told me you were coming," Tommy said, laughing. "I am frosting up a bunch more glasses."

*　　　*　　　*

It had been a Saturday morning on a muggy summer day, when Chris first walked into Gus's bar. He had spent the first part of the morning in his apartment trying to convince himself his life was back on track. Then he had driven out to the beach, walked along the pier, picked up the stench of his Vietnamese experience from the kitchen areas of the mobbed food stands and immediately departed. He drove back into town, another miserable damned day was in the making.

Driving down restaurant row, the sign *Gus's Gastronome* caught his attention. The second line read *Live Life with Gusto*. In smaller print were the magic words *Lounge: from noon*. It was twelve-ten. The small side parking lot held one car. He parked alongside.

The bar was empty, except for the bartender and one man on a bar stool. The lone customer wore white tennis clothes with a white sweater draped over his shoulders, the sleeves wrapped across his chest, a half empty beer glass before him. Chris took a stool to the man's left. The situation almost demanded conversation

"I would hesitate to say this is one of your better days," the tennis player said, noting Chris's somber expression. "Of course, I do not profess to be an expert in such matters."

Chris smiled. The remark was obviously meant to be friendly, and to be honest about it, the guy was right. So far, the day had been less than satisfactory.

"That bad, huh?" The sigh was unintentional.

"Not any worse than some of mine, but I happen to be on a high today. Just won two out of three sets, for the first time I might add, from someone I have been trying to beat for months."

"Is he that good, or are you that bad?" Chris was pleased the conversation was light, and on his favorite sport.

"*She* is that good," the man said as if humbled by the explanation. "It was damned demoralizing, especially since she is the bartender's younger sister." He laughed and motioned behind the bar. "Meet Gus Delveckio, part time bartender, bouncer, concierge, waiter, butler, backup cook, and full time owner of *Gus's Gastronome*. Besides being another healthy and consequently horny Italian, he really believes in living life with gusto. That would be okay, I guess, if he hadn't taught Fellina to be so damned good at tennis. Other than being adamant about proclaiming every politician is on the take, he is a normal rational individual. Me? I am Larry Bertelli, hopefully a better lawyer than tennis player." He leaned forward and held out his hand.

The friendship between Chris and Larry proved a natural. Their friendship with Gus also flourished. All three were energetic, personable, satisfactorily successful, and tennis nuts. Gus was a few years older, but the difference disappeared when he stepped on the court.

*　　　　*　　　　*

"You look as if you're having troubles," Larry said as he watched Chris take a larger than normal sip of wine. "You are not letting that new CEO get to you, are you? I am still holding open the job of head subpoena peddler."

"Tonight, the idea does not sound as bad as the first time you mentioned it," Chris answered. "I will tell you one thing for sure, these last few weeks have been something else." He looked at Larry, leaning back and relaxed. The CIA's concern over trusting one's friends seemed preposterous. Hell, maybe he really was getting paranoid. How could a conversation in generalities with Larry create problems? "Let's move down toward the end of the bar, near the office," he said. "Gus said he would try to slip out and have a drink with us unless business suddenly picked up."

"Great. I'm looking forward to several."

Larry's enthusiasm and spontaneity were catching. Chris agreed that several would be fine. "Got a couple of off-the-wall things on my mind," he said as they settled on the new stools.

"You've got the floor; my attention, anyway."

"Nothing important. In fact, I feel kind of foolish even mentioning them, but we have been seeing each other so seldom lately. Anyway, I've been to a bunch of briefings on business related subjects lately." Chris paused. "Sounds dumb, doesn't it? Hells fire, what other kind do I ever attend? Anyway, some of the discussions pertained to details that I seldom pay attention to. Guess I should, but frankly, it has been the kind of crap I ignore when I see it in the paper or hear about it on the news. Besides, it never concerns me."

"Hey, this sounds serious, at least interestingly serious. What the devil you getting involved in?" Larry sat his glass on the bar

"No, now don't go making an issue out of it. Maybe I said it wrong." Chris raised his hand as if rejecting Larry's remark. "It is just that I was never interested, at least, previously. It is as if I created some kind of shield to keep it out of my mind."

"Well, old friend, let me tell you something. I haven't the foggiest idea what you are talking about, but when we first met, you were having some difficult days. Whatever it is you are considering, or are trying to say, maybe you had a right to put it aside. Try me. I'm terrific on other people's problems. It's my own that get all screwed up."

Chris relaxed. He would keep it casual. Besides, getting an opinion that was not the CIA approved line of patter could be refreshing. It might even put things in a more realistic perspective. "Have you ever heard of a fellow in Europe called *The Eagle*?" he asked.

Larry looked at Chris in disbelief, then almost exploded, but did keep his voice down, "Jesus Christ, Chris. What the hell are you mixed up in?"

"I am not mixed up in anything." Larry's reaction surprised him. "It's just that I heard the name used in a briefing, nothing important, not to me, anyway, but the man's name sure seemed to impress everybody else. Like I said, I had never even heard of him. The whole thing was disconcerting." Chris picked up his wine glass. Maybe discussing generalities was not so smart after all.

"Of course I know who *The Eagle* is," Larry said quietly, "or at least, who most concerned people think he is. I can give you a complete brief on him, damned few facts, but a lot of verbiage and guesses. So can the police, the CIA, the FBI, and most any of the foreign intelligence outfits."

Chris looked at Larry strangely. "Oh?"

"Hey now, wait just a frapin' minute. Don't give me that 'Oh' look of yours. Did you forget what I do for a living? Corporation law. Remember?" Larry glanced around, then said in an undertone, "And that sonofabitch is a corporation unto himself. That is the prevalent opinion at any rate. No one can find any trace of his business connections, but he has so many clandestine operations, and demands such outrageous fees, that those who should know, claim he's got a war chest in the multimillion category, minimum. Kadaffi supposedly gave him more than twenty million for just one operation, and not a penny of it made a ripple in any of the financial centers. It all just seems to disappear. How he launders it is a mystery, but he is obviously a master at doing it. He is a damned terrorist. There is no question about that, but one of a kind, and one who drives authorities crazy. No one has knowingly seen him, has a picture of him, or even an accurate description. That is a tidbit of what I have gleaned from my financial briefs, the corporate rumor mill and good old news print."

Larry looked over Chris's shoulder. Gus had just come out of his office door. "Pull up a stool and join us, Gus. Chris and I were just discussing *The Eagle*."

"That sonofabitch? You must be having some night."

"You know him too?" Chris asked incredulously.

"If you're an Italian, and have family back in the old country, it's the same as asking someone if they ever heard of Giangiacomo Feltrinelli."

"And just who the hell is he?" Chris asked.

"Not is, was. He was one of Italy's leading publishers, one of those fellows with more money than brains," Gus said. "He also wanted to be a terrorist, like *The Eagle*, but blew himself to smithereens while trying to destroy a communications tower. He was rich, but stupid, or careless; but look, I came out to tell you I just had a call from a party of twenty-six. Should be here in about half an hour, so if you don't want to get caught up in what sounds like an extemporaneous wedding party, you had better come in and order before they get here. I thought you might prefer to miss the rush, even if it does reduce your liquid hors d'oeuvres."

Chris pulled into his basement parking spot. For awhile, he had thought Larry was never going to get off the subject of *The Eagle*. Perhaps he should have listened a little more closely to the CIA's suggestions, but it still had been a good night. Always was when the two of them got together. He wondered what would have happened if they had stayed in the bar. They both seemed to be in the mood to tie one on. In fact, the double Drambuie Gus gave them to top off the meal almost got him started again. He stepped off the elevator and headed down the hall, his mind wandering into strange channels. How come Larry and Gus knew so much about terrorism. Could they—? The idea was ridiculous, but the idea did little to settle his mind. Also, Larry stopping in Charleston on his trip back east was just one more incident to jog the imagination.

The reason for the trip sounded logical enough, but it was strange how things all seemed to come at once. According to Larry, his law firm had an account with Union Carbide and he was to check on the perennial lawsuit concerning the tunnel through Gauley mountain below Hawks Nest.

Chris reached for his keys. If he had not visited the place when he was a kid he would have sworn Larry was making up the story.

As he remembered the story from his childhood, Union Carbide dug a tunnel through Gauley mountain to divert water to a hydroelectric generating station they were building. During construction, the rock in the tunnel was found to have a silica content of about ninety-nine percent. Hundreds died from the lung disease, silicosis. Though no one, the company, the contractor, or the state ever admitted liability, there were some large settlements made, and those involved were still sensitive to the issue. Larry claimed that if the same type thing happened today, it would get more coverage than the Bhopal disaster, but since it happened so long ago they could keep it under control.

Chris remembered how he stood near the edge of that towering cliff in the mountains of West Virginia, and looked down into what seemed a bottomless canyon. At that young age it would be normal not to notice anything as insignificant as a tunnel entrance, but he was fast becoming convinced there were a lot of things in life he never noticed. He walked into the kitchen and put a cup of water in the microwave, then poured himself a glass of Cabernet Sauvignon. The coffee could wait.

Chris felt a tinge of doubt creeping in his mind. Did he really have a handle on this whole affair? Sure he did. He and Larry may not have explored all the details of each other's background, but their years of companionship had to be proof of something. Also, Larry's explanation of being so well versed on *The Eagle* was also perfectly rational, and Gus's remarks were also logical. Like Gus said, "I still got family back there."

Chris picked up a magazine, set his glass on the end table and leaned back, the magazine remaining in his lap. One thing he knew for sure, neither Larry nor Gus knew anything about molecular structure. A more satisfied expression drifted across his face. Nor did they know that previously, selenium dioxide, a versatile oxidant for ketones, alkenes, and other compounds was the only selenium reagent in common use by organic chemists; or that shortly thereafter, a method to convert epoxides to allylic alcohols by using a selenium nucleophile was found. Chris chuckled to himself, "Wonder what they would have said if I had tossed that one into the conversation." The wine must be going to his head. He had a nice warm feeling.

He refilled his glass, slipped off his shoes and put his feet on the coffee table. Dahlia was really something else. What a woman! They had managed to continue going to work, but the first four days had left him exhausted. He smiled. Dahlia seemed stronger. The thought reminded him of his trip out to Ontario for a meeting with Randy Blake. The trip may not have produced startling revelations concerning the pollution problem, but it sure should have cleared the air on one point. His inference of his relationship with Dahlia had to have established he was being more than adequately cared for. At least, he hoped there would be no problems. Randy was too valuable an asset to lose. His work on this current project was a good example.

Although Randy had said he had found no specifics to refute the growing belief that selenium was the culprit, he claimed the possibility of selenium being introduced as a substrate, either a nucleophile or electrophile into some undetermined grouping, perhaps by increasing interstack molecular interactions to suppress other transitions, was getting most of his attention. So far it was all hypothesizing, and the checks were producing indeterminate results, but Randy felt he might be on to something. Chris had to agree. The idea was fascinating. New products are found everyday, a large number of them surfacing from the old tried and true WAG system. He held his wine glass to the light, and contemplated the deep red glow. The first man to make wine probably did it by making a wild-assed guess on what to do with left over grape juice. Now that was a good WAG.

But there was one thing about his meeting with Randy that still was troubling. When Randy learned Dahlia was flying to Charleston, he asked if he could go along on the flight. The request was logical, yet it did not seem right. Randy claimed he wanted to visit an aunt and uncle he had not seen in a long time. The explanation would not be unusual for most people, but Randy had said on many occasions he was not anybody's favorite cousin. Why then was he now trying to reestablish himself? Unless—, but how could the telephone conversation with Mrs. Strater have anything to do with it? The possibility of the events being connected was ridiculous. Had to be.

Naturally he had agreed on the trip. Randy had earned approval of any such reasonable request. When he asked Bart about open seats on Dahlia's flight, Bart had said, "If we have a full load, I'll log him on the manifest as a suitcase, and stick him under a seat."

CHAPTER 22

The small pickup truck stopped in the shade of a large eucalyptus tree beside the highway near the Kesterson headquarters complex. The driver took a notebook from his shirt pocket, perhaps checking that he had purchased everything he needed while in Los Banos. After a few minutes he slipped the notebook back in his pocket and continued north. At the intersection with route 140 he turned west, then stopped again by the north entrance to the Kesterson complex.

Near the wide wooden gate to the fenced-off area, was a four-by-six foot sign. It read:

KESTERSON NATIONAL WILDLIFE REFUGE

Jointly managed

U.S. Dept. of Interior's Bureau of Sport

Fisheries & Wildlife, & Bureau of Reclamation

Public Sanctuary is managed by Cal. Dept. of

Fish and Game

Foot Traffic only, Sunrise to Sunset

NO FISHING

That the area would be empty after sunset was of special interest to Carl. He drove the remaining five miles into Gustine. The first restaurant he came to looked good. It was.

While enjoying a country-style meal, including pork chops and oven hot biscuits, he read the local paper. Checking local events was always a pleasant way to pass time. Later, he would check the road to the gun club, make sure it was open, and verify that the back road through the duck ponds, as shown on the map by a dashed line, was navigable. He had all afternoon. *Eagle 4* would be working late, catching up on the time lost from constant questioning by the police.

Carl also liked to read the Help Wanted adds. The long lists of jobs available in a country with so many people, amazed him. But why did so many work so diligently to prove themselves, yet were so reluctant to follow instructions? He had seen it so many times, like Sean O'Connor, who supposedly had been trained to know better.

        *   *   *

Sean swung his feet up on the corner of his desk, and lit a cigarette. He took off his grease stained baseball cap, ran a hand through his black hair, and hooked the cap back on his head. It assumed its usual off center tilt with the bill flipped up, a habit developed to look up while bent over an engine. His boyish face held the satisfied look of someone pleased with himself. He leaned to his left, pulled a bottle of scotch from the bottom drawer. It had been a long day.

For the past few days, his planned off-hand remark to old lady Hasting about the inspection on Clanton Darnel's vehicle being overdue, had put him in the hot seat. More so than expected, but it made little difference. He had been queried by every officious bastard within miles, and each one of the fuckers had gone away empty handed. They kept asking the same stupid damned question. "Why did you imply the vehicle might be unsafe?" They kept asking it over and over. He chuckled. "Because I knew I was going to blow the fucker off the face of the earth," he bragged to himself. Why the hell couldn't at least one of those stupid idiots come up with another question? He poured another shot. How Americans could ruin the nectar of the gods with ice cubes, was unbelievable. He had learned to accept most of their idiotic customs, but watering down a good scotch was an inexcusable lack of culture.

The lighting around the automotive maintenance yard left a few confusing shadows on a night with no moon, but in this quiet rural area, that was no cause for concern. The common joke was, "When the crickets quit chirping, you can hear them walking through the bushes." Tonight was a perfect example, but even the crickets were not moving.

Sean had worked late as planned. "To catch up on my work," was the phrase he had used when *Eagle 3* called. He was not about to have this uproar over Clanton's accident cause him to get too far behind. The few things left to be done could easily be worked into tomorrow's schedule. He poured another shot.

Resting his elbows on the chair arms, he sipped his last drink slowly, secure in the knowledge his attempt on Darnel's life would never be detected. According to the last report the idiot was still on the critical list, still in a coma, and the longer he remained there the less chance he had for survival.

Every time Sean thought about that day, he became irritated. How was he to know the dumb bastard was going to get out of his car? The man could have been wasted on the spot, but he figured that waiting until the bloody meddler was away from the cabin, would increase the possibilities of it looking like an accident. The bottle the stupid idiot picked up, looked like one *Eagle 3* could have used. If so, forensic checks might have established some type connection. But what was so damned irritating, was the nosey bastard got out of his car. Who the hell could plan on that?

Sean set his empty glass on the desk. From all indications, the explosion was being charged off as an accident, so, even if the bastard did survive, what the hell? But the idea he may have made a better decision was sobering. In fact, even the thought that *The Eagle* may disapprove was chilling. He imagined he saw a shadow flash across the glass in the office door, then quickly regained his composure. Years of work with the Provisional Wing of the Irish Republican Army, and what he called his finishing school, working with *The Eagle*, had made him a professional.

The Eagle said to notice, evaluate, and react or ignore. Sean relaxed. His talk yesterday with Alexander Blanchard, or *Eagle 3* when they used their team designations, was the usual dull thing. Alexander was a quiet one, cold, calculating, not much reaction to anything. Christ, if the world went up in flames, that tall bastard probably would sit there and watch it burn, with that slow knowing smile crossing his skinny fucking face. To hell with it all. He decided on one more good belt, gulped it down in a satisfied swallow, and put the bottle away. He would sleep good tonight.

Sean glanced at his watch, surprised he had been sitting there the better part of an hour. No wonder he was getting sleepy. He shut off the light, locked the office, and walked over to the maintenance dock. The switch for the maintenance yard flood lights was on the near wall of the maintenance stall. He snapped it off. The perimeter lights for the four corners of the complex were on a timer. They would remain on until daybreak.

Sean walked back towards his car. He heard a soft rustle, started to spin. He was too slow.

Carl's left arm locked Sean's head. His right arm came around Sean's chest and flashed upward. The lightning swift movement drove the long thin blade into the soft tissue under Sean's chin, up to the dorsal cavity, penetrating the cerebrum. There was no feeling for Sean, only a blinding shaft of light in his brain. The light enfolded him, his muscles relaxed.

Carl released the handle and caught the body, leaving the blade in place to prevent the escape of blood. Holding Sean with his left arm, he hurriedly removed the keys from Sean's pocket, then placed him in a body bag before telltale marks could be made. He gently laid the bag on the hard surfaced driveway.

Slipping on a new pair of surgical gloves, Carl made a search of the office. Good, there was no incriminating evidence. He put a few drops of scotch on the outside of Sean's glass, waited until the drops reached the desk blotter, then set the bottle upright in the partially closed drawer. He locked the office and went to Sean's car. Placing the car keys under the mat on the driver's side, he stood back and surveyed the area. It was done. Only the apartment remained to be searched. He tossed the body bag lightly over his shoulder and disappeared into the black shadows behind the compound.

An hour later, a camper truck that was parked on the dry weather road on the back side of the project, started moving. It proceeded southward into Los Banos. It stopped in the north end of town near a large apartment house. A half hour later, it headed east on highway 152.

Carl looked at the odometer. Closer to Fresno, he would stop and reconnect the cable. When he turned in the vehicle, the mileage would agree with the distance of the trip he had discussed with the girl in the rental agency, an overnight stay in Sequoia National Park. Carl picked the canceled park entrance ticket with the proper date from the three he had prepared, and dropped it on the seat. He checked his watch. In Fresno he would park in the shopping center, sleep for a few hours, then pick up some cardboard boxes. The clothes and small appliances would go to the Catholic thrift shop near the shopping center, the suitcase and shoes to the Salvation Army collection container on the edge of the parking area. After turning in the camper, he would catch the commuter flight from Fresno Air Terminal, where *Eagle 3* had dropped him off the night before. In Los Angeles, he would put the empty body bag and stiletto in a plastic sack and drop it in the hotel trash. If anyone ever did unearth Sean O'Connor's body from that muddy swamp, decomposition would have removed any trace of foul play. He passed the city limit sign. Good. He was starting to tire. Fortunately, three to four hours sleep would sustain him.

From Los Angeles, he planned on taking a circuitous route to Charleston, West Virginia. He would check in with the doctor, or *Eagle 2*, and some good answers had better be forthcoming.

CHAPTER 23

The early morning sun had already heated the air in the Los Angeles basin, restarting yesterday's Santa Anna Winds.

Dahlia, Randy Blake, and five other passengers were walking toward the Corporation's Lear jet.

"You are planning to visit relatives?" Dahlia asked. The dry wind blew hot in her face.

"Yes," Randy answered. "I plan to visit my aunt and Uncle. They moved to Charleston three years ago, maybe a little more, but to be perfectly honest, I used them as an excuse more than anything else when I discussed the trip with Mr. Braxton. I really just wanted to get away for a few days. This consistently mild climate gets to me sometimes. It is so darned monotonous for someone brought up in Minnesota. There, you may find snow under your feet or maybe up to your elbows, but certainly not confined to the top of a picturesque mountain peak." He swung his suit coat over his shoulder. "I really am not very close to them. In fact, I may end up in a hotel and do nothing but read and relax, but I had some leave I had to either take or lose, so thought I would give this a try. Your friend Chris was a big help." He hoped the unintended reference to 'her' friend Chris had sounded casual. He had not intended to make it so personal.

"I am glad you could get away," Dahlia said, surprised by the involved answer to a casual question. She wasn't that interested, and what was this 'her friend' nonsense? Surely he couldn't be, she smirked inwardly, jealous. Preposterous. "Well, I can not think of any reason you should not go, especially since there are empty seats. The plane is going, regardless."

"That is what I was hoping when I first had the idea, and I guess it worked, at least, going this direction. Coming back could be a problem, but Bart said he can take up to ten, and the plane is seldom completely full. I didn't know there were degrees to the term, full."

To Dahlia, the flight, as always, was a thrill. Being released from the need to stand in lock-step to get on a commercial flight was a pleasure, and each time they taxied in after landing, her imagination of how the gleaming aircraft must look from the passenger lounge created an aura she found hard to ignore.

The flight went quickly. After landing, when they taxied in toward the Charleston terminal she watched out the window for the specific purpose of checking the surrounding mountains. When Chris drove her to the airport this morning, he told how the construction crews had to level the top of a mountain to find a flat spot big enough for the airport. Maybe so, but she felt he sometimes said some things just to impress her. He should relax. She had to admit though, acting normal was also difficult for her. She felt both supercharged and weak when near him, wanting to throw herself at him, yet feeling as if she were ready to collapse. Her normal calm mind turned into a muddled jumble of discombobulated gibberish. She forced herself back to reality. It was time to get organized.

As Chris promised, George Buchanan, the local plant manager had a driver waiting at the gate to take her to the Marriott. The hotel was supposed to be centrally located and have every service she could need. That is what Chris said. Then, just like a man, he had added that if he could join her they would switch to the Red Rover Inn, a place he preferred for its informality and ease of access.

"Why don't you ride in with me?" Dahlia asked as she and Randy walked through the concourse. "It should make things easier, regardless of where you decide to stay."

"Thanks anyway," Randy said, "but I will call from here. I told my uncle I would, and I really should stay with them, at least for the night. I don't see how I could do otherwise, but even if things don't work out, there is no problem. It is only three or four miles into the city." He wanted to be by himself, make his own plans. Besides, Dahlia had mentioned Chris might fly in, and the way she seemingly tried to cover up the remark puzzled him. Chris had not been subtle when he discussed her.

"I would not mind waiting while you make the call."

"No, really, you go ahead."

"As you wish," Dahlia said. "When will you be going back? I should be ready in three or four days. You mentioned you could use a ride."

"Yes, I would like that if it is possible. I can go most anytime, really."

"Give me a call, then. I will be at the Marriott, on Lee Street. I understand it is near the Civic Center. Let me know, and I will remind the home office you are here when I call to confirm my own schedule. Oh yes," She said a bit hesitantly, "if I move to another hotel, I will leave a message at the desk."

"Thanks. I'll be sure to check in with you, probably day after tomorrow. That okay?"

"Were your accommodations satisfactory?"

It was the next morning. Dahlia had just walked into George Buchanan's office.

"Very nice, thank you. The flowers were a thoughtful touch."

"Flowers?" Mr. Buchanan paused, then smiled. "Either the Marriott is seriously trying to improve its image, or you have a hidden admirer, and if you will permit a personal observation, a very discerning one."

Dahlia felt foolish. It had to be as she first thought. Chris sent them. But since there was no card, well, she would check again.

"What a charming way to explain it," she said. Her expression betrayed her embarrassment

Mr. Buchanan seemingly did not notice. "Thank you. Won't you sit down, please? We have been looking forward to your visit. Your reputation has preceded you. Hopefully we will be able to learn from your expertise. My old college professor used to say that good accounting provides the eyes and ears of management."

Dahlia smiled. "You sound as if you have a background in the field."

Mr. Buchanan laughed. "If you are referring to actual accounting procedures, I must confess my knowledge is limited. One course on Principles, Systems, and Concepts, plus one concentrated seminar on Management Accounting is the extent of any formal training. I admit I am fascinated with the rapid advancements in automated data processing, though. I was informed of your expertise in that area."

"It is true, electronic equipment has added a new dimension," Dahlia said, "but the basic input must still be entered by an individual, a fact some people tend to forget." She paused. "That could possibly be the cause of the confusion in your laboratory records," she added as if having considered the problem previously.

"Could be," Mr. Buchanan said. "Those people seem to enjoy operating on their own terms." The resigned look on his face expressed much more than his words.

"Perhaps you should integrate the research chemicals into the overall process, instead of leaving them under Operating Materials and Supplies. Then again, that could skew other cost factors." Dahlia smiled. "But from your expression, I would say we agree on one basic point. Research people never seem to be captivated with cost accounting details."

Mr. Buchanan laughed aloud. "That is certainly one way of describing it. What kind of a schedule did you have planned? I presume you would like to look around, see the plant, meet the staff?"

"Yes, all that, but first I must make a call if you don't mind. I need to set up one outside appointment. Mr. Braxton asked me to get some material for him, and I really should do it before I get too involved in the details here."

"Of course. Do you need privacy?"

"Oh no, there is no need for that. In fact, you may know the lady, a Mrs. Strater. I understand her husband, Jack, was a moving force in the success of the original company, back before it became part of *Knutte, Ancell & Ferrole.*"

"I doubt if you could find anyone around here who is not familiar with the name." Mr. Buchanan exclaimed. "He was an institution in his own right. Use the phone over there on the table by the window." He pointed. "While you do that, I will alert some of the staff."

Mr. Buchanan, and Dahlia, walked down the corridor. She was still upset, both with herself, and with Chris. To have left herself so wide open was her own foolish action, but for Chris to set her up as he did was hard to ignore. He may be loveable and strong and gentle, but he obviously had a few rough edges. When she went back to the room she would take that flower arrangement apart, piece by piece. If there was not a card down in there somewhere, he better have one awfully good explanation. One thing she knew, hotels seldom provide an arrangement that size. Still, flowers are a thoughtful way to express one's self, she thought warmly.

Whether the first stop was by coincidence or careful planning, Dahlia was not sure. The research department was a large open room with three long work benches filled with the normal Bunsen burners, test tubes, strange looking flasks, and lines of labeled bottles. Dahlia glanced around. There was a commonality in laboratories that detracted from the importance of the work involved. She always had a feeling that if someone picked up one of the rooms and shook it, when it settled down, it would look the same, and there still would be no logical pattern to it all.

"Miss Pauley, here is a young man I think you should meet," Mr. Buchanan said. "You said you were going to visit Mrs. Strater. Well, this young fellow was Jack's personal assistant, or as close as anyone ever came to filling the position. He is Patrick Riley. Mrs. Strater still calls him occasionally, so I guess he can't be all bad."

As Dahlia and Mr. Buchanan left the lab, and walked along the sidewalk leading to the main production facilities, Dahlia could not lose the feeling she had experienced when talking to Patrick Riley. He seemed ill at ease, or tense, or secretive, maybe even scared. The feeling may not have been justified, but it was there. She was reminded of her mother's remark, "The men in the family may out number us, but we have an inner sense." Her mother was a smart woman.

Dahlia drove back to the hotel for lunch. She had told Ethel Strater she would arrive no later than one-thirty, and she wanted to freshen up before going.

*   *   *

Pat Riley *was* upset. He tried to figure out this new development. Why was Ms. Pauley going out to see Mrs. Strater? Was it because of the break in and Mrs. Strater being sent to the hospital? Sure, the attack was a terrible thing, but did that rate a visit by someone from corporate headquarters, all the way from California?

Pat tried to remember what Mrs. Strater's exact words had been when she told him about calling Mr. Braxton. She never did say what they talked about. In fact, she had sounded sneaky about the whole affair. That is why he had mentioned it to Graig. It could only mean one thing. Mrs. Strater had found Mr. Strater's research papers, and it wouldn't surprise him if his own notes were with them somewhere.

Maybe Mrs. Strater did not know what she had, Pat thought. Then again, why else would she call all the way out to California? Another disturbing thought suddenly surfaced, maybe she did not trust him. Maybe he was purposely being left out of the picture. Well, more than one person can play that kind of game. The thought upset him. He would call her, soft soap her, get a few facts. He should be able to trick her into saying something. She was so naive. But there was something else, maybe even more important. Was Pauley's visit here specifically to check on the lab shortages? Why else would she stop here, first thing? He really needed to talk to Graig again. Lunch would be a good time.

* * *

Dahlia made a mental note as she drove out of the Marriot's underground garage, she needed to get on Washington Street to drive out to the Edgewood area. Has to be the older part of the city, she mused. The map showed the area was centrally located, had an Edgewood Country Club, an Edgewood Drive, and an Edgewood Acres. She smiled. Probably also had an Edgewood High School, and an Edgewood Bowling Alley.

"Come in Ms. Pauley. You did say Dahlia, didn't you? What a pretty name! I can see why your mother gave it to you. You're as pretty as the flower."

"Thank you," Dahlia said. She followed Mrs. Strater into the house. "But if I confessed my first name was Willawanette, would it destroy the illusion?"

Mrs. Strater's laugh filled the room, her eyes twinkled. Nothing could spoil her joy of having a new and exciting visit from a new and exciting acquaintance. "Oh, pshaw, dear. Don't let that worry you. We all have a cross to bear." She laughed again. "With a name like Ethel, you can only imagine what my middle one must be; but you will have to imagine. I will never tell. Here, sit here on the couch," she said, motioning toward the sofa. "I will get the tea. Now don't object. I know the timing is bad, but I have the chance so seldom. I will be right back."

Dahlia was shocked to learn of the circumstances surrounding the attack on Ethel, and of her stay in the hospital.

"Yes, it was nice of the girls to worry about me," Ethel said. "When I failed to return to the bridge game and didn't answer the phone, two of the girls came by to check up on me. I was awake, but still sitting in the middle of the floor when they arrived. Guess I figured I didn't have anywhere to go. Doctor Poindexter said being quiet was the best thing I could have done, even if my head was too hard to be hurt very bad; but he kept me in Kanawha Valley Memorial a few extra days. He claimed they needed the money. That is probably the reason Mr. Braxton could not reach me. I wasn't released until just before noon, Saturday."

"Do they know about this down at the plant?" Dahlia asked, incredulously.

"Oh, I suppose so," Ethel said. "I told Patrick. He is such a nice young man, but there was no reason to call anyone else. They are all so busy. Anyway, I am kind of stubborn when it comes to Jack's work. I will just stick by what my friend Jason Blair said to do, wait for Mr. Braxton to tell me what to do."

"I am certain Mr. Braxton would love to hear from you, Ethel. And I know he will be shocked to hear what happened. Let me get him on the phone. I will reverse the charges, and you can mention about my being here." Dahlia had been wondering how she might work into the real reason for her visit. This would make it easy.

"Oh, that would be fun. He sounds like such a sincere man."

At three-forty-five Dahlia drove back down the hill, and turned right on Washington Boulevard, toward the Dunbar bridge. If the map was accurate, she should be able to make a quick check at the lab, and arrange things for first thing in the morning. The problems they were having could not possibly be sustained for so long a time if they were really trying. Even bumbling chemists have to have a tolerance level

somewhere. Either that, or this group was extremely lax, or downright—
. Well, she should not pass judgement before she examined the evidence.

Dahlia had another reason for returning to the plant, though
reluctant to admit it. On the way back to her hotel, she would drive by
the Red Rover Inn and see what Chris found so interesting.

Dahlia was surprised at the extensive number of supplies and
chemicals in the laboratory. A quick check of the last inventory
indicated the possibility of many production type items being carried
that could more properly be charged off to other areas. There should be
little trouble in correcting the discrepancies. From the few brief
comments, it would also appear that the personnel maintaining the
supplies needed a short refresher course in basic fundamentals. A girl's
voice came over the intercom, "Ms. Pauley, you have a call on line four.
Ms. Pauley, line four, please."

"I am afraid our only phone is out in the main room," the technician
said. "We have been trying to get an extension, but so far have been
unsuccessful." He shrugged.

"That will be fine," Dahlia said. She walked out and picked up the
phone. "Hello?...I thought this might be you...Yes, I have it." She
laughed. "No. No difficulty at all. As usual, you were very
persuasive...Yes, I'll be careful...I will...Believe me, I will!" She laughed.
"With my life if necessary...Where?...You would never guess. She may
be old, but senility hasn't touched that woman. She is clever...Yes, she
had quite an experience...Day after tomorrow? Sounds great...Very
well. I will see you then." She hung up the phone.

Pat Riley was standing at the next work bench. He had tried not to be
obvious. Now he knew he was right. Every damned thing he had told
Graig was correct, down to the last comma. On top of that, she had the
papers in her possession. He needed to get in touch with Graig again.

Dahlia walked back to the supply room. The same feeling as when she was talking to Pat Riley this morning came over her again. Was her imagination getting the best of her? Was he just pretending to work while listening to her conversation? It had to be her imagination. What possible reason could he have for being interested in what she said?

CHAPTER 24

Dahlia Pauley's intuitive feeling about Patrick Riley's interest and concern was justified. The over protective nature of his father may have led to Pat's original misguided actions, but the end result was a series of naive mistakes exceeding anything Dahlia could have imagined.

When Pat was in college, his father soon learned Pat's Academic standing could produce difficulties in obtaining a prime job at graduation. Being a pragmatic man, as well as a State Assemblyman, he insured *Plastiko Inc., Knutte, Ancell & Ferrole's* predecessor, received his favorable attention whenever State approval was needed on a project. When Pat graduated from the University of Southern California, his application received quick approval from the company.

Pat had hoped for a job in southern California, but he knew his father would not understand his refusing the local assignment, and he quietly accepted the position. A secondary consideration was, he had received no other job offers. None-the-less, he resolved that after he developed an acceptable resume, and no longer felt obligated to his dad, he would head west. Nothing could match the golden female bodies on the golden sun drenched beaches of California.

Like most people at *Plastiko*, Pat soon noticed Jack Strater was a most unusual man. One morning over coffee, he voiced his thought to Dick Schooley, a fellow chemist.

"I know I'm the new kid on the block," he said with a smile, "but it sure seems Mr. Strater writes his own rules around here. Not that there is anything wrong with it," he added quickly, "I like the man, even if he is a little odd. And smart? He is fantastic. Makes me feel like I might do a lot better in another profession."

Dick laughed, "Didn't take you long, did it? You are right. He does do as he damned well pleases, and as you may have also noticed, Walt Couser really runs the place. Jack may be head honcho on paper, but without Walt, the routine work around here would fall flat on its face."

"The brass don't object?"

"Used to, but you can only bitch so long. Jack's insistence on following his own hunches, and working without restriction, including theirs, is just as strong as his dedication. Like you said, he is a brilliant man and they know it. You probably heard, he is the one who developed the first plastic soft drink and whiskey bottles. Being first was worth a fortune to the company and nothing impresses a board of directors more than a money making idea."

"Yeah, I heard."

"Incidentally, he seems to have taken a liking to you. He seldom, if ever, uses any of us in his work. We were surprised he started letting you help him. I would say that's quite a feather in your cap."

"Oh? Well! I didn't realize."

Dick's remark had pleased Pat. Maybe he was doing better than he thought. Sometimes he felt he was playing the part of a gopher, go for this and go for that. Yet in one area, he knew he was good, taking notes. Knowing he had a tendency to get confused, he had developed the habit early in college of writing everything down. After Dick's remark, he began attaching more importance to his good fortune. The complex formulas and intricate matrices were beyond him, but the pattern seemed to form a logical sequence

Pat's imagination began working overtime.

Maybe the inside office joke about the plastic wine bottle was true. Maybe he had been picked as a protege to help finish the project. The facts added reality. If he could get more involved, maybe he could show his dad the money spent on education was not wasted. Another thing, having Mr. Strater for a mentor could be a big step up the corporate ladder.

The more Pat thought about the idea of being a partner, the more intrigued he became. He even started keeping a separate set of notes. Not at work, but notes he would summarize when he returned to his apartment. Remembering the complicated procedures was difficult, but he was being fairly accurate.

He also noticed, the supply room personnel normally ignored the check out procedures when he picked up things for Mr. Strater. The idea of taking an added amount for his own use, crossed his mind. If he could experiment in his spare time, he may be able to offer a suggestion or two. A secondary idea soon developed. If he took a few chemicals back to his apartment, to use with his limited equipment and extra notes, it might work to the advantage of both of them.

A short time later, Pat met Graig Mersick, the Production Control officer for the corporation. The two immediately became friends. Both were bachelors, both thought hill-billy music should be stuffed back in those squeaky fiddles, both deplored the excessive number of Mondays and sad lack of Saturdays; and both wished there was some way to get to the World Series Play Off without the boring months of build up. It was a solid, friendly, comfortable, relationship.

Of the two, Pat was the more reserved. After a few cocktails, he could be outgoing and friendly, but normally he kept to himself rather than fight the social scene. As he told Graig: "At five six, and a hundred and thirty-five pounds, I don't expect to create a sensation when I walk in a room, but damnation, people could at least say hello, make an effort. I don't give a hoot whether they like me or not, but they could meet me half way. If not, screw 'em, who needs 'em?" He could talk that way to Graig. Graig was not the overbearing obnoxious type.

Graig, some fifteen years older, was also a bachelor who proclaimed enjoyment in the status as long as sexual abstinence was not a related requirement. He was just short of six feet, blonde, quiet without being retiring, and conservative in dress, though knowledgeable of the latest fads.

Though the two were different in character, Graig was forceful, firm, determined, outgoing, athletic, and sociable while Pat was quiet, reticent, shy, and anti-social, they meshed perfectly. They enjoyed their new friendship, spending much of their free time fishing and cruising on the Kanawha River in Graig's houseboat where Graig lived full time. The boat was a beauty. It was the type Pat had dreamed of owning since he was a kid.

One evening they pulled into Graig's dock space after a trip down river to the locks. Graig closed the fuel cocks to idle the lines dry while Pat poured two beers to toast the sunset. They met on the bow and leaned back in the canvas chairs to enjoy their evening ritual, listening for the sound of the sun when it set. To date, they had heard nothing, but the beer was always good. This evening was no exception.

There were no sounds. The birds were tired, the trees relaxed, the air humid, the Kanawha River clear and quiet. Graig's remarks had the inflection of an afterthought, an apology for an intrusion into the peacefulness, "I've had this idea about a method to purify water for a long time," he said hesitantly. "The compound would not only purify, but also could be used to neutralize some of these chemical spills we seem to be having with increased frequency." He paused as if reflecting. "I have not worked with the idea for a long time, but lately I've been thinking. Maybe you and I could play around with it. It would give us something to do. Could prove to be interesting."

"Sounds good." Pat chuckled. "Might prove a little difficult without a lab, though. The stuff I've got sure wouldn't hack it." He leaned back and crossed his feet over the front railing, then bolted upright as something jarred the dock hard enough to cause the boat to rock.

"Don't worry," Graig said. He listened to a roaring expletive about a Vodka and Tonic being lost as he walked over and stepped onto the still swaying dock. Pat watched him wave a greeting to someone behind them. He came back to his chair, smiling. "Comes down every month or so. Maintains his boat won't park right."

"I noticed the space was empty when we came in," Pat said. "Hope it was cheap vodka."

"Not for that man. Probably has it flown in from Russia. He is the one I was telling you about. His father bought up most of South Charleston when it was nothing but a railroad yard." The two sat quietly, smiling, listening to the loud remarks about 'a stupid damned barge'. A few bumps later the man apparently got his boat parked. The movement of the dock subsided.

"I know what I could do," Graig said as if pleased with a sudden thought. "You know the room I use for storage, next to the head? But I guess I keep it locked most of the time, don't I? Anyway, I could open that, clean out the junk, give the stuff to the Salvation Army, as I've been planning to do for months. We could use that space for a lab. It's not large, but big enough. We would definitely have one thing working for us. If something turns out wrong, we can flush away the mistake." They both laughed.

"You know," Graig continued, "Maybe we really should. I was more or less kidding when I started, but it is a good idea. And as I said, I have already done some work." He paused and chuckled again. "Like Jack Strater and his wine bottle, I guess. But hey, with your help, maybe we could get a winner. One thing for sure, if we did pull it off, the world would damned well know who we were. I think I'll fix up the room."

Pat liked the idea. A more extensive laboratory could also work to his advantage. But he was surprised at how fast the equipment was installed. The following week, Graig took the boat to Cincinnati. When he returned, everything was in place, almost as if the equipment had been there previously.

To partially off-set his feeling of inadequacy in providing so little to the enterprise, Pat began bringing in a few chemicals from work. When

Graig said nothing, he gradually added to their supplies until the practice became routine. Eventually, Pat even decided to share the notes he made from his work with Mr. Strater. Graig expressed surprise when he first saw them, but then laughingly agreed, saying, "Either we are stupid, or there are some missing links."

One evening as they sat on the bow, bundled up against approaching winter, but still enjoying their beer, Pat tried to sound casual. "I might have to stop picking up chemicals for awhile."

"Oh?"

"The other day Mr. Strater glanced at the charges against his account and he got all upset. He claimed the supply people were charging him with stuff he didn't use. Said he really didn't give a damn, but from the looks of the screwed up records, the front office might have a legitimate complaint. Said he would have to check it out one of these days."

"Well, if he is starting to talk that way, maybe you should," Graig said absently.

*   *   *

It was four-thirty in the morning, no moon. The lone individual on the sidewalk in the Edgewood section of Charleston stopped when he reached the street light. He turned slowly, looked back at the houses lining the darkened suburban street, then disappeared around the corner. A few minutes later the muffled sounds of an automobile leaving the area drifted across the predawn silence

An hour later, in the kitchen area of the two story house, a light appeared. It was the only light visible until Jack Strater tensed his body against the early morning chill, opened the rear hall door, and turned on the garage light. He used the garage door opener to raise the door about three feet, hurried to his yellow Chevy coupe, pumped the throttle to get a smooth idle, then hurried back to the kitchen. He knew he should have worn his coat. Ethel's remark would probably be correct one of these days. She kept saying, "Go ahead. Catch your death of cold, you stubborn old goat." But he could get out and back by the time he could put on a jacket and get it buttoned. And with Ethel still in bed and the coffee good and hot, the process simplified itself.

He was getting so damned close. In fact, the change he had jotted down last night may just be the answer, but there was no need to take the notes to the office. Once he wrote something down, he would not forget. There were advantages to a photographic memory. He would add the new powder to the mix as soon as he got to the plant. A more refined acrylonitrile derivative may be required, or a different valence, but other than that he should have it nailed. Jason Blair's remark came to his mind, "Tight as a damn drum." Jack smiled. His old friend would be happy for him

He slipped on his jacket and walked down the hall, hunkered up his shoulders in anticipation of the chill. 'Hound' (What else would a logical, practical man name a lanky, brown hound dog?) walked along beside him, but was smart enough to turn before the chilled blast of air came through the door.

The dog, as usual, trotted back to the den, to the heating register by the chair. The floor there was warmer, had a scent of friendship, closeness. He heard the muffled sound of the car door shut as he completed his final turn before curling up. The floor jumped up and hit him as his loud yelp, Ethel's scream, and the blast of the explosion filled the neighborhood.

The garage exploded in a ball of flame.

One neighbor said there was a loud boom, another said the noise made a big 'varoom' sound. All agreed the flash of light lit up the neighborhood. The fire department, responding within four and a half minutes, found the garage door against a tree across the street.

*   *   *

Pat Riley was devastated. He may have used Mr. Strater as a foil to sneak out chemicals, but he had grown fond of the man. A sense of guilt and emptiness overtook him, as if he may have somehow added to the cause of the accident.

Graig explained how activity would help ease Pat's sorrow, and suggested he look through Mr. Strater's notes. The search produced only one important fact, which Pat discussed with no one except Graig. The notes he had made for Mr. Strater during their afternoon sessions were missing. He could damned well recognize his own notes. The two quietly agreed to ignore the situation. For him to raise the issue, may start an investigation into the excessive chemicals Mr. Strater had supposedly used.

No longer could Pat walk out of the supply room without signing for supplies, but familiarity with the procedures made it easy to obtain the items he and Graig needed. He had planned to stop, but the availability was too simple to ignore. Taking a few extra grams, each time, over a period of days was not difficult. Soon he was again using the room as his main source of supply.

When *Knutte, Ancell & Ferrole* purchased *Plastiko Inc.* Graig Mersick's expertise was quickly recognized. He was assigned to reviewing production programs of *KAF* plants around the country, traveling even more, covering a much larger territory. That he seemed happiest when heading west was a feeling Pat readily understood. Pat began laying his own plans

He would use Graig's influence to get transferred to California, after he had time to properly set the stage. Damned if he was going to go all that distance, then end up on another mountain, or out in the desert. He checked through the personnel roster, looking for others who might help him. His eye caught the name, Randolph Blake: Manager, Research Laboratory, Ontario, California. "Well I'll be damned." There was a man he had known extremely well, unfortunately.

In his senior year, he and Randy had gone out on the town, drank excessively, and before the night was finished, had indulged in a raucous hour of homosexual activity. Much of the evening was vague in Pat's memory, but he was aware of the extent of their activity, and also was aware that Randy seemed reticent about continuing the friendship. From Pat's viewpoint that was fine. The episode was a stupid, irrational fiasco, one to be forgotten. He wanted no further part of that type activity, drunk, sober, sane, or insane.

Pat sat quietly, looking at the paper. No doubt Randy had earned his present position. He was smart, had a mind like a steel trap, was number three in their class, and used to brag about never forgetting a face or name. Remembering the last fact was sobering. That did not help his chances for a transfer, to that area anyway. Pat laughed to himself, "Unless the guy has turned gay and needs another lover."

Damned if he wanted a transfer that bad.

CHAPTER 25

Randy Blake's Uncle Edward did not like what he called a bunch of goddamned queers.

"Is it true that California is the land of fruit and nuts?" he asked, turning on to South Main. "I didn't want to mention it last night. Your Aunt Martha is such a prude." He laughed. "I don't think she even knows what those guys do to each other."

Randy felt his muscles tense, but answered evenly. "Never thought much about it. Why do you ask?"

"Don't try to kid me, Randy. You know what I'm talkin' about. All those queer sonofabitches in the movie business out there in Los Angeles, and that big gay community up in San Francisco. They are in the news all the time. The place must be loaded with 'em."

"Well, I guess those are two places where there are many such people, but then again, there are all different types of people everywhere."

"Yeah, but not that type and not that damned different. I would know those guys anywhere. Even seen one or two of 'em around here, swishin' back and forth, talkin' like a damn girl." He turned into a parking lot. "Here is the car rental place I mentioned. I'll wait while you go check. You don't have to leave, you know. You could stay with us at night. Be a lot cheaper than stayin' in some hotel."

"I know, and I do appreciate the offer, Uncle Edward. But since it's the company that suddenly decided they want me to work, they will foot the bill. Wouldn't be fair to you and Aunt Martha if I just dropped in at bed time. I'll be right back." He went in the office, returning in only a few minutes. "It is all taken care of, Uncle Edward. They had one, and I can drop it off at the airport when I leave."

Randy watched his uncle drive away. As expected, they had nothing of common interest to talk about last night except family history, and that had taken less than twenty minutes. They were nice, but one night was enough. He had told them the company decided to set up some last minute meetings when they learned he was coming to the area. He felt a little guilty about making up the story, but even worse about telling them the saved leave time would enable him to come back again soon.

Driving through the city, he noted the Marriott was centrally located, just as Dahlia said, but he did not want her looking over his shoulder. He would try to get in the Red Rover Inn. Chris always spoke highly of it. He was glad he had taken time to check his map. Using the bridge in Dunbar would give him a chance to drive through the city

From the bridge he glimpsed South Charleston jammed between the hills and the river bank. That he should drive past the plant suddenly seemed obvious. Not to run into Randy, that would be stupid, but to come this close and not even look, might be difficult to explain when he returned to California. There were Corporate personnel who could easily interpret it as a lack of interest in the company.

The plant was larger than he had expected. Maybe it was the sloping tile roofs on the one and two story brick buildings. Whatever it was, the place had that old permanent look, like those places back East. He laughed to himself. "Hell, that's where I am, for a Californian, anyhow."

The entrance had two wide sliding gates separated by a guard shack, apparently remaining open during the day. Probably all the time, he decided from his parked position about half way down the block. At least, the guard didn't appear interested in who entered or left. The man was obviously there for information not security.

After watching a few minutes, he drove slowly around the block. The plant filled the entire block. He made a second lap, marveling at the large parking areas and wide sidewalks behind the iron fence. Only in an older facility would they waste so much ground. Now they'd stick in a couple more buildings, or raze the place and build a complete new complex.

The idea of going in, perhaps even walking around the place, kept prodding his thoughts. But how would he explain his presence if Pat saw him? Thank God, he didn't really have to attend any meetings. He drove back to MacCorkle Avenue.

The Red Rover Inn did look like a nice place. He should have known. Chris never sold himself short. He pulled in and parked. At this time of day there were plenty of spaces. The overnight customers had departed, and it was too early for afternoon arrivals. He even had to wait for his room to be made up, so decided on a leisurely walk.

Again, Chris was right. The shops and restaurants were within walking distance. What a mind blowing experience for someone from California? Browsing in a drug store, he bought two Louis L'Amour westerns. Probably read them sometime before, he thought briefly, but they never went out of style. Provided nothing else changed, he would spend the day reading and relaxing, maybe drive by Pat's apartment tomorrow evening. Last night's visit, and his uncle's stupid comments this morning, had been enough strain. He needed to lay back and unwind, revitalize his courage. Now that he was here, he was not nearly as confident as when he first thought up the idea of a possible meeting with Pat.

CHAPTER 26

Greg Mersick was furious. Pat Riley was starting to lose all semblance of control. The idiot had made two damned frantic calls in one day. During the first, he had acted like a stupid school kid (German or American they were all the same), and during the second he was the typical overbearing American, talking without thinking, demanding without reason, and recommending without logic. That was not the worst of it. The fool had figured out why Mrs. Strater had called Christopher Braxton

Graig drove into the carport. Pat's frantic prattling had jarred memories of the day Ethel Strater was supposed to have played bridge. If she had not returned home, he would have that damned formula, and this entire mess would have been avoided. He should have let her fall on her face, would have served her right. He grasped for self control. Useless reminiscing wasted time, and Pat was his immediate concern. No telling what the idiot would come up with, now that he had guessed one thing right. Graig locked the car, then made his usual check for scratches and dents. There was comfort in sticking to a standard ritual. The car could use a wash job, but otherwise was okay. Next week he would have Garcia detail it, personally, inside and out. He glanced at his wristwatch, plenty of time. He still had ten minutes.

"Hi, Graig." The heavy set man in droopy gray sweats was jogging on the cinder track next to the walk. It was Glenn Trausper from one of the houses bordering the park. "Don't look so damned solemn," he wheezed. "We all have a bad day now and then."

Graig gave a halfhearted smile and raised a hand as if in no mood to argue. He opened his entrance gate, walked down the ramp, and paused by the utility pole, his senses back on edge. Yes, the telephone jack was connected. He stepped up on the boat deck and again checked his watch. He still had three minutes, time to review a few details.

Maybe Pat was raving needlessly about a lot of things but he was probably correct about one. Ms. Pauley must have Jack Strater's research papers. Why else would she drive out to the woman's home? That was a package he could put to good use.

At exactly five-thirteen he picked up the phone and dialed. After one ring he hung up. Thirty seconds later he dialed again, and again after one ring, hung up. He waited. Thirty seconds later his phone rang.

"Hello?"

"Is this Graig Mersick?"

"The one and only." Graig's voice sounded pleasant. "Are you free?" He was talking to *Eagle 1*, next in line to *The Eagle*.

"I'm the one."

Graig's voice lowered in bitterness. "Then maybe you can tell me what is going on with that crazy Pat Riley."

"I noticed he was nervous and upset, like something might be bothering him. What has happened? Did you talk to him?"

"Talk! He has already called twice today, the last time about an hour ago. Is he still around?"

"Calm down, now. I don't spend my time watching after him. I presume he is either home or on his way. You know his habits better than I. What seems to be his problem?"

Graig explained the two phone calls. Pat was worried about Ms. Pauley's auditing the supply account and he thought she had gone out to Jack Strater's house to pick up the man's old research papers about a nonporous plastic. "And of course you know, Pat and I have been working on a related idea."

"I was aware you were spending time on some project, but I never thought you considered it a major effort."

"Not a major effort, maybe." Graig did not want to sound as if he were slighting their basic mission. "But it sure would be a good thing to have. Could be worth a fortune."

"Perhaps, but you must be aware we are behind schedule in our own project. I hope your secondary project is not interfering."

"Of course not," Graig said. "But damn it, when you think she might have the answer in her possession it's a thought difficult to ignore."

"Perhaps, but let's get back to business. Why did you call?"

"I wanted to talk about Pat, and be sure you understand what he is doing. He is really hypertensive about Ms. Pauley's visit. If he were to accidentally figure out our true purpose, we may have to take action."

"I hope you were not foolish enough to tell him anything." *Eagle 1's* voice suddenly turned grim.

"Of course not. Do you think I'm some sort of klutz?"

"Klutz? You mean fool don't you?"

"I presume your remark was meant to correct my grammar," Graig said tersely, then finished the remark with a short laugh. He could not afford to upset *Eagle 1* with a side issue of his own making. "Forget that. I've had a rough day. I just wanted to let you know, Pat is not acting very stable."

"Do you think he needs to be removed?"

"No, not yet, anyway." The uneasy feeling in the back of his mind, that he should not have mentioned those papers would not disappear. "But I did want you to know the possibility exists. If he falls apart, and he has a damned good start, we may have to move fast."

"Well, he is your friend. Keep a close check on him. If he starts getting paranoid and making irresponsible accusations, we will decide then."

Graig opened the refrigerator, took out a beer, then put it aside, not today. Americans could gag on that stuff if they wanted, but there was no need to drink it when he was alone. He longed for a Munich everyday standard. Any of them beat this tasteless brew, if you wanted to call it brew. He would even take a Munich draft in one of those dumb glass boots the beer parlors used to trick tourists. Tourists always point the toe up. He took a wine glass from the refrigerator, poured a glass of Liebfraumilch. His thoughts turned to one of *The Eagle's* favorite comments: "Failure is never an alternative."

The thought brought up a good question. Had he let his search for Jack Strater's research papers create a problem? The idea that Pat or Mr. Braxton might obtain them with little or no effort was also disconcerting. Then again, if the papers were now to suddenly disappear, would *Eagle 1* now assume he had them? He should have never mentioned the papers to *Eagle 1*. But if he were going to be accused anyway, maybe now would be the time to act. The thoughts conflicted.

The thought of "when in doubt do something" also came to mind.

CHAPTER 27

At three o'clock in the morning Charleston was quiet. A street sweeper truck worked its way slowly along the curb on Lee Street. Three taxi drivers, chatting on the front fender of the middle vehicle, climbed in their cars and circled in the empty street to let the truck work its way past the Marriott Hotel

In the hotel lobby the cleaning crew had started work. The few guests coming through the entrance door walked directly to the elevator, most looking sorry for their excesses of the evening. Hopefully, bed would help.

The well dressed man in the dark suit stopped to glance at the headlines of a newspaper on the end table. His dark fedora may have sat lower than normal, but not enough to attract attention. Nor would anyone know he was the man dressed as a delivery man from the flower shop next door, who had stopped by the front desk earlier to get Ms. Pauley's room number. At the time, he had carried a large floral arrangement which he tossed in the hotel dumpster when he left through the employee entrance.

The man laid the newspaper back on the table, idly scanned the lobby, then entered an elevator. On the fourth floor, he held the door open as if waiting for someone to get on. Feigning surprise that no one entered, he checked the hallway. It was empty. He stepped forward, turned to his right, walked slowly, his hands in his pockets, his head slightly bowed as if lost in deep thought. On his hands a pair of skin-tone vinyl medical gloves provided the sensitivity and non-slip sureness for the task ahead.

Ms. Pauley's room was on the left side of the hall, the entrance door in an alcove near the end of the hall. Two entrance doors were in the small alcove, a feature designed to provide privacy for groups who wanted private, but interconnecting suites. An arrangement for illegal entry could not have been easier.

Of one thing, Graig Mersick was certain, there would be no mistakes tonight. One way or the other he would get that report. If he could get in, find the envelope and get out undetected, fine; but regardless, he would have it. There would be no bumbling old lady returning home to interrupt him this time. What he was doing may have no effect on what *The Eagle* expected of him, but it would certainly insure his fame after that project was completed, or perhaps called off. The delays to *The Eagle's* project may have been extensive, but that had always been a possibility. He thought of Pat Riley's ranting about developing an acceptable wine bottle. Who ever worried about that trivia? Think what plastic could do for weapons: light, rustproof, and unaffected by water. Armies would demand them. The possibilities were endless.

Dahlia rolled over, raised her head. She lay motionless, listening. She cracked her lips to breathe through her mouth, then realized her mistake, the change in sound could be a give-away. Even so, she knew better than to try to simulate the slow, deep breathing of sleep. That sound could not be mimicked. She lay quietly, listening.

The vision of her instructor in defense training flashed through her mind. He had been short, thin, like a steel wire, had a silly looking crew cut, and had strutted back and forth across the platform like a bantam rooster. At the time she had been amused.

*You will be scared....*He was right....*You will imagine all sorts of things....*Maybe he knew what he was talking about after all....*And though ninety-nine times out of a hundred most of the problem will be* *your imagination, don't forget, you are betting your life on the remaining one percent....* God, but it would be nice to be back in that auditorium.

Dahlia lay listening. There was nothing, only a feeling. Slowly she turned her head. Was that a shadow or an object in the dark by the dresser? She watched. Nothing moved. She waited. She could not be sure, but some of the tension started to leave her. The entire day she had been imagining things; first, Pat Riley, now this. Mom had said, "Women have a sense that men never understand." Whatever Mom had been referring to, was sure here tonight. She looked again at what could be a shadow against the wall. This was ridiculous. She reached for the light. There was a rustle beside her. The nearness and intensity caused the same shock of terror she had experienced as a little girl when she flushed a covey of quail from the tall grass behind the barn and ducked as they escaped around her. It was the last sound she would hear. A blinding light flashed through her brain.

CHAPTER 28

Who needed food? It may be lunch time, but what he needed was a drink. If that Pauley woman started digging too deep, things could get sticky real fast.

It was in the middle of the night, last night, when Pat suddenly woke and realized why Graig found it so easy to pass the whole thing off. Graig was not the one with his prick hanging out in the breeze. He, good old Patrick Riley, was the one who had been stealing the chemicals. Pat shut down his equipment and picked up his suit coat. As he walked toward the door, Dick Schooley came hurrying in.

"You better wait a minute."

The sound in Dick's voice caught everyone's attention. Dick continued on to the center of the room, leaned back against a work bench, took a deep breath, then exhaled as if regaining his composure. "You all know that Ms. Pauley, the woman who was here yesterday? You know, the pretty one who flew in from the coast." He turned toward Pat. "You know, the one you talked to yesterday morning. The one who came in here with Mr. Buchanan."

"Of course I know." Pat said. What was all this nonsense? "There was only one. So?"

"She is dead," Dick said. It was apparent he had difficulty accepting his own statement. He walked to the end of the bench, turned, walked back toward Pat. "You are so lucky you were out," he added as if searching for something to say. "They asked for you first, you know. My God, what a morning? Murdered. That is what she was. No doubt about it. Murdered." He talked to no one in particular. The words tumbled forth. "Hit on the head, then suffocated, with her own pillow. Like I said, there is just no doubt about it." He took his cup out of his drawer, walked over to the coffee pot, sat the cup on the table, then walked back without filling it.

No one moved. They stood quietly, looking at Dick, startled, staring. The supply technicians, watching through the glass partition, came out of their room. One started to speak, the other held up his hand.

Pat felt himself being pulled into the center of the conversation. God. Now what? Weren't things bad enough? "Me? Why me?" he exclaimed loudly. "No one said anything to me. Where was I? I didn't know anything about it. Murdered? Are you kidding? That'd be one damn big joke."

"Joke? Believe me, Pat. It is no joke." Dick's voice held an edge. "I have not been—."

"Okay. Let's settle down," Walt Couser said quietly. The thought pattern needed changed. He turned to Pat. "The rest of us knew I sent Dick to the hotel to check on Ms. Pauley. You were over in the main plant when word came down, I sent Dick in your place. Mr. Buchanan mentioned your name since you talked with her yesterday, but he didn't seem to really care who went. Nor did it seem important enough to mention when you returned. Guess the others felt the same." He turned back to Dick. "I was wondering why you were gone so long."

Dick explained what he knew about the tragedy. How he had convinced hotel security to check Dahlia's room after he learned she still had her room key with her and every attempt to locate her had proven unsuccessful. How they did find her around ten-thirty and all hell broke loose, and how it took him until now to get away from the police and all their questions. And that was after they knew he was the one who convinced the hotel people to look for her in the first place.

Pat Riley's thoughts began racing. What was happening? Yesterday the woman was a problem. Today she was dead. He may have worried about her being here, but he sure had not planned on her being dead, even if she did have the letter. Could someone else have overheard her phone call yesterday? It was stupid not to have looked around, but he had wanted to act as if he were busy minding his own business. Then again, anyone could have heard. There were extensions all over the building, and her call *was* announced over the intercom. Yes, it could have been anyone. The only other person he knew, who knew she picked up something from Mrs. Strater, was Graig. He knew that, because he told Graig himself. But Graig? But wait a minute.

Thoughts came rushing. Graig was also the one he told about Mrs. Strater calling Mr. Braxton. And that was before the break-in when Mrs. Strater was banged on the head. Come to think of it, he also told Graig about Mr. Strater's plan to check into the supply room problem, and that was just before Mr. Strater's accident. Coincidence? But Graig? Nah! Ridiculous.

Pat looked at the others. No one seemed to have anything to say. Death leaves so little room for conversation in its early moments. He turned toward the door. "I am going to lunch."

Pat pulled into the service station near the clover leaf, parked by the public phone, and dialed Graig's office. Incredulous! Graig was taking the day off! He had only one choice.

Pat looked through the large front window as he hopped onto the deck of Graig's houseboat. Through the partially opened drapes he could see Graig sitting at the table reading a letter.

Graig looked surprised as he opened the door. "I would say I was glad to see you, but why are you wasting a good lunch hour by driving down here?"

"I wasn't hungry, and we need to talk," Pat exclaimed. He noted the envelope in Graig's hand. "What are you reading?"

"What kind of question is that? Obviously it's a letter. What's your problem? Are you getting yourself worked up again? What is it? Ms. Pauley's accident?"

"You know about it?" Pat looked startled. "It only happened an hour or so ago. I thought you were here all morning."

"Is this some kind of game? Of course I know. I checked in with my office a little while ago. How else would I know? I am no damned mind reader. You better sit down. I thought after our talk last night, you might settle down. Keep it up, and you'll get around to where you start thinking you caused it."

Pat started to speak, then sat down. "Maybe you're right." He was not being very diplomatic, and Graig was not the type to be pushed around. "But it was not an accident. She was murdered."

"Oh?"

"You didn't know?"

"Of course not. Becky said she had just heard about it herself. We assumed it had to be an accident. What happened?"

Pat knew Graig was the unemotional type, but he had no idea the knowledge of a murder would bring so little reaction. The guy should show some emotion. Murders don't occur every damned day, at least, not around here. But when he stopped to consider everything, it all was perfectly logical. Perhaps he was over-reacting. He tried to force himself to relax, explain what he knew. The longer he talked, the better he felt.

As Pat talked, Graig made some sandwiches, and opened two cans of cola. He tossed a bag of potato chips beside the plate of sandwiches, and took a jar of pickles out of the refrigerator.

Graig stood in the door as Pat stepped off the boat onto the dock. "Let's meet at the Gigi tonight. Around seven? A few drinks might be a good attitude adjustment tonic for you. I would think your nerves could stand the pleasant shock."

Pat smiled. "Maybe you're right. See you about seven."

During the trip back to the lab, Pat found his thoughts again creating doubts. Graig should have let him look at that letter. Then again, who lets you read their mail? Maybe an advertisement, but not their personal mail. But it didn't look like a fancy advertising flyer. It looked like something he might have seen before.

CHAPTER 29

"Mr. Braxton?"

"Yes, Betty." Chris was in his office.

"I have Mr. Kirkpatrick on line three."

Chris leaned forward and punched the speaker button. "Yes, Paul. What can I do for you?"

"I need to see you, Chris. We have a problem."

"Be right there, sir."

Chris hurried through the front office. "Betty, I will be in Mr. Kirkpatrick's office." Paul's statement had not been a request.

Chris sat in the chair, stunned.

"I, well, I find it hard to believe. I just talked to her yesterday, in the afternoon. There was no indication of anything unusual. Certainly, not this. She sounded—." His voice broke. "Fine," he said quietly.

"It does seem unbelievable," Paul said. "And I am terribly sorry, Chris. I know you two were friends. George Buchanan said everyone back in Charleston is also in a state of shock. According to him, there was absolutely no indication. Dahlia had set up appointments, and apparently made arrangements for a normal day. He said he sent a Mr. Schooley to check on her, after she failed to come in and he couldn't contact her by phone. Apparently, after Schooley had the same results and noted her key was not in her box." he hesitated. "Do you want the details?"

"Absolutely."

"She received a blow to the left side of her head. Then apparently and quite needlessly, since the blow was sufficient to render her unconscious, she was suffocated. There was no evidence of a struggle or, of other possible actions. Robbery seems ruled out. Nothing was missing, her purse, money, watch, rings, necklaces, all seemed to be untouched. We both know who her real boss was, and I suppose being part of the CIA does generate increased danger, but I am at a loss to see how, especially in this case. There doesn't seem to be the slightest reason, at least nothing obvious."

"Was the CIA notified?" Chris asked.

"I don't know, but I assume so."

Chris's face muscles tensed, his eyes narrowed. Frustration surged through him. Much the same as in NAM, but in NAM he could take out his frustration in physical activity. It may often have been useless activity, but it was action, a physical release. "Like you once said, Paul, assume, is spelled, ass…u…me."

Paul Kirkpatrick said nothing. The friendship must have been closer than he realized.

When Chris walked back through his outer office, Betty started to remind him of his four o'clock conference, then said nothing. She finished the line she was typing, turned back to her desk, reached for her shorthand notebook.

"Betty?" Chris pressed the button on his intercom.

"Yes sir?"

"Get me on the first flight to Charleston. Charleston, West Virginia. Arrange for a car to run me by my condo on the way to the airport. Book me into the Red Rover Inn, in my old room if possible, and let me know when it's set up, please."

"Yes sir. When will you be ready to go?"

"Now. Oh yes, I am buying my own ticket. You have my card number, and call Personnel, have them put me on emergency leave for a few days."

"Understand." She laid her notebook on the desk. The conference became a secondary thought. Either Mr. Blanchard could take it, or it would be delayed. Those details could be approached after she got Mr. Braxton on his way. Whatever he and Paul Kirkpatrick were involved in must be getting out of hand.

Chris swung around in his chair to face his computer. He would make certain Jay Gilbert and the CIA troops knew about Dahlia. This was no time for assuming. Something was screwed up. What was that famous phrase? When in doubt, do something? Punt? Cut bait? Shout back? Screw 'em all? He was not about to do nothing. Now was the time to see if Jay Gilbert's emergency plan was all talk, or had substance. He began typing a note to send to himself.

To: J.C.Braxton
Ref Tab c to my previous notes. Ontario lab can not find last report from Charleston. Worried about tie-in with Ms. Pauley's death. Must remember to find Jason Blair, old boss, in RV, headed west. JCB.

Now he would see if that crap about the letters a, b, and c had any validity. They were within the first twenty. He swung back to his desk. "How are you doing, Betty?"

"The car is waiting in the basement by the elevator. Your ticket for a five o'clock departure will be at Eastern's desk. You will have to switch to Piedmont in St. Louis, but that's only a fifteen minute delay. Just a minute."

Chris could hear her talking. She came back on the line.

"Okay, you have a room at the Red Rover Inn. They apologized, but your usual room was taken an hour ago. It is six-thirty back there, you know, time for travelers to be getting located for the night."

"I'll be right out," Chris said. He swung back toward his computer, rechecked his note, logged on the office line, and immediately tapped the 'Enter' key. He stopped by Betty's desk. "If by chance, someone shows up asking for me, tell them I had to go, unexpectedly. I'll explain later."

Twelve minutes after Chris departed, two gentlemen walked in the office. They asked to see Mr. Braxton. Betty was talking to Alexander Blanchard about the scheduled conference. "He is out at the present time, had to leave unexpectedly." she said.

One of the men took a leather shield from his coat pocket, and flipped open the cover. "As you can see, we are government agents," he said, "and without trying to be too forward, I must insist on checking his office."

"Well, there is no reason. I have already told you he is not here. He had to go to Charleston, unexpectedly."

"West Virginia?"

"Yes." She watched the second man start toward Chris's office door. "Where is he going?" she asked, watching him open the door.

"Mam, I told you we must check his office."

Alexander Blanchard moved forward. "Now just a minute."

"Please do not cause problems, sir. You have your job. We have ours. And right now, government business comes first."

Alexander exploded. "You bastards think you own the whole damned world. Well let me tell you something. You hide behind those tin badges like the sneaky group of self-righteous pricks you are. You can't come in here like some obnoxious, officious bureaucrat, and tell us what to do." Alexander was livid with rage.

Betty stood back, aghast. She had thought Mr. Blanchard may not be too stable, but this outburst was beyond her wildest imagination.

The man next to Betty grabbed Alexander by the front of his shirt to push him toward a chair.

The man suddenly found himself flat on his back with Alexander's knee in his throat.

"Don't ever—." Alex was glaring down at the man, but the scowl on his face suddenly relaxed, and he slowly stood up. There was an icy stare in his eyes, but he stood quietly, unmoving. He had heard the metallic click when the man by the door snapped off the safety on his pistol. As

Alexander stepped back, the man reset the safety, waited until his partner stood up, then put the weapon back in the holster under his arm.

Betty stood limp, leaning against her desk. "Please, everybody," she said weakly. "Mr. Braxton is gone. He is really gone. Check the room if you wish, but he really is on his way to Charleston; Charleston, West Virginia."

When Chris boarded Eastern flight #102, he had a window seat. Having arrived at the airport with no time to spare, he knew nothing of the incident back in his office; nor did he know the man in the seat behind him was a CIA agent.

CHAPTER 30

"Who is this?" To *Eagle 1* the voice sounded like Graig Mersick's, but more stressful

"This is Graig, damn it."

Eagle 1 hurriedly clicked on the scrambler. "How am I supposed to be certain without asking, Mr. Mersick? And I might add, you do not sound normal. In fact, I rather doubt your actual identity. Can you offer some verification?"

"How does Libyan sand dunes and supply shortages, or big damned houseboats strike you? Hell's fire, you know who I am. Are you clear?"

"Now I am, fortunately, and I sincerely hope I covered that last outburst. Why a call this time of the evening? You sound excited. We are to clear ourselves first, remember?"

"Yes, I know, but I needed to call. You were not expecting *The Eagle* were you?" Graig tried to shrug off the remark he knew he deserved.

"No, but who does? He is there when you turn around and see him. Incidentally, remember his last visit?" This was a good opportunity to nudge Graig about his research. "The man was not too happy."

"I'm glad you know what he is thinking," Graig answered. "I never have the vaguest idea. Anyway, I called to let you know I agree with you, about not being seen talking together for the next few days. Guess that is why you are number one and I am number two, but there is another reason I called, one that won't wait."

"Oh? Very well, but I would appreciate your making it brief. I already will be running a little late."

"I'll be brief. I talked to Pat Riley again, and I am concerned, now more than ever. He may have made it easy to get supplies and operate outside the corporation, but now he thinks Ms. Pauley had figured out what he has been doing." Graig was careful not to mention the research papers he took from Dahlia's brief case. That could be explained later, when the timing was better.

"Then it is fortunate someone removed her for us, isn't it?"

"Yes, it is." Graig said, not expecting such a direct inference so quickly. Now he definitely needed to keep last night's actions quiet, at least for awhile. "But Pat is becoming extremely nervous, and as I said yesterday, not acting at all stable."

"So?"

"Well, hell. Yesterday you implied we may have to quiet him, if he became unmanageable."

"And?"

This discussion was not going as planned. *Eagle 1* was beginning to act like the stubborn ass he could be from time to time. "Well, damn it, if you thought that way yesterday, why not the same way today?"

"Let's discuss this intelligently now. I did not recommend Mr. Riley be eliminated yesterday. I asked you what you thought about such action. We also discussed paranoia yesterday. I hope I am not detecting any in your present remarks. What is it you want to do, or me to do, or what is it that is on your mind?"

The man was right, Graig decided. Losing his own self-control would only complicate matters, and things were bad enough.

"You are right. Maybe I am a little too uptight, but I want to be certain you understand Pat might get me involved in his supply room problem, and if he does. Well, it might cause problems that could interfere with our project."

"Now we are discussing a point that has some relevance. Are you making progress? I know you are to have complete control in the research area, but we seem to have been at a standstill for some time now."

That is twice now that he has sounded off, Graig thought. "I will do the worrying about the research," he said coldly. "You just be certain the team members are ready. Do you have readouts on the drainage systems, and the locations plotted so you can place the product for maximum effectiveness?"

"Perhaps we do need to meet," *Eagle 1* said. "Are you okay? You said Pat Riley was upset, but it seems to me you may be more so." His tone reflected both concern and impatience. "Unless you have something that is vital let's continue this discussion tomorrow evening. I will be gone most of the day. We can resolve any differences when we meet."

"Okay. Tomorrow night, then." Graig decided it was just as well he was being shut off. Ms. Pauley's death could never be pinned on him, but even a suggestion of it may be too much. *The Eagle* had made it very clear he would not accept interference with the mission. It was a thought that could not be ignored. He glanced at his watch. It was almost time to meet Pat.

*   *   *

Randy Blake entered the lobby of the Belair Apartments. He took a newspaper from the rack beside the revolving door. The last thing he needed after two novels was more reading, but he needed something to make sitting in the empty lobby appear normal. He walked over to a couch in the far corner and sat down, not certain what his next step should be. Now that he was here, the idea of calling Pat on the house phone and saying, "Here I am," was obviously ridiculous. There had to be a more sane approach.

As he unfolded the paper, the bold print on the front page jumped out at him:

KNUTTE ACCOUNTANT MURDERED!

Randy's reaction was predictable. My God, this can't be. He almost shouted the thought aloud.

The article was brief. It said the reason for the murder was unknown and no clues had been found, Mr. Buchanan, the local plant manager, had provided Dahlia Pauley's background file: education, position, why she was in Charleston, etc., but there was little concerning the incident itself, except to state it occurred in her room at the Marriott.

Randy dropped the paper in his lap, glanced around the lobby with a look of disbelief, then picked up the paper and read the article again. Suddenly his real reason for sitting there sounded as absurd to him as it would sound to anyone else. The trip could turn into a disaster if he became involved. What if he were questioned? Then again, why should he be? How could he be a suspect? He forced himself to sit back and try to relax.

It was only a few minutes later, a little before seven, when the elevator door opened and Pat Riley stepped out. He looked good, trim, slender, neatly dressed in an English tweed jacket and tan trousers. He was a little older, naturally, but even more noticeable was his expression. Whatever was bothering him was all consuming. He glanced neither left nor right, walked straight to the entrance and out the revolving door, a definite destination in mind. Randy could not help noticing that Pat's walk had not changed, like a loping duck. Pat managed to throw each leg forward, instead of smoothly placing one in front of the other.

Randy debated. Should he follow? This thing about Ms. Pauley was demoralizing. In the back of his mind, he knew what he should do. He should go back to his hotel room; but, he was here. He should at least go outside and check. Pat would not be looking back, not with the expression he had on his face. He was concentrating on where he was going, nothing else.

The front portico was empty. Randy stepped out slowly. Pat was about forty yards down the sidewalk, to the right. Farther down the block, above a canvas awning extending out to the curb, was a small neon sign that read GIGI. No other signs were near, so unless Pat was headed for his car, that had to be his destination.

Randy watched until Pat entered the club, then started walking. A bar would be a perfect place to accidentally meet.

Partially opening the door, Randy noted the normal bar darkness. He stepped in, turning his back to the room as he closed the door. It was the standard small bar. Whether in New York, Central Kansas, or California, they were the same: dimly lit, music from a sound system, small tables, and stacks of glasses sparkling in the back-bar mirror. The room was not crowded, but there was enough activity that his movements should not be a distraction. He took a table in the far corner where the light was dim

Pat had joined a man at the bar. The two talked quietly.

Randy ordered a scotch. He needed one. God knows, this was going to be a night he would not forget. Logic told him to return to the inn, but he knew himself. Leaving now would make him hate himself later. He must learn to face such challenges if he hoped to maintain his sanity.

Pat and his companion did not appear to be having a very pleasant evening. They would sit quietly for a few minutes apparently lost in thought, then renew their discussion. From their actions they seemed to disagree as much as agree. The conversation was obviously not a smooth one. The knowledge made him feel better until he remembered his own position. It was degrading to sit there like a spy. He could walk up and speak, but he knew he wouldn't. He watched the two order another round. He did the same.

It was close to an hour later when the older man sat back as if not believing what he heard. At first he acted as if he might be angry, but then he laughed and threw his arm around Pat, the problem apparently resolved. After another round of drinks they both laughed and stood to leave.

Randy paid his own bill and hurried out in time to catch them entering the apartment building. The man had looked familiar, but he had never been able to get a good fullface look.

The lobby was empty when Randy entered, the paper still on the end table where he had left it. He sat down, toyed with the paper, started to leave, then sat back, unable to resist checking on how long Pat's friend would remain. A feeling of guilt crept over him. He turned off the lamp, hoping the dim light would make him less conspicuous.

Close to twenty minutes passed before the man returned to the lobby. As the elevator door opened, Randy saw him clearly. Sure, he knew who the man was. As he used to brag to Pat, he never forgot a face. Now he knew how the friendship developed. They both worked for the corporation, but why would Pat want to run around with somebody that old?

Randy sat quietly, and reconsidered his position. Perhaps he should tell Pat he was here. It was not yet nine o'clock, and he may never get such a chance again. But he could not release the thought he might be questioned about Dahlia Pauley's death, if only because he flew in with her. No, his idea of getting together with Pat was now out of the question. He drove back to the inn.

Lying back in his bed, Pat stared into space. He had a perfectly logical reason for being here. Why was he feeling self-conscious? For spying on Pat? That was what he was doing, but was it because of that, or what he had in mind when he flew back here? Thank, God, nothing happened. He could talk to anyone with a clear conscience, and be perfectly honest about knowing nothing about Ms. Pauley's murder. If by chance he were questioned, he would claim he was in his room reading for the entire time. That way, nothing could go amiss.

CHAPTER 31

The transfer to Piedmont Airlines in St. Louis went without a hitch for Chris. The desk agent had assured him his luggage would not be lost in the quick transfer between planes, but he was relieved when it appeared on the luggage rack in Charleston.

That the rental car Betty had reserved was also waiting, was another plus. He tossed his luggage in the back seat, and headed for the Red Rover Inn.

He felt his tenseness start to ease when he turned in to the parking area. Being here, gave him a better sense of control. Not that he knew of any constructive action he could take, but he was here, and he would do something.

Except for the desk clerk and a man vacuuming an overstuffed chair by the doors leading out to the pool area, the lobby looked to be empty. Chris turned toward the reception desk. The digital display behind the counter indicated one-fifteen. Not bad, four hours and forty-five minutes, plus half-an-hour drive from the airport, not bad at all; and he was neither tired nor sleepy. It may be one-fifteen locally, but his internal clock was still running on California time, ten-fifteen.

As he walked toward the reception desk, he glanced through the closed glass doors of the cocktail lounge. The bright ceiling lights outlined the empty chairs and booths in a garish silence. Just as well, he decided. A night cap would have been good, but he needed an early start. Another thought, unless the inn had recently changed its policy, he could have something in his room.

"Reservation for Mr. Braxton, please," Chris said. He sat his bag on the floor and folded his suit bag on top. "My secretary scheduled me for a late arrival."

The lady responded immediately. "Yes sir, Mr. Braxton. We have been expecting you. You have room one-nine-seven, across the lobby." She pointed. "Through the archway by the elevator, and about half way down the hall, on the left. If you will sign in, I will get your key." She tapped the bell.

"Yes, I am familiar with the room arrangement." He picked up the pen, "I would like to leave a call for six-thirty."

"Certainly, sir." She made a note, then remarked as if reminding him of the time, "Only about five hours from now."

"I'll catch up tomorrow night," he answered with a smile. He waived off the bell hop. The boy seemed pleased to go back to his chair, as opposed to the receptionist who seemed filled with energy, apparently glad to break the monotony of the long night shift.

Walking down the hall, his thoughts returned to Dahlia. Arriving and signing in had been a welcome relief from his struggle to make sense of her death. Logic suggested there was a connection between the CIA and what happened. It was hard to think otherwise, but how, unless she was also working on another case? The thought provoking question had occurred so often he was beginning to feel he may have to accept it, but if so, it must be unrelated to anything he knew. Also, the idea that Clanton Darnel's injuries in an explosion, or Mrs. Strater's injuries during a robbery, or, as occurred to him during the flight, Mr. Strater being killed almost two years ago might all be related events, did not make sense either. But one thing he did know, logical reasons be damned, there was an answer somewhere and he intended to find it. He set his bag on the hallway carpet and unlocked the door. As the door swung open, he noticed the room lights were on. Faint sounds from the TV drifted into the hall. He stepped inside, almost certain of what he would find.

"Come in, Chris."

Jay Gilbert sat in a chair by the table. "Let me pour you a reasonably hot coffee. The front desk called to say you were on the way." He opened his thermos and took another cup from the plastic top.

"I thought that woman on the desk was unusually active," Chris exclaimed. "Hold the coffee a minute. Smells good, but let me check something first." He put his bag on the luggage rack, hung his suit bag in the closet, and walked over to the small refrigerator built into the wall. He pulled out a beer. "One of fifteen reasons for staying here." He smiled. "Honor system. This place still believes in such things." He sat down, popped the tab, leaned back in his chair, took a long swallow, and sighed. "That first gulp is always the best, isn't it? The rest could be iced tea as far as I am concerned, but not that first gulp. I am not surprised to find you here, you know. When did you arrive?"

"About two hours ago," Jay answered. "In town, that is. I've been here about thirty minutes. Thought we needed to get eyeball to eyeball. Things are occurring with increasing frequency."

Chris looked at Jay. With an open collar, his shirt sleeves turned up, and a cup of coffee in his hand, the man looked almost normal, the steel spring, ready-to-release tension not so tight, not gone, but not so evident. Perhaps the one-on-one circumstances had something to do with it, that and the late hour.

"I sent you a message," Chris said.

Jay's immediate reaction astounded Chris. For the first time since he had known the man, Jay actually laughed aloud; not a full length guffaw laugh, more like one chopped off in mid effort.

"That I know, and I have an agent in L.A. who is convinced your assistant is a hell of a lot more qualified than you ever imagined."

"Oh?"

Jay gave a capsule version of the incident.

"We are running a check now, and should have Blanchard's status confirmed soon. Then we'll see if my pissed off agent, who is now a much more humble man, is correct in his opinion. If he is, and he may very well be, it may take a day or two to pinpoint just who Mr. Blanchard really is. But that is only part of my reason for being here. There are things you should know before you decide to do whatever it is you intend to do while you're here. Especially, if Blanchard is more than he professes. If he is, he may have guessed your real reason for visiting Kesterson, but there are even more important things. For starters, Clanton Darnel, the fellow injured at Kesterson has regained consciousness." He paused to let Chris regroup his thoughts.

"Darnel maintains there is no way that explosion could have been an accident. He swears everything on his car was shut off, and had been for at least a minute before it blew. He also said if he had not decided to take another water sample, he would be dead by now. Of course, everything else being equal, he is right; but another thing, the mechanic at the Kesterson complex is missing. The man disappeared the other night without a trace, not one damned single trace." Jay poured himself some more coffee as he talked.

"There is also a high probability, he, Sean O'Connor was his name, maybe you remember him, was involved in the attempt on Clanton Darnel's life. If so, his disappearance could be a result of his own planning, or possibly ordered by someone else; but those are only guesses. His car was in the parking lot with the keys tucked under the floor mat, as if someone was supposed to pick it up, but the police impounded it so we may never know. Also, his clothes and personal belongings are missing from his apartment. It is possible he decided to skip, but personally, I doubt he will ever be found. All the missing circumstances are too perfectly missing. Everything is too clean, too professional. Which brings me to my biggest worry."

Biggest worry or not, Chris thought, what has this got to do with Dahlia? The name Sean O'Connor escaped him at the moment. Not that he much cared, but he withheld comment. Once again he was on the hind teat.

"British SAS, the Brits highly trained intelligence unit, Special Air Service, feels *The Eagle* is in this country," Jay said. "The rumor is, he is here for a specific reason. You do remember my mentioning the name, don't you?"

Chris nodded. "Oh yes. It is your contention he is behind this whole deal."

"Precisely, and if my contention is valid, and if he is here, and if the reason as suggested by the SAS is to bring some project to fruition, I have a major problem. I have already tightened security at the main entry points, but with so many international airports around the country it is a difficult situation."

Chris walked over to the refrigerator and opened another beer. Maybe it was the long day or the series of events or the time change or he was tired, but to him, this involved dissertation was a lot of self-centered diatribe, with the emphasis on self-centered.

"You have a problem?" he tried to sound in control. "Perhaps so. I know next to nothing about your organization, nor am I interested in changing that status, but you have a lot of 'ifs' lined up back-to-back. But, leaving that aside, let's get even more basic, you have not said a single thing about Dahlia's death. Do you people just write a person off when they are killed? As I understand it, if she had not been one of your people, it would have looked like a normal robbery, except nothing was taken. How could she possibly be in trouble here? This place surely could not be connected with your operation out west. Did anyone check her belongings? And while I'm at it, did anyone find an envelope addressed to me? Dahlia told me she had one. I can think of a million things to consider besides hypothesizing about some damned mythical European terrorist."

Jay waited a moment. "I can understand your being upset, Chris. Perhaps I was too blunt. Probably was. Somebody once said it is a mechanism we develop to cope with unpleasantness. One thing for sure, it does occur too often, but we have to keep trying, and I was hoping you would mention that letter. It is missing."

"Oh?" There was a quizzical look on Chris's face as he spoke. "You knew about it then."

"You'll probably be more upset than ever, but yes." Jay knew his next comments would not be well received. "We have been cognizant of most of your actions, and conversations, since you and Dahlia have been together. Only the most," he searched for the word, "personal moments were turned off. I doubt it will make you feel better, but Dahlia was not aware of the monitoring either. This was her first mission. We had to be certain." Jay paused for a moment, apparently evaluating Chris's reaction. He knew his comments were not being easily accepted, but also knew his explanation would be ignored if false. Chris would immediately see through a sham. He continued.

"As is rather obvious, I am being perhaps unacceptably honest, hoping you will be honest with me. There are a lot of blank spaces in the scenario we are developing around Dahlia's murder, and an important consideration must be that letter, or paper, or whatever it is, or was. It is the only thing missing that we know of. How much do you know about it?"

Chris was furious, and the look on his face showed it. He sat quietly, trying to decide how to answer without sounding irrational. Perhaps the monitoring was essential in the CIA's mind, but that did not make the act any more palatable. A memory of the Air Force colonel who had been his mentor in Intelligence in NAM, flashed in his mind. The colonel's favorite phrase had been, "Tell the truth whenever you can. It is that much less you have to remember." Perhaps Jay attended the same school.

"I have no specifics," Chris finally said. A tirade of invectives would resolve nothing. "I have an opinion but nothing based on fact. That's why I mentioned Jason Blair in my message. To my knowledge, Mr. Blair is the only person who might know, except for Mrs. Strater. Frankly, I don't think it has anything to do with Dahlia's death. However, I do think it is significant that Mr. Blair wanted Mrs. Strater to contact me. That should be indicative of something."

"We agree. There must be some tie in," Jay said. "But either way, we have the state police searching. "We talked to Mrs. Strater, and she was cooperative," he smiled, shaking his head, "except for that letter. That, she refused to discuss. Said we must talk to you or Jason Blair. She showed us two post cards he sent her, so we have a good idea of where he might be. May nail him by morning if he stopped in a regular camp site. Of course, if he pulled into some offbeat shopping center, or takes a detour out into the boondocks, it could take a little longer."

Chris had to give Jay credit. He had been busy. "Anybody else you can tell me about?"

"No one of interest to you. Two things though before we wrap up this conversation. I know this will be of interest. Somebody obtained Dahlia's room number by posing as a florist's delivery man. At least, the flowers never reached her room and no florist admits to dispatching an order. For awhile we were confused, until the hotel explained the bouquet in her room was present when she arrived. Yours? We could not find a card. Anyway, that means the incident was not staged by a rank amateur. We are running a check for finger prints, but that is probably a lost cause also. From the looks of the place and a check of her belongings, it would seem nothing was touched except those papers."

Jay shook his empty cup over the waste basket and screwed the top back on the thermos. "My last remark is actually more of a question than anything else. What do you know about a Patrick Riley? He works in the lab in the local plant, here in South Charleston. Dahlia expressed mixed emotions about him."

"At last you have asked a question for which I have a factual answer," Chris exclaimed. "I don't know one damned thing about the man."

Chris climbed into bed. He hoped the beer would make him drop off, but his thoughts kept jarring him awake. They came rushing at him through the darkness, blaring at his subconscious. Fact: Alex Blanchard must have caused a memorable scene back in the L.A. office. Funny how Betty had said she sensed something different in the man, but what was the man's true status? Fact: Dahlia was gone. How? He didn't know, yet. Fact: Randy Blake was here. He had forgotten about that. But how could Randy have anything to do with it? Jealousy? Ridiculous. Fact: Larry was in the city somewhere and if he was on schedule, probably shacked up at this late hour. Fact: Jason Blair must know something that would help, or at least provide information that could lead to some good guesses. Chris wondered if his old friend was finding his retirement years as relaxing and enjoyable as planned. It must be pleasant to get up in the morning, and approach each new day with no stress...no strain...no nothing...drive along in the warm sunshine...enjoying the wide open spaces...the fluffy white clouds...in the...deep...blue....

CHAPTER 32

The waitress turned Chris's cup right side up and filled it with steaming hot coffee. Chris picked up the cup, sipped, smiled at the waitress, set the cup back in the saucer and sat back. The day was now officially open.

"Two eggs over-easy, hash browns, one of your delicious sausage patties, and some hot biscuits." Chris did not need a menu. He never missed the chance to eat here, at least once. The restaurant was famous for its sausage, and the biscuits were as good as any.

He had hoped his thoughts would become more clear in the bright morning sunlight, but neither the smiling faces nor bustling activity seemed to provide much clarity

Jay Gilbert's question last night about a Patrick Riley still intrigued him. Apparently, Dahlia had mixed emotions about the man, whatever that meant. Maybe George Buchanan would offer an opinion when they got together a little later this morning. But first, he had to call Mrs. Strater. She should be up by the time he returned to his room. Hopefully, she would tell him something about the letter. Of course, she may be hesitant about discussing it over the phone, especially to someone she had not met face to face. Not that he blamed her. To be physically attacked would make anyone think twice. If necessary, he might be able to run out and see her before going to the plant. Buchanan would probably understand.

The reality of Dahlia's death still eluded him. Like reading about an accident in the newspaper, detachment was still providing a barrier. There would be no protection though when he visited the funeral home. How would her parents accept him? Should he explain their relationship? Sure, he had loved her. Everything happened so fast, but it had to be real. The feeling came from too deep inside to be otherwise, like some uncontrollable surging force demanding her nearness.

He remembered his mother explaining love was like beautiful music. Well, even the final movement of Handel's *Messiah* could not approach the sensation he had felt. Their relationship had been something special, something to be treasured. He tried to compare his feelings for Dahlia with those for Ruth, which were equally strong, but different. He came up with nothing.

Well, so much for the letter. Chris sat back on his bed and dropped the phone in the cradle. Mrs. Strater had tried to be helpful, but she insisted she was only a housewife and knew nothing about "all the little gibberish things" in her husband's notes. Chris believed her. She did bring up one interesting point though. Patrick Riley was working as her husband's assistant when her husband's accident occurred, and she still talked to him. "I told Patrick about getting hit on the head," she had said, "and about my stay in the hospital. And yes, about calling you, but I sure never said anything about what was in those notes, mainly because I didn't have the faintest idea, unless it had something to do with wine." Chris leaned back on one elbow. No wonder Jay asked about Pat Riley. He needed to talk to Jason Blair. Jay Gilbert obviously knew a lot more than he was admitting, not lying, just not telling everything. Then again, Jay should know such things. It went with his line of work.

Chris picked up the phone again and dialed the number Jay gave him last night.

"Plaza Fashions." The feminine voice was pleasant.

"May I speak to Nancy Schaefer? This is Mr. Braxton."

"One moment, please."

Chris waited.

"I am sorry. Miss Schaefer did not come in today."

"Perhaps you could help me then. I am looking for a lady's robe in the price range of ninety-six to sixty-nine dollars." Jay had stressed the larger number must come first.

The voice turned factual. "Yes, Mr. Braxton. What can I do for you?"

"Has Jason Blair been located?"

"Just a moment." There was a long break. "Mr. Braxton?"

"Yes."

"Mr. Blair has been contacted, and will call you at Mr. Callahan's office around one-thirty this afternoon. If you are not available, we have arranged to have the call switched to Mr. Gilbert. He is acquainted with Mr. Blair and will relay any information to you. He thought it best to have a back up. Is there anything else?"

Chris picked up his suit coat and walked out the door, shutting it with some force. "That damned Jay knows a multitude of things he is not divulging," Chris mumbled as he walked down the hall.

"Go right in, Mr. Braxton. Mr. Buchanan is expecting you." Chris was moved by the lady's seeming concern.

Mr. Buchanan walked forward, extending his hand. "Please have a chair Mr. Braxton. Whoever said 'These are the times that try men's souls' must have had our corporation in mind."

"Yes, she was a lovely women, one who will be sorely missed, especially by those of us who knew her personally."

Mr. Buchanan studied Chris before answering. "I must agree. I knew her only briefly, but her charm and zest for life were apparent at first glance. However, now there are other complications to this seemingly endless nightmare."

Chris's face opened in question. Mr. Buchanan read the expression.

"I didn't think you would know. It was only a half an hour ago that we learned about it ourselves. The news is running rampant around the plant."

"What are you talking about?" Chris asked quizzically.

"We have a Pat Riley who works for us, or did. This morning his car pool companion, Jed Taylor, who lives two floors above him, went to Pat's room after waiting in the lobby for fifteen minutes. He found Pat, Mr. Riley, on the floor, in his living room, dead. Must have happened last night. He was garroted with a wire, then stabbed."

CHAPTER 33

"Hello. I am Vicki. May I help you?" The girl raised her arm and tossed her auburn hair back off her face.

Carl Eagleman's memory flashed to his childhood, the image as clear as if his mother were standing before him, but again the flood of pleasant memories was shattered by the memories of her violent death. He had given up trying to eradicate the thoughts. He forced himself back to reality. "I was advised your company may be able to resolve my problem," he said evenly.

The similarity would not leave him. The young girl must be in high school. Were not loose fitting sweaters, pleated skirts, and flat soled shoes high school attire? Yet if so, how could she be working at midmorning on a week day? He watched her erupt toward him.

The truck rental agency Carl had chosen was on South Central Avenue in Huntington, West Virginia. The sun streaming through the window made his double-breasted pin-strip suit uncomfortably warm. With a sport coat he could have forgotten the tie without being improperly dressed. He must insure Olga include such clothing in his next wardrobe.

"I don't know what you are moving," the girl answered with an infectious laugh, "but unless it's something awfully big I'd say you could carry it yourself." He's what is called a gorgeous hunk, she thought admiringly. His dark penetrating eyes seemed to hold her, yet revealed nothing. She would not mention the feeling when she saw her husband this evening.

She watched Carl smile, noting it was pleasant, but slow to develop, as if placed on his face. She glanced aside.

Carl read her uneasiness, and tried to ease her plight. "Thank you for the compliment, but I am moving my daughter's possessions. She is transferring to the university in Charleston. The distance is excessive, even for someone my size." His smile remained pleasant, but unchanged.

"Is she out at Marshall? I am attending night school there," she added, not waiting for an answer. "Is she in one of the dorms? Maybe I know her."

"She attends the college, but does not live in a dormitory," Carl said. "She resides with her aunt, which, and I am only assuming, is why she is dissatisfied. I hope this change will solve the problem."

"Wish I could attend full time," the girl said wistfully. "It would take a lot less time to get my degree. I am going to be a nurse."

"A very honorable profession," Carl answered.

"My boss already warned me once about trying to be funny," she said, referring to her earlier comments. This man's presence merited respect. Next time she would think before talking, as her daddy used to constantly suggest. "Here, let me show you the different type vehicles we have." She spread a folder on the counter. "Sounds like our small seven footer, what some men call a pickup with a box on the back is what you need."

"I will be happy to accept whatever you recommend," Carl said easily. He wished he could touch her, feel her warmth. He had never seen anyone who reminded him so much of his mother. "May I get one now? I need to load my daughter's items today, even though I may not be able to put them in her new quarters for two or three days?"

"A man who moved his daughter here to go to Marshall, turned one in last night," she exclaimed. Her eyes lit up. "Seems as if we all want to be somewhere else, doesn't it?" She glanced at the wall clock. "Ten forty-five? Just a minute. I will check. It should be ready by now." She turned toward the door behind her. "I'll be right back."

Her voice sounded hollow in what must have been the garage, the faint answer indistinguishable. She came back in, smiling.

"You're in luck. They go so fast." She put a paper on the counter. "If you will just fill out this form. You do have a credit card, don't you? It makes everything so much easier."

"Most certainly, which do you prefer?" He removed the thin leather case from his inner coat pocket.

"Any kind. Anyone will do, and your drivers license, naturally. Nothing works without that."

"Surely. Here you are."

"Thank you, Mr.," she checked his Ohio drivers license, "Burlson." Her eyes brightened. "Are you from Cincinnati?" She bubbled with enthusiasm. "I just love that city, especially their baseball team. My brother's trying to work up through their system."

The sign on Highway 74 indicated *Charleston 175 miles*. Carl automatically started to convert the miles to kilometers before reminding himself the odometer was set for miles. He would be in Charleston by early evening, easily, even if he took time to enjoy the scenery. This was the type country he appreciated, mountains, land with some character.

The sporting goods store the girl had recommended had carried every item he wanted, bed roll, overnight kit, towels, a heavy canvas bag. They even had cotton shirts and trousers in his size. He purchased two sets. Driving a U-Haul truck while dressed in a dark suit was sure to attract attention. Changing, in the shell on back, had been simple.

Carl's thoughts returned to the young girl's stare when he had smiled. He must remember the stiffness in his cheek muscles was still noticeable. Dr. Eschadero had been correct, it would take time to get back to normal. He could wait. What he enjoyed most was the choice of having a clean shaven face whenever he desired. Of course, being able to mix in a crowd without being categorized as the man with the beard, and having the ability to use more aliases were the important considerations.

Carl could not forget the young girl's similarity to his mother. Hopefully, his reactions had not created an attitude she would remember. But if she did, he still should be covered. Last night he had entered the college's administration building and inserted a card for his imaginary daughter in the registrar's files. If for some reason the girl did check, the registrar would find the record. The incident would be forgotten.

The rising West Virginia mountains reminded Carl of his Kurdish friend, Azerki. That Azerki was now as effective and respected a leader as his father had been was no surprise. Azerki was smart, had always thirsted for knowledge, and read constantly. Carl wondered if it might not have been Azerki who taught him the true value of reading, where the knowledge of the universe waits for those willing to look.

Carl visited his friend, at least once a year. To him the Kurdish life style was still the most satisfying existence he had experienced. For him it was easy to understand why he could not convince Azerki to travel outside his native area. Occasionally, Azerki would accompany one of his three sons to Sulaimaniya, the city where he and Carl first met, but that was his limit, except for his trips to Baghdad, where he authorized and verified the movement of monies in the numerous accounts of a Karl Izgur, a most illusive man. According to the meager information available, Mr. Izgur was a successful, but reclusive, member of the Kurdahnka tribe, who, because of his many interests in varied countries was seldom available.

Carl tried to provide compensating financial benefits for Azerki, but Azerki would accept only the funds he could use for medicine and books for his people. As he told Carl, "I have the best horses, the best woman, the tribe's loyalty, and a warm tent. Allah gives the protection of the mountains, a high plateau filled with abundant life, and the boundless sky, all of which will remain as long as our tribe treats them wisely. What else is there?" Carl had no answer. As a Christian he had been taught Allah was not the one to be given credit for all the good things in the world, but he had yet to find a sensible way to differentiate. Blind faith seemed such a weak argument.

Carl watched the cars moving along the wide ribbon of concrete, and compared it to the dirt road in front of his mother's house. He broke into a slight smile at the thought. It had to be that girl that was triggering all the memories. His thoughts went back to Azerki.

It would be good to rejoin the tribe and roam the high plateau again. He looked forward to the day when he would return for good. The thought was comforting.

For the last few days, Carl had begun thinking he may have waited too long to cancel the Kesterson project. That woman killed in Charleston, and Alexander Blanchard losing his temper with those two agents was sure to focus attention on the *Knutte Corporation*. It was not a good situation. He must make a decision soon. The thought of time brought up another consideration.

Alexander should presently be somewhere between Guam and the Philippines, en route to Ankara. Knowing the mind of the typical CIA agent, Carl was certain they would first check the flights to Europe. So, if everything worked as planned, Alexander would be in and out of Manila before the CIA sent his picture and ID that direction. Still, from a practical point of view, it did not make much difference. The most the Manila office could do was tail him. He had done nothing the CIA knew about, except nearly strangle one of their agents. Carl chuckled to himself. That part of the story would undoubtedly be minimized in reports back to headquarters.

But there was nothing humorous about the other conditions involved. Having the CIA around was a hazard. Ninety-five percent of them were professional, and if Jay Gilbert was involved, the odds on having trouble jumped to ninety-nine percent. That man must never sleep. Not only was he deadly accurate in his evaluations, deadly in pursuit, and merciless, he was a most worthy opponent.

Carl's thoughts turned to the coming evening in Charleston. Perhaps there would be some redeeming reasons for Doctor Becheimer's strange actions during the last few weeks. That the doctor had never easily accepted a secondary role was understandable, even somewhat expected, but that was not the present concern. Definitive comments concerning progress were needed now. Unexplained delays would no longer be acceptable.

It would seem the doctor may have diverted his attention from the primary mission.

CHAPTER 34

For Chris, the raucous outburst as he walked into the lobby of the Red Rover lobby was as welcome as it was unmistakable.

"Chris! What the hell are you doing here?"

Chris waved and smiled, but lacking Larry's uninhibited nature waited until they were closer before returning the greeting.

"Larry! I was wondering where you were. It never occurred to me you might be here."

"You think you've got a lock on this flea bag?" Larry laughed. "Hell's fire, you talk about the place so much I had to give it a go." He practically pulled Chris toward his sofa. "Sit your body down. Just finished an early lunch and was checking the news. Got nothing until one o'clock so there is no hurry. When did you get in?"

"Last night. How about you?"

"Been here two days, but as you know my friend, I am supposed to be here. The question is, what are you doing here? Don't tell me *Knutte* suddenly went belly up. If any one could get it off its aft section, you'd get my vote, but I wouldn't think you would start here. What's up? That dark suit looks like you're headed to church."

"Didn't you read about Dahlia Pauley?" Chris looked surprised at Larry's comments.

Larry missed the expression. "Sure, the paper's covered with it. A terrible thing. Must be a shock to the corporation. Did they send—?" Larry suddenly realized. "Good Lord, don't tell me she is the one you—. Jesus. I am sorry old buddy. Hey, now I do feel like a stupid ass, but you never said. I did not realize. Is there anything I can do?" Larry was caught completely off-guard. During their last telephone conversation Chris had mentioned a new friend, but Larry did not press the point. He knew Chris did not accept relationships lightly.

"No, there is not much anyone can do. And now there has been another murder. Maybe there's no connection. It is all so absolutely unbelievable. But someone is going to pay." Even he was startled by the bitterness in his remarks. Larry did not deserve that. He forced himself to regain control. "I was hoping you would show up. I need someone to talk to about this whole mess; but not now. Could we make it later?"

"Your call, old buddy. I will be there."

"Dinner?"

"You got it."

"How about meeting in the bar, seven, seven-fifteen? It will give us time for a short one, maybe two."

"I will be waiting."

Chris felt better as he headed down the hall. Larry always was a boot in the butt, but he had better hurry if he wanted to change before going back to the plant. He would skip lunch. He did not want Jason Blair's call being transferred to Jay Gilbert. There was already too much secondhand information floating around.

"Chris, I would like you to meet Assemblyman Erin Riley, Patrick's father." George Buchanan turned to Assemblyman Riley. "Erin, this is J. Christopher Braxton, Vice President of our Environmental Division."

Chris noted the man's handshake was firm, confident. "I am terribly sorry about your son, Mr. Riley."

"Thank you, sir." Mr. Riley's voice matched his handshake. "I appreciate your concern. It is incomprehensible, a damned crime, a miserable, dirty, damned, cowardly crime." The flood of words seemed as much a release of tension as condemnation.

"You are so right," Chris answered. "And for two such incidents to occur in as many days is beyond belief."

"I talked to the police a little while ago," Mr. Buchanan interjected. "They said they have no evidence, but are looking into the possibility of a link between the two cases."

"Has to be," Mr. Riley said firmly. "And I would bet the farm that our Mister Graig Mersick had a hand in it."

"Now Erin," Mr. Buchanan broke in. "I know you don't like the man, but that is no cause to accuse him of something this serious."

"Don't you 'now Erin' me, George. I know a set up when I see one. Graig Mersick was too buddy-buddy with Pat, too agreeable. Pat may have been an only child and maybe spoiled, but Mersick, was using him. For what? That, I don't know. I couldn't get Pat to admit anything, but something happened. Pat just kept saying, 'One of these days you'll see, Dad,' well." His voice broke. He waited, then spoke. "Forgive me, Mr. Braxton. I honestly didn't come here with anything in mind. Just had to get out, and somehow ended up here. I tend to talk when I am at a loss or upset. Maybe it does come from years of political ploy." He turned to Mr. Buchanan. "I will go now, George. Call me if you learn anything."

His presence lingered in the room.

"You have to have compassion for a man like that," Chris said. "It is natural to want to blame somebody. If I could pick out someone to blame, maybe I would not feel so frustrated."

"Well, he has expressed his opinion of Mr. Mersick more than once," Mr. Buchanan answered. "He always was the positive type, and saying pretty much what he thinks, but I can't agree with him this time. Graig may be quiet, but he's a good man, dependable, reliable, and does good work." He walked around his desk and sat down. "So, you want to check some files? That is easily done, down the hall, first door on the right. Anyone in particular? I could have the files brought in here without any trouble."

"That won't be necessary. Especially since I have no real reason for checking," Chris said. "Checking the files just seems a logical approach. I have already been asked about Pat Riley, and look what happened to him."

"Oh? How did you get his name?"

Chris checked himself. If Jay Gilbert wanted to go public, fine, but it was not his place to reveal the connection. "When I talked to Mrs. Strater this morning, she said she often talked to Pat, even suggested I might profit by talking to him myself." For a moment, he had found himself stuck with his talk with Jay Gilbert, last night.

"Oh? I knew the two talked, but I wonder why she said that?"

"Good question. I may check with her again, especially now. Could be, she had some idea in mind."

"You may use my phone if you wish."

"No," Chris answered, "I would rather make a quick check of the files before I get the phone call I am expecting. It might prove helpful."

Only two files really interested Chris, Pat Riley's and Graig Mersick's. Maybe neither would reveal much. Mr. Buchanan claimed the files were not too extensive, original resumes, effectiveness reports, and a few miscellaneous details, but what other choice did he have? Jay Gilbert was not divulging anything. He picked up Pat Riley's file. Good, at least there was a picture.

Patrick Mulvaney Riley: 26, five foot six, one-hundred thirty-five pounds, USC graduate, nothing significant that he could see. Chris flipped to the next page. Jack Strater had given him a satisfactory rating: methodical, accurate, quiet, dependable, reserved. There was nothing derogatory or detracting. The remaining few remarks revealed little. He put the folder back in the drawer, and pulled out Graig Mersick's. It was considerably thicker.

Graig Mersick: 42, five-foot eleven-and-a-half, one-hundred eighty pounds. From the 8 x 10 photo, the strong lines in his face indicated he was in excellent shape. No doubt about his background. It was complete, chronological and complete. The file even contained a thermofax copy of his birth certificate: born on a farm in northern Michigan. According to the file, after his baby sister died, his stepfather abandoned the family, never to be seen again, and the mother moved back in with her parents on their farm in the southern part of the state. Soon after, she died of pneumonia. The grandparents, German immigrants, raised him. After high school he went to Oregon where he worked in a lumber camp, then south to San Diego where he worked on a fishing trawler until deciding to attend San Diego State College. The inheritance from his grandparents farm land had made him financially independent. After graduating he moved to Philadelphia and completed a masters in molecular science. He tried working on his own for three years before moving to *Plastiko* where an innate talent for revising production techniques earned him recognition. *Knutte, Ancell & Ferrole* had since promoted him to Chief of Production Control

Chris looked at the report again. What an enviable record? The references were impeccable. He opened the clip, took out the picture, ran off a copy. The man was almost too good to be true, and what an unusual home address, Box 224, River Road.

He quickly thumbed through the files of the other men in the research department. Nothing.

"Find anything?"

"Afraid not," Chris said with an apologetic smile. "But then, I really didn't expect to. I had little in mind when I started and finished much the same way. If anything surfaced, I would say it was Mr. Mersick's address."

"Oh?"

Chris chuckled. "Box 224, River Road? That kind of address could either be a shanty or an estate."

George Buchanan broke out in a laugh. "Never thought of it that way, but you are right, especially farther south in magnolia country. But here? Well, you're in for a surprise. Graig may not have an estate, but he certainly has a house worthy of notice. It is a houseboat, but not in the usual sense. It is really something else, sixty or seventy feet, as I recall. At any rate, it is big, but I guess he can afford it. He inherited a sizeable sum from his grandparents. I sometimes wonder if the easy money is not what irritates Pat's father so much. Erin was of the generation who 'earned every dime' and 'walked ten miles to school in blinding snow storms.'"

"I know the type. My father was in the same group," Chris said. "I noted the part about the inheritance. Incidentally, I was surprised by the thoroughness of his file. None of the others were that thick and complete."

"You are right. It was his idea. He claimed he was too poor a housekeeper to keep track of it himself. Of course, I give that idea little credence. He is as methodical and accurate as an engine, but the request wasn't an inconvenience, so—." Mr. Buchanan chuckled. "Well, sometimes older bachelors get set in their ways, and need to be humored."

"Have you set an age limit?" Chris asked wryly, then laughed aloud as he watched Buchanan's look of frustration.

Mr. Buchanan laughed. "Now I know how Ms. Pauley must have felt the other morning when she thanked me for the flowers."

"Oh?" The conversation suddenly lost its semblance of humor.

Mr. Buchanan explained what had happened.

"That is one of those classic cases where the culprit gets the comeuppance he deserves," Chris said dryly. He explained how he had purposely left out the card, thinking it would be so damned cute to make her guess who sent them. "Stupid, downright stupid. How could anyone be so thoughtless?" There was a deep hurt within him.

Mr. Buchanan saw the dilemma. "We must not look back and fault our intent because of changed events," he said softly. "Life is difficult enough when we face it head on." His secretary's voice came over the intercom. "Mr. Buchanan. There is an incoming call for Mr. Braxton. Shall I put it to your phone?"

Chris walked out of the plant feeling as confused as ever. His talk with Jason Blair had been no great help. That Jay had queried Jason before recruiting him was something he had already surmised. Jason's laughing comment about issuing a glowing recommendation without knowing a thing about the mission placated his ego somewhat, but so what. But Wait. Another of Jason's comments set off an alarm. Sure! It had to be! According to Jason, Jack Strater's papers apparently contained an answer to the formula he had been searching for. A person who could understand that importance, and also be in a position to learn of its existence must be involved. Damnation! He was making headway. The person must be some type of chemist. Someone at the plant?

He looked for his rental car. No wonder he couldn't find it. He was standing next to it. He inserted the key, but found the door unlocked. Strange. He seldom forgot. Then he noted the folded paper on the passenger side of the front seat. It was short: "Stop at the antacid section of J & J Drugs. Study labels. Don't know me." Chris's adrenalin surged.

Chris marveled at the seemingly endless row of pills tablets capsules syrups and powders used to replace a spoonful of baking soda. Jay Gilbert appeared beside him, picked up a bottle and held it out as if asking for an opinion. "Thought you might be interested to learn your assistant, Alexander Blanchard, has departed our fair country. Careful now, you are offering an opinion on those tablets."

Chris glanced over, then took the bottle. "I really haven't bought your story, you know, and if Alex was so far out of line, why didn't your people grab him? Why so damned secretive?"

"First, there is no point in advertising our relationship; and as for your Alexander, all the man did was embarrass one of my top agents. We are still not sure why he took off, but if he is tied in with *The Eagle* the appearance of my men may have suggested your trip to Kesterson was more than casual research. The idea can't be treated lightly."

Chris put the bottle back on the shelf, picked up another and handed it to Jay. "You are not making me feel very secure."

"Seems you do tend to draw a crowd," Jay chuckled softly. "I also note two of your friends from California are here."

"Hold on, now. Don't tell me you suspect them."

"Who knows? We have been checking. Did you know Patrick Riley and your Mr. Blake were classmates in college? And you do know Blake is as queer as a three dollar bill don't you?"

Chris laughed his first good laugh in the last two days. He watched Jay return the box to the shelf and choose a bottle of liquid. "It is nice to be certain. Were they roommates?"

"No. They were on different floors, but another thing, how well do you know your friend Bertelli?"

"Now just a damned minute." Chris exclaimed.

"OK." Jay decided to keep it casual. "I was just asking. We have not found much on him." At the last second Jay decided not to discuss the man's defection to Canada to dodge the draft for NAM, especially here.

"I have no idea why you're having difficulty," Chris exclaimed. "You had no trouble with anybody else's background. Maybe he is just too fast on his feet for your people."

Jay sat the bottle back on the shelf. "I will get back to you when I have more information. Be careful. When, or if, things begin to unwind, they can move pretty damned fast."

As Chris unlocked his room, the phone was ringing. He did not hurry. Something was goofed up. With all the crap the CIA had found about everybody else, it was strange they had found nothing on Larry. He tossed his room key on the table and picked up the phone.

"Hello?"

"Chris?"

"Yes."

"Randy Blake, here, Chris."

"Thought I recognized your voice, Randy. Where are you?"

"Here in the Inn. Saw you this morning but knew you were busy. I would like to talk to you, now, soon if I may. I need help or advice or something. I am in over my head."

Chris hesitated. This room was not the place. He had already decided it was bugged. Jay had firmly established that his people had no qualms about listening to anyone or anything.

Randy misunderstood the pause. "It's serious Chris. I didn't want to bother you but this is important."

"I was not trying to put you off, Randy. Just trying to think of a good place we could meet. I know. How about out by the pool? We can relax while we talk? The place was practically empty when I came in."

"Fine. I'll get a couple of beers and meet you there."

"OK, but give me a minute for a pit stop."

CHAPTER 35

In the pool, a young boy and girl played with a large multicolored ball, their loud laughs and yells accompanied with flailing arms and splashing water. Nearby, a middle aged woman quietly read a paperback, content the two lone occupants were self-occupied.

The sky was crystal clear. A large circular thermometer on the perimeter fence read seventy-eight degrees. The air held September's mystic touch of approaching winter, which probably accounted for the lack of sun bathers, Chris thought briefly.

Randy sat at the far end of the pool, two beers and a sack of chips on the table beside him. He smiled and waved in recognition to Chris, but his expression belied any feeling of enjoyment.

"It is good to see you, Randy," Chris said as he approached, "but from the expression behind the smile, I would say you understated your trouble, or troubles." Could Dahlia have made a remark that suddenly took on a new meaning for Randy? The idea buoyed his thoughts, but why so damned scared?

"I well may have. In fact, I probably did." The smile had faded from Randy's face as Chris spoke.

"Surely it can't be that bad, can it?" Chris sat down and began pouring his beer. The gulf between them seemed to widen. Maybe he was being too negative. He smiled. "Look, I was happy you called. Had even hoped we might get together, especially since you flew here with Ms. Pauley. You must know she is the reason for my being here. I doubt that has anything to do with your present concern, though."

"I figured as much when I saw you this morning," Randy answered, "and thought you might have questions. But before we get into that, I have something I would like you to hear. And I want you to know before I begin that if I had known what I was seeing when I saw it, I would probably have acted differently. At least, I hope so; but if you'll hear me out, and I can get it all to make any sense, I am sure you'll be surprised."

"If it is as screwed up as you're making it sound, I guess I will be," Chris said. He sat back quietly as Randy began his story.

The police questioned him late this morning, and he had lied, flat out lied. He told them he spent the entire time in his room, reading and relaxing, even claiming he did not know a Patrick Riley. Naturally, he said he had flown here with Ms. Pauley, and just as honestly he told them he knew nothing about her death. Also, when they questioned him about some papers she had he was still okay, but from there on, everything went downhill.

Chris sat back in amazement. Especially after Randy explained his true reason for making the trip, and the events of last night at Pat Riley's apartment complex. Randy's fear was damned well justified. The whole thing was ridiculous. How the press would treat it was one thing, but withholding evidence was another. Randy had seen Pat Riley's murderer. That started a whole new ball game.

"You told the police nothing about what actually happened?" Chris asked. A thought began brewing.

"No. When they first started questioning me, I did not even know Pat had been murdered. Then after I got caught in my web of lies, I was too scared to change anything."

"That really was not too smart, Randy. I am afraid there is no other way to categorize it, but why did they question you? Did they say? Did they think you were involved, or was it because you flew here with Dahlia?"

Randy had a peculiar look on his face. "I thought maybe you gave them my name."

"Me? Of course not, I didn't mention your name to anyone, had no reason to. No one asked. Were there any people other than the police present when you were questioned?"

"I have no idea. You mean from the Corporation?" He hesitated. "I don't think so. They all looked like cops to me, but the longer we talked, the worse it became. They kept looking at me, strange like, while I just kept saying that I stayed in my room, reading. You are so right. How dumb can I be? They must have known I was lying."

"You are certain you told no one about this, absolutely no one, except me?" The thought was becoming an idea in Chris's mind.

"No one," Randy answered. "I was too scared. You know what the press would do with that kind of story. I am still scared, but at least I'm smart enough to know what I should do. I just decided I would feel better if I told you first. I owe you and the company that much. Then again, maybe I'm using that as a crutch."

A bright light flashed in Chris's mind. "Wait here while I run back to the room. I've got something I want you to see."

Chris hurried to his room. He nodded quickly to the man having trouble with his door lock across the hall, then inserted the key in his own lock.

Damn. Apparently, Randy's call had upset him more than he realized. The door was unlocked. He withdrew the key, and went inside, going directly to the bureau. Graig Mersick's picture was in the top drawer but was outside the envelope. Must have forgotten to put it back, he decided hastily. This time he made sure he released the safety latch as he hurried out. The fellow across the hall had apparently resolved his problem. He was gone.

Had Chris looked behind his shower curtain, he would have seen the man he almost caught searching his room. His fast jog back to his room had not allowed the look-out time to give adequate warning.

"Here, look at this," Chris said dropping the picture on the table.
Randy picked it up.

"He's the man I saw," Randy said without hesitation. "I knew who it was as soon as he stepped off the elevator last night, but what are you doing with his picture?"

CHAPTER 36

Suddenly, everything was so damned obvious.

The more Chris thought of Graig Mersick, of Dahlia's concern over Pat Riley's strange attitude, and of Randy's bizarre story, the more he was certain. Mr. Strater's research papers had to have led to Dahlia's death. Jason Blair's quick evaluation of Jack Strater's research paper when he visited Mrs. Strater in Charleston damned near confirmed it.

How could he possibly have taken so long to see it? But he already knew the answer to that stupid thought. No problem has a solution until the unknown quantities surface, then solving the equation becomes a simple matter of addition and subtraction

He leaned back in his chair, his face pulled in thought. Pat Riley learned Dahlia had the letter. Maybe Dahlia even said something to Pat about it. Mrs. Strater had probably already mentioned the letter to Pat (She said she hadn't, but she seemed to tell him most everything else), and Pat would have guessed what it contained. To top that, even if Pat was originally in doubt, it wouldn't take a mental giant to figure out there had to be a damned good reason to hand carry the letter instead of tossing it in the mail. That fact would have been the clincher. Pat knew Dahlia had the lost research files.

Chris subconsciously reached in his shirt pocket. What the devil was he doing? He had not had a cigarette since NAM, but he was glad the pocket was empty.

To him, the picture of what had happened was clear. As Pat was stealing the letter from Dahlia's room, Dahlia awoke and saw him. Pat panicked and hit her on the head. In his fright he smothered her to insure she remained quiet. Then Graig Mersick (no wonder Pat's father didn't like the man) learned Pat had the papers and killed him.

Even Pat's father said Mersick was a devious S.O.B. who dominated Pat. Mersick may have an outstanding personnel record in his file, but considering his struggle in growing up, he also had to have plenty of street smarts, the type knowledge not found in school curriculums. One thing was obvious, the man knew how to act on a once-in-a-lifetime opportunity. Pat's father was right. His son may have been a little spoiled, and was not as pure as the driven snow, but he damned well had been used.

Chris's sudden thought that his own call to Dahlia might have started this whole chain reaction stabbed his gut. He had to do something, but what? Wait for Randy to act? Hopefully Randy would remain quiet until morning as promised, but Randy was so confused he might do anything. Another thing, the police would see through Randy's story soon enough (if they had ever believed it) and once they were sure about their legal coverage, would be back after him. Yet, what if Randy came up with some other off-the-wall explanation? Jay had already confirmed Randy was queer. Did that make a difference? Suppose I blurt out the story, and Randy denies the whole thing, Chris thought. Who does what to whom in that case? Chris tried to regroup his thoughts. If he was going to do something it had to be soon, before Randy took off on another tangent. Sure, there were professionals working on the case, systematic diplomatic bureaucratic officials with systematic procedures, producing diplomatic and bureaucratic answers. What he needed were answers to plain old obvious truths, now, without waiting for bureaucracy to run its course. There was nothing unlawful in that. He walked to the window, pulled back the curtain. Why not tonight?

The dark clouds rolling in over the mountains reminded him of similar sights when visiting his grand-father's house in the small mining town of Elk Ridge, not too far away. He let the curtain fall back in place. It would be dark soon. He went over to the bed and propped himself up on the pillows to give himself time to firm up a plan. He was not trying to take the law into his own hands, he just wanted some answers before everything became lost in legalized jargon.

Chris slipped on a sweater, picked up his raincoat and rechecked the window. When those type of clouds rolled in, you might as well get ready. It was going to rain. Using the hallway exit at the end of the building, he headed across the parking lot.

He glanced at his watch. Still twenty minutes before he and Larry were to meet. He would have called Larry if his phone was not tapped, but Larry would understand. Anyway, by the time Larry finished his second martini he probably would have located a more charming and curvaceous dinner companion.

"Evening Chris."

"Jay! God, you startled me." Chris put his car keys back in his pocket. Shit. Now he had Jay on his back again. Could not he go anywhere without the man being there?

"Got a date?" Jay's angular face held a benign smirk.

Chris tried not to show concern, but why should he? He was only going for a drive. "One silly question deserves another, I guess. Is this a business visit or another of your social calls?"

"Both, I was coming to see you."

"And we meet here in the parking lot? That's spooky."

"Oh come on, now. Even spooks have to park somewhere." Jay acted as if the inference were intentional. "We don't all ride brooms. I decided to touch base and let you know you will have a replacement problem when you get back to California. Your Mr. Blanchard is on the last leg of a flight to Istanbul. Should be landing in the next hour or so."

"Istanbul?" Chris said amazed. "Along with everything else, he must be a damned fast traveler."

"Istanbul," Jay said slowly, caressing the syllables. "I always liked that name. Has a mystic quality: turbans, crusades, massive walls, seductive women, snake charmers, intrigue. I've spent many a pleasant day there. It is just as fascinating as the brochures make it sound."

Chris laughed. He might as well be polite. Jay would leave when ready, not before. Chris knew the man for what he was, a thorough, dedicated, intelligent man, with unrivaled tenacity, and his reason for being here did make sense.

"I didn't know you were affected by such exotic thoughts," Chris said. "I am surprised. However, since you are in a reflective mood, what does the name, Charleston, remind you of?"

"Rain." Jay's answer was immediate.

Chris looked at the sky. The clouds were even darker, and the chilled evening air matched the dampness.

"I have to agree, but even the local TV weatherman could call this one. Do you have anything else on your list of things to divulge? Each time I see you, your revelations amaze me." Chris looked at Jay quizzically. "And you know, I have the strange feeling you were there when the police questioned Randy Blake this morning. In fact, I would bet on it."

"If I agree, would you tell me what he wanted to see you about this afternoon?"

Chris looked at Jay in disbelief. If there had been any doubt about his phone being tapped, that comment removed it, but there was no point in broadcasting the thought. "Damn it man, how did you know we got together? I only left him a couple of hours ago."

"I keep reminding you, Chris, that is my job. Like yours, some parts are good, others less so. What did he say about the picture of Graig Mersick?"

"I'll be damned. You are too—, just too much." Having no privacy whatsoever was getting to be a definite irritant. Chris's voice developed an edge. "Mr. Randolph Blake said the guy in the picture looked like a thin Lower Slobovian, a white Russian Moscovich, or a Lithuanian Mongoloid, take your choice." He had tried to sound ridiculous and was painfully aware he had succeeded. Then he sighed audibly as if resigned to the truth, "I was just showing Randy a picture of the guy. George Buchanan told me Mr. Mersick was Pat Riley's friend. Now look, I came out to take a drive, and unless you have some reason why I should not, I intend to. I appreciate your keeping me informed, but this surveillance crap is getting tiresome. I may be overstating my case a little, but at least, when I am in my car I don't feel like the proverbial fish in a bowl."

"Just thought I would touch base, Chris. Sorry about annoying you, but now that we know your man Blanchard has a good chance of being one of *The Eagle's* men we are even more concerned about your safety. I will try to be more considerate. Enjoy your drive. If you are like me, you like driving in the rain. It is relaxing, puts you in your own little world."

Jay turned and walked away, as if returning to his own car. Passing between two of the others, he tapped the door panel on his left. The agent, prone on the front seat, glanced at his wristwatch and gave himself fifteen seconds before sitting up. He faked a stretch. It may be almost dark, but parking lot lights sometimes reveal images with unexpected clarity. He added a long yawn. If it started raining, his job of tailing Mr. Braxton would be easier. Mr. Gilbert had said, "Keep the man out of trouble." That should be simple. Who knew enough in this case to get into trouble?

Chris watched Jay start across the lot, then got in his car and pulled out. He drove onto Highway 64. That would give him a straight shot at the bridge and the Lee Street off-ramp. The freeway also would make it easier for his tail to follow him. There certainly would be one.

If his plan was going to work, he needed to know exactly where the man was, so he could lose him when the time came.

CHAPTER 37

Jay Gilbert stood beside his car and watched Chris leave, then watched his new assistant, a recent graduate of the CIA training program, pull out and follow. The kid was too close. He shrugged. Maybe the Chief's gentle admonition was deserved. Maybe he was too critical on occasion. On balance, the young man was doing a good job, and tonight's task tonight was not that difficult.

Jay hoped he was wrong, but he was sure Chris had some bird brain idea in his craw, could even end up acting on his own unless something, or someone, intervened. Jay almost winced. He had seen that determined look on too many frustrated faces and witnessed too many debacles to think anything else. Maybe his foresight would pay off. If the kid was as good as his academic record suggested, he should be able to keep Chris in line.

Better yet, the Chief's admonition resurfaced, maybe Chris was smart enough to know better, but what bothered him most was maybe Dahlia's presence had simplified recruiting him, but now her absence was creating an opposite problem. Why couldn't the man stay in his room? It was amazing how people with perfectly good intentions screwed up so often. A venereal disease lecture from his Marine Corp days flashed in his mind. "Keep your pecker in your pants" had been the medical officer's counsel. Another of those foolproof but oversimplified solutions, he thought disconsolately. He turned toward the inn.

Aside from Graig Mersick, and probably one other person he could not yet identify, Jay felt the Red Rover Inn held most of the main characters in this operation. He may not know when the show was going to start, or how, but it would, and soon, unless it was the dampness getting into his bones. He walked over to a comfortable looking couch, sat back, worked himself into the cushions and tried to force himself to relax.

Had Jay known who was now present in the city, his bones really would have ached.

*   *   *

When *The Eagle* called him from a gasoline station on the edge of Charleston, *Eagle 1* had recommended the two of them meet at the *Chateau du* Boeuf. *Eagle 1's* usual table on the second floor provided an excellent view of the downtown area and also seclusion.

Carl spread his napkin on his lap, looked around, and smiled. "Very nice. It is a little different from our camp in the Libyan desert, is it not?" He wanted his old friend to relax. Tonight could well be crucial to the mission, and straight forward information was a necessity. He looked out at the black sky. "We seldom faced these type conditions though. Sand perhaps but not rain."

"Very true. They said on television that a storm was on the way. We are fortunate to have arrived before it started." *Eagle 1* wanted to sound casual. He did not think he had reason to worry, but one could never be certain. That *The Eagle* was not satisfied with the progress of the mission, generated several possibilities, some not pleasant to consider. He also was most definitely aware *The Eagle* had never yet let friendship interfere with business decisions.

"Yes, I heard similar reports during my drive here from Huntington. I believe the term was 'wide spread thunderstorms'. I regret I gave you so little notice, but I suppose you are used to that by now."

"Absolutely no problem, Mr.—?"

"Burlson, from Cincinnati," Carl answered. "I will change it after I turn in my rental vehicle."

"Understand. I had a theater engagement this evening, but your arrival certainly created no problem. In fact, I am happy you came. I am not an enthusiast for string ensembles. I mention it only because I am so formally attired. Should I know the details concerning your daughter?"

"If any of your acquaintances should see us and you feel an explanation is necessary, you can say she will be attending the university this semester, but if this is the most exposure we will have, I doubt that will be necessary." Carl felt he had used enough small talk. "I am sure you remember my original briefing concerning the necessity for placing the mission above other priorities?"

"I assure you—."

Carl lifted his hand to wave off the remark. "No, I am not concerned with your work. It is *Eagle 2*, or Graig Mersick, if you prefer. He is the concern I do not appreciate. I know I designed this project around his expertise, and am aware that minor delays in a project of this magnitude are inevitable, but constant excuses? That is what I am now receiving. Look up the word in a dictionary. You will find it implies a person attempting to prove himself faultless. I do not accept such a premise. Further, I am beginning to wonder if his delays may not be from distractions unrelated to our mission."

"I appreciate your concern, sir. We have been waiting for an extended period." Perspiration was beginning to show around *Eagle 1's* collar. *The Eagle* may be a friend of long standing, but the course of this type conversation could easily lead to a conclusion that more than one man was at fault

Carl seemed intent on pressing his point. "I do not wish to seem too abrupt, but we must get to specifics, and to the most honest of answers. I intend to contact the doctor later, but do not let that concern you. He and I will discuss our alternatives at that time."

"I understand," *Eagle 1* answered, somewhat relieved. If he had previously had doubts about telling his friend everything he knew, or even suspected, the feeling was now gone. Graig's inordinate interest in the papers Ms. Pauley had obtained, to the point where Graig's intent could easily be questioned, could no longer be ignored. The thought had crossed his mind several times since he and Graig talked.

Now was not the time to withhold such information.

CHAPTER 38

The map had indicated the highway would make a sweeping left turn just before the bridge, and the second off-ramp would get him to Pennsylvania Avenue. Chris moved into the right lane. Missing that off-ramp could ruin his timing.

In his rearview mirror he watched the black car move in behind the van following him. Good. The black car had been with him since the parking lot. Had to be Jay's man, and hopefully the man was smart enough to have guessed the destination by now, especially after the lane change. If so, he may drop back another car or two. That would help. Extra time would increase the odds of his plan working smoothly.

In the black car that Chris had spotted, the young CIA agent was pleased with his maneuver. The minivan in front camouflaged his car, but Braxton's green Chevy was visible through the van's large windows. Braxton had to be headed for the Marriott. Funny how people do that, he thought with a knowing smile. There is nothing they can do or change, yet they still have to check. He thought back to his college lecture on *Psychological Reactions to Stress in a Criminal Environment*. The instructor was right, people do return to the scene of a crime to reenforce the reality of the event. No need to crowd. If Braxton took the Lee Street off-ramp, he had it nailed.

Large splats of rain hit the windshield as Chris turned down the ramp to the underground parking beneath the hotel. Good. His tail was about three cars back. The extra time would help. At the foot of the ramp he made a quick check. To his right was an empty slot. He swung in, switched off the ignition, grabbed his raincoat, ran to the next row of vehicles and ducked down.

A few seconds later the black car came down the ramp and pulled into an empty slot six or so cars further in.

The CIA agent jumped out of his car, looked for his target, then hurried toward the bank of elevators, checking the indicators. Mr. Braxton must have been lucky enough to catch the elevator stopped on the main floor. The supper crowd always jammed them. He ran for the stairs. With that kind of crowd, he could get to the fourth floor and be in place when Braxton arrived. He had not been on first string track for nothing. Regardless, Braxton could not get in the room. The police still had control, and the room would be locked. It was after seven. Amateurs just don't think ahead. He smirked as he ran for the door.

Chris, seeing the agent enter the stairway, ran back to the ramp and up to the street. The few splats had turned into a downpour. Thirty odd yards to his right was the last taxi in the waiting line for the hotel entrance. Throwing himself in the back seat, he slammed the door and fell back.

"Looks like it's going to be another one of those nights, don't it?" the cabby said unperturbed. Any type entrance was acceptable in this type weather. He flicked up the flag on the meter. "You're supposed to wear that coat, not carry it, you know."

"I knew I had it for a reason," Chris exclaimed breathing heavily. When this ordeal was over he was going to get serious about getting in shape. "I will see if the damned thing works when I get out." He leaned back, raised himself and straightened his trousers.

"Any place in particular, or are you just looking for an expensive place to stay dry?"

Chris was worried more about the agent coming out the front entrance than the cabby's sense of humor. A few seconds on the fourth floor and he would be back to ground level like water off a cliff.

"If you can get away from here fast, it'll be worth an extra five," Chris said hurriedly. "I am trying to lose an overly enthusiastic female. I doubt that she'll find me in this cloudburst, but the line is moving up damned fast, and if I am caught I'd have a hard time explaining what I am doing in your cab. The thought that I was trying to give her the slip may even enter her three martini mind."

"Say no more, we're the same as gone. No wonder you didn't have time for the coat." He leaned out his window, waved his arm and forced his way into traffic.

Chris looked back through the downpour. No one rushed frantically out of the hotel entrance.

"Did we make it?"

"God, I hope so."

"Where to now? We're running on your nickel."

"River Road. 224 River Road."

"You got it. That's along the river, you know, over in South Charleston."

The agent, rushing up the stairs to get ahead of Chris, hit the fourth floor at a dead run. When he chose the stairs, he forgot about the high ceilings in lobbies and mezzanines. By the time he had a good start, even his poor math skills had recomputed the total as at least eight full flights.

He did a decent job of using controlled breathing as he forced himself to walk down the hall toward the elevators, but it was a struggle. The indicators showed one elevator still on the third floor, the others either moving down, or at higher floors. Good. He had made it. But when the third floor elevator started moving upward, it did not stop. Damn. He ran down the hall to Ms. Pauley's room. It was locked. He ran forward and hit the elevator button. When the first one arrived, he jumped in, pushed the emergency to clear the programmed stops and dropped directly to the basement, explaining to the crowd he was responding to an emergency. In the basement he leaped out and ran to Chris's car. It was unlocked, the ignition key still in place. He was furious. Mr. Gilbert should have told him he might be suckered. His fury suddenly subsided.

The thought of what Jay Gilbert's reaction would be was sobering.

CHAPTER 39

Jay Gilbert stared at the television in the lounge, neither seeing nor listening. There was no need, he had scanned the UPI, AP, and Reuter teletypes before leaving the local office. What Chris Braxton was doing, or planning to do, was his current problem.

A TV commercial showing a mother tucking her baby in a crib brought his eye's back to life. As the scene unfolded, the feeling he had never learned to accept stabbed at him again. He and his wife's only child had been stillborn, then a year later his wife was killed by a terrorist seeking revenge for a failure the man blamed on Jay. That the man was later killed by one of his own kind was small solace. As Jay had since accepted, his only salvation was to push the memory aside by considering the present.

Alexander Blanchard? The man should have landed in Istanbul by now and probably was staying at the new Hilton Hotel, a distinct contrast from the nearby ancient shops of the underground Grand Bazaar. The Bazaar, a maze of underground shops, offered every imaginable item from hammered brass and delicate silks to hand carved Meerschaum pipes and basic sex. It was an area that had not noticeably changed since Richard the Lion Hearted passed through on his crusade to Palestine. Jay wondered if those noble souls had felt the same omnipresent sense of eternal destiny as he when he stood in the huge dining room of the Hilton and looked out over the ageless Bosporous. They must have. Time may change physical things but not gut reactions.

Jay's reminiscing lead him back to what he called the low points of an otherwise acceptable career, events that could have been glorious successes with only the slightest change. Three times he had been within reach of *The Eagle*, but could not, or did not, successfully respond.

The first involved a tragedy of international importance that occurred in Istanbul. The day was the first of February, shortly after dark. Mehmet Ali Agca, a Turkish peasant hid in one of the narrow streets and murdered Turkey's foremost editor, Abdi Ipekci, returning home from work. There had been no street lights, and a light snow blurred the scene, so the few witnesses were understandably vague about the shadowy figures who quickly escaped in a getaway car.

When the police revealed the complicated financing used to support the event, Jay had immediately seen the hand of *The Eagle*. Accounts in several cities were involved. Jay immediately flew to the area and began building a case, confident of where the trail would lead. But just when Jay was certain his information would prove *The Eagle* was involved, Ali Agca confessed, surrendering voluntarily, supposedly out of a feeling of deep remorse. The man was imprisoned, the authorities were happy, and the case was closed. Frustrated, Jay returned home. Some months later Ali Agca escaped by a plan arranged by an outside source. Jay was certain he knew that source.

Later still, Ali Agca again regained international recognition by attempting to kill the Pope. The investigation revealed Ali Agca had been financed and guided by the Bulgarians.

It was the thought of Bulgaria that reminded Jay of his next missed opportunity, in the city of Sofia.

Bulgaria's powerful export-import agency *Kintex*, whose covert smuggling operation was much more profitable than its routine procedures, had generated the opportunity. The agency insured illegal shipments traveling overland between Europe and Turkey would proceed safely without inspection if certain conditions were met. If the move was by sea, a *Kintex* patrol boat would direct the boat to a transfer area, all operations under the strict control of the Kintex agent.

It was after a smuggling operation at sea that Jay's contact in the port of Varna learned *The Eagle* was to be in Sofia for a meeting in the Pliska Hotel.

To get in the hotel would have been no great task, but to be caught as an intelligence agent would have been disastrous. The huge marbled halls were a recognized meeting place for subversives and dope smuggling rings.

Jay was not foolish enough to believe he could apprehend *The Eagle* under such conditions, but he had hoped he could pin some type identification on the man for later use. However, the needed arrangements could not be established in time, and Jay spent a frustrated three days pacing the floor of a hotel room in Athens, Greece while the opportunity vanished.

But the most maddening experience occurred for Jay when, after returning home from another trip to Istanbul, he learned that while he had been staying at the Hilton, *The Eagle* had attended a meeting with a German scientist by the name of Becheimer on the third floor of the older, though equally famous *Pera Palas Hotel*. Intelligence pieced together the information after learning of a small time terrorist being eliminated while posing as a waiter in the hotel.

Jay folded the paper and dropped it on the end table. The more he thought of that last incident, the more he wondered if it may not have been the start of this entire exercise.

He had checked out the name. A German scientist by the name of Standartenfuhrer Jurgen Von Becheimer had developed a gas during World War II, a gas that was extremely difficult to detect. The man had since died, but he had a son, and that son had dropped out of sight soon after that meeting. Was it all happenstance? The events had to be related. He could feel it. Perhaps the lack of concrete evidence was what made it all so convincing.

Jay stood up and walked to the motel entrance. The strength of the storm had actually increased. Where the devil was Chris? The guy had to be up no good. No rational person would drive around aimlessly in this kind of weather. Yet, why hadn't his own young assistant checked in? He returned to his sofa in time to see Larry Bertelli, Chris's lawyer friend, walk out of the bar and look around, a worried look on his face.

Jay's observation was correct. Larry Bertelli was worried. It was not like Chris to be late. Larry walked over to the house phone. "Room 197, please." He waited. Chris must be in the shower. Either that, or on his way. One thing for sure, the guy was not outside. Look at that damned rain. He started back toward the lounge, then stopped. A man, about his own age walked up and smiled.

"Aren't you Larry Bertelli?"

"That I am," Larry answered. Neat, clean, precise, flashed in Larry's mind.

"I thought I recognized you. I know this is unusual, but I am also a friend of Chris Braxton. He once showed me a picture of you two taken on a fishing trip. I am Randy Blake, manager of *Knutte's* Ontario plant out in California." He paused, as if searching for the correct words. "Considering the terrible circumstances our firm is experiencing, I assume you have heard the news, I thought you might accept my rather bold intrusion."

"Yes, I remember Chris mentioning you. That was a terrible thing to have happen, wasn't it? Absolutely terrible. I read about it, but didn't know Chris was involved until this morning. Did your headquarters send a team? Chris never said. We only spoke briefly."

"No, being here is pure coincidence. I am on vacation."

Larry's face turned more serious. "Well, the fact is, I am waiting for Chris now. We were to meet for dinner, but he is already a half an hour late, and as you probably know, that is not like him. Can't imagine what happened. I called his room." Larry's expression turned back to a smile. "Well, look. How about joining me in the bar while I wait."

"I am sure he will show up, soon," Randy answered, "and I don't mind if I do. I would enjoy something, and I do have time before my engagement." The remark was a lie, but he needed an excuse to leave when Chris showed up. After their recent meeting, trying to act nonchalant would not work. Another thought crossed his mind. Mr. Bertelli may have a good reason to worry. When Chris had that picture of Graig Mersick, he suddenly started looking like he had something in mind. It was a look uncharacteristic of Chris, devious. Maybe that is why Chris suggested he not say anything to the police until tomorrow.

Jay sat quietly and watched the two men enter the bar. Why would those two be getting together? He could not hear their conversation, but from their actions they looked as if they could be meeting for the first time. Well, if so, they apparently hit it off rather well, but nothing in their backgrounds indicated they had anything in common. He watched as they disappeared through the door. Now what? His electronic alert signal beneath his belt stung his waist. It was uncomfortable, but better than the untimely sound of a beeper. He walked over to the outside phones and called Tom Brennan in the command post.

"He did what?" Jay's face cringed in disbelief. "Well at least he is honest. How long ago? ...Any indication in Christopher Braxton's car as to where he went?...Didn't think there would be." Jay noticed the two men in the bar. "Pull out that file I started on Graig Mersick ...Yes, I'll wait...Got it?...What's his address, and what's a good way to get there? This rain storm's a bitch... Yes, from the Red Rover...Yeah. I'm ready...Wait a minute, not so fast. Turn left on what?...OK, I've got it...What do I want him to do now? That's easy. Call him back to the office and have him read the damned manual...Don't laugh. I am not in the mood. On second thought, better let him know such things can happen once in awhile…No. I'll call you later."

Jay hung up. He needed some information before charging out into a dark and stormy night, and he needed it now. Why the hell can't people leave well enough alone? He headed into the bar.

*   *   *

Eagle 1 watched the drenching rain wash down the city as he and *The Eagle* finished their coffee. He normally enjoyed the restful sight, but tonight was not one of those times.

"Should my conversation with *Eagle 2* indicate drastic action is needed, I would expect you to remain in your present position until a change is warranted," Carl said evenly. "There is no need to draw attention to our work by an unexpected change on your part."

"I would enjoy remaining here. My life style is most comfortable." *Eagle 1* hoped his words had not sounded affected. He certainly was not comfortable with the inferences in the conversation. "It was unfortunate Mr. Blanchard had to lose his temper and reveal himself. Had he remained in place there may have been other alternatives."

"Yes. My evaluation that he could maintain his self-control was incorrect, but he can still be useful. He is a dedicated man. Incidentally, before we leave, let me congratulate you. The café-au-lait was delicious. I am sure that is why you chose the place. I wonder why the Americans find it so difficult to prepare?"

Eagle 1 drove toward the theater, then turned toward home. Citing business reasons would be simple enough to justify his absence. Besides, the thought of Graig Mersick's future was excitement enough for one evening. But whatever happened, he knew the decision would be fair. *The Eagle* was not a cruel man. Though he never hesitated to take action when needed, the man was capable of great compassion. His mind flashed back to his own wife's death after her lengthy illness. *The Eagle* had paid the hospital bills and established trust funds to educate his four children. Yes, the man could have compassion, but *Eagle 1's* sense of foreboding for Graig Mersick would not go away.

However, the man was an arrogant German.

CHAPTER 40

Except for the storage areas along each end of the double-sided carport, the flat roof was supported by metal poles between every other parking space. There were seven spaces per side. The cab driver pulled under the overhang on the side nearest the long entrance driveway. The rain had not lessened.

"This is as close as I can get unless you've got an assault boat handy." The cabby turned and threw his arm over the back of the seat. "With one of those I could of slid you right in living room." He laughed to brush off his pride in his military service. "The houseboats are over there in all that dark, behind those fuzzy little blurs of light on the fence gates."

"Sounds like you were in NAM, too," Chris said, familiar with the use of assault landing craft in the marsh areas.

"Twice, didn't get it right the first time and had to go back. How about you?"

"Towards the end, 'til we surrendered."

"You feel that way too, huh?"

"Surrendered, gave up, quit, backed off, flat-ass lost; pick one."

"Yeah. Well, this rain should be familiar then, but it won't last forever like it did out there. Here, it stops as fast as it starts, but it'll get you as wet when you get in it. Remember that yucky crap we—?" he stopped and chuckled. "Well, anyway, do you know where you're going? It is mighty damned dark out there."

"Not really." A shaded light by a rack of mailboxes, and the cabby's fuzzy row of gate lights was all he could see.

There was a hint of a pale glow from Charleston's lights across the river, but the rain was doing a good job of suppressing most help from that area.

The cabby aimed his finger. "There's a walk over there by that light by those mailboxes. Leads down along some bushes to a wire mesh fence. Turn right and follow along it." He laughed. "Not that you've got a choice. Anyway, it leads along those gate lights you can barely see. The dock is on the other side. It's one of those wooden floating things, pretty nice, about ten feet wide, and runs parallel to the bank. Got four boats to a section as I remember. Carried a woman's luggage out there one time. The dock numbers are on the gates. But you'll see all that for yourself when you get there." He pointed again, a little to the right

"That chunk of darkness is a recreation field," he said, laughing at his description of the hidden area, then stopped. "Well I'll be damned, look at that." A quarter moon broke through a small opening, the resultant pale gray light creating a maze of obscure forms in the large open area. "Like I said, on and off like a fucking faucet. It'll probably quit in a few minutes, just as fast as it started, but there's sure no way of knowing for sure."

"I could stand the shock of a little less rain," Chris said, hoping the cabby was correct. He leaned forward. "Here, will a twenty cover it?"

"Not tonight my friend. There's nine-sixty on the meter, the five for the fast exit at the hotel, and I'll include a forty cent tip to make the change easier. Here's your five. We've both had enough problems in the past without trying to screw each other financially. Tonight may not be the right time, but as the saying goes, have a nice day."

Chris stood under the carport, the drone of the rain a restful sound. Some foreign type car across from him and a small camper on the far corner at the far end were the only vehicles present. As the cabby circled to leave, his lights flashed on the camper. It was a U-Haul.

The cabby drove back along the narrow driveway and turned on to the street.

The most common tie that binds, Chris reflected: camaraderie, one of the pleasant denominators of war, but tonight was no time to philosophize.

The drone on the roof softened. Chris glanced skyward. Small patches of stars appeared. As his eyes adjusted, blurred shapes appeared along the shore. The wire mesh fence was still invisible, but box-like shapes of what had to be houseboats began taking shape.

The clouds opened more. He glanced to his right. In the distance, the silhouette of a long line of trees with tall metal looking poles at the right end of them came into focus. Almost had to be a tennis court, he decided. Left of that were what must be two volley ball courts. The random other shapes spread around the far end of the open space must be playground equipment, swings, slides, picnic tables, grills, barbecues, that kind of stuff. The faint images were too far and too dark to be certain, but the open area just the other side of the cinder track was easy to decipher. Had to be a soft ball diamond. It was too small for hard ball. The cinder track along the edge of the parking area? It must circle the entire area. All in all, it was a nice little community layout.

Over by the street, rain softened lights in a row of houses indicated most people were home for the evening. Where all rational people should be on such a miserable night, Chris reflected briefly.

Chris turned up his raincoat collar, wrapped it against the dampness and walked over to the mailboxes. Most of the name plates were blank. That was normal, when he stopped to consider. People seldom had mail sent to this type of place. He checked the few names present. Graig Mersick's was the last one, lower right hand corner, clear, neat, hand printed.

As he started down the walk, a ridiculous thought surfaced. He had noticed all the address numbers on the mail boxes were even. Where were the odd numbers, across the river?

At the fence he turned right. Like the cabby said, he had no choice. At the first gate light he stopped and checked. The latch was the old spring type, it latched when passing the closed position, regardless of which direction the gate swung. He leaned forward to shield his eyes from the gate light. In the glow from across the river, the houseboat immediately in front of him looked to be twenty-five or thirty feet long. What was

Mersick's? Sixty, seventy feet? Must be huge. He tried to make out the wooden dock at the end the long wooden ramp leading down to it, but it was lost in the river darkness.

The rain must be dampening sound, he decided. Since the cabby left he had heard nothing. That was good. The less activity the better. All he needed was some small kid to come running along, asking questions. Just then, the muffled sound of an automobile engine broke the silence. He turned. A small truck passed beneath the street light by the driveway entrance. He tried to get a second look, but it had quickly disappeared into the darkness.

Strange. At first glance he thought it had resembled the U-Haul he had seen when the cabby circled, but he had seen no one. Had to be some other vehicle.

*   *   *

The Eagle was pleased he had taken the time to wait before acting. Waiting in the visitor's parking space established two things: except for the arrival of the taxi there was no local activity, the rain was solving that detail, and he had recognized Mr. Braxton from a visit with *Eagle 3*. Even more importantly, Braxton's arrival established another validating consideration. There was only one person in this isolated area who could cause a *Knutte* corporate executive from California to show up on a miserable night like tonight. The mission was either compromised, or would have to be further delayed. Neither hypothesis was acceptable. He drove to the end of the houses, switched off the engine and coasted to a stop. From there, he could leave quickly without worrying about being blocked when the panic started.

That Mr. Braxton may have to be eliminated was unfortunate. But such was life, or death.

CHAPTER 41

Back in the Red Rover Inn, Jay Gilbert knew he might be grasping at straws. Chris's two friends may know nothing, but experience was telling him one or the other did, and he needed that information now. Why else was Chris out on some damned tangent on a night like this? Worse, how could an inexperienced man like Chris know his actions might give away an entire operation? Answers, damn it, he needed answers not questions.

"Do you gentleman mind if I interrupt?" Larry and Randy were sitting at the bar, their questioning looks expected. "I know I have you both at a disadvantage, but let me begin by explaining I work for the government." Jay flipped open the leather folder displaying his ID and shield.

"Those are pretty good references," Larry said, "but I hope your reasons are not personal. We were doing nothing more than enjoying an interesting conversation. I would say your presence practically guarantees a continuance, as we lawyers are known to say."

"Fine with me," Randy added. Why would a government agent appear in a place like this, this late in the evening, and in a miserable downpour? Wasn't this morning's fiasco enough for one day? "Perhaps we should move to a table." Hopefully, taking part in the conversation would help him control his composure.

Jay nodded. "One where we can talk privately, without wasting time if you don't mind." He nodded. "How about the booth beneath that big picture in back? Should be quiet, there."

Jay was almost certain where Chris had gone, but that was like being almost pregnant. There is no halfway, and charging out into the rain on a guess would be his last resort. Not that he considered these two men to be especially trustworthy. One, he already knew was a liar. Maybe he didn't know why, but Blake had damned well been lying this morning. As for the other, well, he would see. Maybe he could pit one against the other, or if Blake discovered how serious the situation actually was, he might quit his cat and mouse game and admit whatever he was trying to hide. Someone had to reveal something, soon. Chris may be screwing up and needing help. Later might be too late. This was no kid's game.

*   *   *

Through a break in the bushes along the shoreline Chris got a clear look at Graig Mersick's boat. Like Mr. Buchanan had said, it was huge. The back part of the boat was dark, but up forward the boat's interior lights cast a soft glow through the windows. A twinge of apprehension flowed through Chris. Everything was too easy. If his premise about what the man had done was true, an unannounced approach was not reasonable. There would be some type of alarm, a buzzer, or something, and surprise was the only thing he had going for him. He had better reconsider.

He took his hand off the gate latch, and walked back to the center gate to let himself in.

The sloping ramp swayed slightly. He stopped. The gate lights had destroyed his night vision. He waited for his eyes to adjust, thankful for his combat training, then moved slowly down to the dock. Mersick must be the only boat owner present, he decided. There were no other lights showing, not even a deck light, and it was too early for people to retire

Chris moved forward slowly. If the cabby was right, there were three connected sections. When he came to the break, he stopped, bent down. The heavy chain allowed about two inches of play.

The same feeling of caution he had developed in NAM began creeping through him. He knew better than to fight it. Who can explain the indefinable? Quietly, he studied the intersection. In the dim light he saw nothing but the feeling persisted. Don't cross over.

Think. Study. Correlate. Compare. Patience. All the words he had learned from experience flashed in his mind. He waited. One would surface. He had been there too often, fighting a battle with his senses, as the day he felt the presence of that sniper in the tree. He still felt someone had looked down and guided him that day, but what was true then was still true. Caution said to place the surging energy on hold. Was there something? Compare.

He stood and slowly walked to the other end of the section. The memory that the absence of objects was the most difficult thing to detect rushed over him; like a missing branch, a cleared area, or a mine that was not there. Or was it? He squatted, studied, absorbing every detail he could see in the faint light. Then he worked his way back to the other intersection. What could possibly be different? But wait! Had he noticed a difference, or had he imagined? He went back to double-check.

Yes! And he understood that difference. His opinion of Graig Mersick was now a damned fact. Graig Mersick was not the average ordinary boat owner or the average ordinary corporate employee or the average ordinary anybody. No ordinary person would install an electric eye warning system to alert himself of approaching visitors, not on an open boat dock. A device on the gate? Maybe, so he would know when guests were arriving, but down here on the dock? Not unless he definitely had something to hide.

Chris went back to check again. There had been no poles on that first section. These two innocent looking foot high poles on either edge of Mersick's section controlled an electric beam, to set off an alarm when anyone walked through it. The possibility of a back up system was possible, but that was a chance he would have to take. He did not have all night.

Standing next to the pole on the left side, Chris put his left foot on the edge of the dock and faced the river. Slowly, he lifted his right leg around the back side of the pole and placed it on the other section. Shifting his weight to his right foot, he swung his left leg around the pole and turned, accepting the awkwardness of the maneuver as necessary to escape detection. It should have worked regardless of which direction the system functioned. He stood quietly, waiting; then waited another minute, mentally counting, knowing how time compresses itself under tension. The silence was heavy. He moved forward. That he might be fantasizing flashed in his mind but the idea died under sound reasoning. Everything he had figured was falling into place and was being reenforced at every turn. He was right.

At the back edge of the boat he stood quietly. What did they call the stern, the fantail? Nothing significant there, two chairs, a small table, and a canvas canopy hooked to a series of metal poles. Two extra heavy metal rods extended down into the water. Had to be dual rudders. A ladder on the cabin wall led up through a cutout in the canopy. There were no structures up on top deck that he could see.

He moved even more slowly. To be caught creeping alongside the boat would be more dangerous than being noticed on the open dock. Mersick would have every right to consider him an intruder. What the hell? He was.

Ahead was a small window, the curtain partially open. He moved away from the boat, hoping the distance would hide any reflected movement if Mersick happened to glance out.

As he started to step quickly by the window, the sight catching his eye caused him to freeze. Through open facing hallway doors he could see Mersick working at a bench on the far side of the boat, his back to the door. The room had to be a laboratory, and from the little shelving in sight, well stocked.

Chris stood transfixed, his blood racing. The pieces of his puzzle slammed together in absolute certainty. Mersick would check a paper, then make additions to a mixture before him. He was totally engrossed. Chris understood why. Those were Jack Strater's missing papers, and Mersick was checking out Jack Strater's long lost formula!

*   *   *

After his pickup had coasted to a stop, Carl sat quietly to insure his presence was of no interest to those living nearby. He took a package from the floor on the passenger side, climbed out, softly clicked the door closed, then crossed the street. A split-rail fence separated the trees and thick underbrush from the dirt access road along the back edge of the park. He worked his way through the trees to the river bank, then crouched behind a bush near the walk. Mr. Braxton's appearance out of the darkness was as expected, but his turning to leave was a surprise. Then he saw Braxton enter the next gate. If he works his way back, I have no choice, Carl decided. The man is involved. A charge next to the petrol tank, one by the propane, and one outside the lab would leave nothing but a hole in the water. Setting the timers for an eight minute delay would give him ample time to get out of the area. He moved nearer the boat, watched and waited. To use the center gate and side-step *Eagle 2's* dock alarm was not the technique of a bumbling corporate executive. The man knew exactly what he was trying to accomplish. Carl hoped he did come back. It was good that he also would be eliminated.

CHAPTER 42

"Dumb damn idiots!"

Jay Gilbert hurried out the front entrance of the Red Rover Inn. He tried to remain calm, not attract attention, but the couple who had just dashed under the portico could not help notice Jay's frustrated actions.

The man looked at his wife and laughed. "Wonder why he's so upset? He has been in where it's dry."

"PYOA," Jay mumbled caustically, hunching his shoulders as he ran toward his car, "protect your own ass." To make matters worse, he had to stop and fumble for his keys. "There has to be truth in such old sayings, so many people use them. Guess that is what Randy Blake thought he was doing."

Jay remembered when his friend was fired from National Telephone after twenty-four years of loyal service. "Your only loyalty is to your family. It's screw or be screwed," was the way his friend explained it. Could be. He jammed the car into reverse, backed out, headed toward the river and grabbed his microphone. It was time for his old friend, Tom Brennan, to once again help him get organized. "Hello, Papa Bear. Give me a growl."

"You sound perturbed Baby Bear. Speak."

"Papa Bear. This is Baby Bear, about two miles back. I am getting hungry. In all this mucky weather why don't we stop?"

I am getting hungry was an open channel call for aid. The code names, like Papa Bear, varied, but also prescribed the type pattern of conversation to expect.

"I am ready, Baby Bear. Glad to hear that alarm in your stomach finally went off. What do you recommend? Over."

"Remember that spot I mentioned awhile back, the one by the river? Let's chow down there. The more I think about it, the more interesting it sounds."

"As long as you buy, I am not about to object. Over."

"Tell you what Papa Bear, I will even spring for Fuzzy Wuzzy, if you can get him on that powerhouse you are carrying, and if he can make it in time to meet us in the parking lot. Think you can raise him? Tell him dessert is included. Over."

"Roger Baby Bear. He must be on corporate frequency, but I think I can raise him. And unless I miss my guess, he'll beat you there. He needs something like this to pick up his spirits."

"Roger." Jay put down the mike, noting the rain had almost stopped. His mind flashed back to the conversation in the lounge with Larry Bertelli and Randy Blake. The first part had gone as expected, nothing of value had occurred. But when he explained, within what he considered acceptable limits, that Chris may be getting to a place beyond his expertise, the two men became more cooperative. Larry Bertelli had acted confused, or at least seemed so. Randy Blake had tried the same tactic, but did not carry it off.

Jay reminded Blake of the interrogation this morning.

"I thought I recognized you." Randy answered, speaking with the inflection of a man who was the last to know. "Chris asked me if there was anyone there besides the police. He knew you were there, didn't he?"

"Police? What were you doing with the police?" Larry exclaimed.

"Any reason they should not talk to him?" Jay answered, ignoring the second question. "He did fly here with Ms. Pauley, you know. Questioning him was an obvious requirement."

Larry hesitated, trying to clarify his confusion. Everything was getting out of control. "You're right, I guess. It is just that this whole mess seems so confusing, so unrelated to anything else. I didn't know any of us were involved until I saw Chris this morning, and now look what's going on." He turned to Randy. "Did you know? How did the police act, decent? They can be a real pain in the ass."

Jay Gilbert broke in to stop the idle chatter. He needed information, now, and he could see Randy Blake was shaken, the same as this morning, but more nervous. All the man needed was a push. Jay looked squarely at him, his voice slow and clear. He did not want to be misunderstood. "What did you say about that picture of Graig Mersick, the one Christopher Braxton showed you this afternoon?"

Randy looked shocked. "How did you know?"

"Forget that for now. What did you say?"

Larry grimaced. "You're as bad as the damned cops." Then noticed the look on Randy Blake's face, a look of resignation, defeat. The man was broken. Larry saw it the same moment Jay held up his hand.

Jay wanted to be irritated with Larry Bertelli, but the man was right. He was being obnoxious. He looked at Randy Blake, his countenance calm. His voice rose in intensity. "Well, what did you say?" Randy then answered.

"If the man had been honest when the police first questioned him," Jay said to himself, "all this could have been avoided." He held his note pad under the dash light and decided to turn right at the next corner. He was glad Tom Brennan was in the office. He may not need back-up, but Tom would have South Charleston's police force off its rusty-dusty and running within thirty seconds. Years ago, when he was giving Tom his field training, they had agreed 'dessert is included' was a request for emergency equipment. He could only imagine how the young agent who screwed up earlier had been motivated.

CHAPTER 43

Chris put his weight on the deck gradually, worried the boat might rock, alerting Mersick. He should be okay with a boat this size but was not sure. He never even knew there were houseboats this large. Another thing, how did sound carry? On open water a small tap sometimes resounded like a shot

Light from inside the houseboat filtered through the closed drapes on the waist-high windows and center door in the forward cabin wall. A soft glow spread across the open deck.

The deck was about twenty feet across, a little less in length. Two metal tables with matching chairs occupied the center of the area. Some folded canvas chairs, looking to be no more than six in the dim light, leaned against the guard rail on the far side. Other than those items the area appeared clear.

Along the edge of the deck, evenly spaced columns formed the posts for the guard rail and support for the upper deck. The upper deck covered all but the last few feet of the bow. It was all very neat, expensive looking.

Chris walked softly, trying not to give the appearance of creeping. If the lights suddenly flashed on, his position would be awkward enough without looking like a damned burglar. At the door he hesitated. To knock while standing on a boat seemed so weird. He searched briefly for a door bell then knocked. As he did, the idea that Graig Mersick's personnel file might be a complete forgery flashed across his mind. What a time to think of that, he grimaced. Then again, so what? It probably was.

The deck lights flashed on. Light flooded the area, bright but not blinding. A window curtain move slightly. The door opened.

Chris was surprised at the size of the man before him. Mersick's file indicated they were the same height, then he noted the interior floor was an inch or so above deck level.

"Yes?" Graig Mersick regarded Chris hesitantly, obviously not pleased by the interruption. He leaned forward, apparently to see if there were others.

"I am Christopher Braxton, Mr. Mersick, Vice President of the Environmental Control Division of our corporation." He smiled as broadly as possible. Any person would be suspicious under these conditions. He held out a business card and his wallet with his California driver's license displayed. "I am sorry to bother you. I know this is a most inconvenient time, but I am representing Mr. Izon, our CEO, and am trying to crowd as much as possible into the short time I will be here. Mr. Buchanan told me you were a friend of Pat Riley's. Perhaps he told you I was in the area." Hopefully, the remarks had not sounded too hurried.

Graig Mersick looked at the card, glanced at the driver's license, then dropped the card in his shirt pocket. "Yes, of course, Mr. Braxton. Come in. No, Mr. Buchanan never said anything."

Graig Mersick may have displayed no outward evidence of tension, but thoughts were rushing through his head. He needed to get back to his lab. The results he had been getting were exciting, unexpected, some even startling. At one point, the mixture had practically flashed to a different consistence, then jelled instead of thinning as the heat increased. He needed to recheck that note about unexpected radicals. The solution had been approaching a critical stage. He could feel it.

When he heard the knock, he had turned off the heat under the mixture. There was no way of knowing what would have happened if he had left it on. Could have blown sky high. Then again, letting it cool might also ruin the entire cycle, and his supply of chemicals was critical. He had to cut this damned visit short.

"You surprised me. I have a warning device on the entrance gate so I can light up the area for visitors. I guess it is not working."

"I did notice your gate light seemed rather weak. Perhaps the rain shorted out part of your system," Chris answered. "That was some downpour."

"Apparently so, but electricity is usually either on or off. May I take your coat?"

Chris felt he detected an edge in the remark. "No thank you. I really don't intend to be long. Just a few questions."

"Well, at least, you will have time to sit down." Graig motioned to a chair. He sat in the chair, opposite.

After a few remarks about the corporation and some verbal sparring to establish dialogue, Chris turned the conversation toward Dahlia's visit. More importantly, toward Graig's relationship with Pat Riley.

"Yes, Pat and I were close friends," Graig said. "His death was a great personal loss for me. That was a terrible thing for someone to do. To Ms. Pauley, also. Two people, in as many days, terrible."

Chris looked at the man. The words were right but the tone not genuine. There was no look of remorse. The gray-green eyes were hollow. A cold steady unblinking stare filled the man's face.

"Did you meet Ms. Pauley before her accident?" Chris asked.

"Accident? I was told—."

Chris interrupted. "It sounds better that way."

"You are right. It does. No, I never met her. Her work had nothing to do with my area. But I was scheduled to meet her yesterday, for the standard recognition contact, in the afternoon, if I remember my secretary correctly."

"I believe you called in sick."

"Yes, I was about to mention that. Must have been a touch of the flu."

This conversation was leading nowhere, Chris fumed. Somehow he had to turn it toward those papers, probably laying open on the bench in the lab. The thought made it difficult to maintain control. "Did Pat Riley call you yesterday?" Chris thought he saw a reaction in Graig's eyes. Only a twinge, but something had occurred.

"No, no reason he should. Well, maybe, yes, now that you ask, he did call, during the afternoon." Graig looked at Chris. What the hell was the man getting at? These were not Corporation VP type questions. Braxton acted like he knew something, was searching.

Graig opened the table drawer beside him, reached in, moved a paper to one side, took out a pack of cigarettes. The Makarov pistol was where he put it this morning, under the note pad. He could not miss at this range, but he must remember the safety was on. He held out the pack. "Cigarette?"

"No thanks. I can understand why my next question might strike you as strange," Chris said straightforwardly, "but the day before Ms. Pauley died, she and I talked on the phone, and I have since learned she was in the lab where Mr. Riley worked while we were having our discussion. We talked about a formula for a new product. I thought if Mr. Riley did overhear the discussion, he may have said something. I understand you and he were close friends." Now he had the conversation going right. Now he could get to his point. "Did Mr. Riley, by chance, mention anything about it?"

"No. But why should someone else's project, or information, be of concern to him, or either of us for that matter? This is all getting very confusing Mr. Braxton. Now that I have had time to reflect, Pat's call yesterday concerned nothing more than my health, which I appreciated, and as you can see, is now quite satisfactory." Graig studied Chris closely. The man was really pushing.

"Well, I must be honest, Mr. Mersick. When I first came down on the dock, I noticed you left a side window uncovered." Chris nodded toward the side of the boat. "Your boat is so big and impressive I just had to walk over and take a peak before I knocked. I apologize for my boldness, but besides being impressed with the boat, I was surprised by the laboratory where you were working. For a man of your background a lab is certainly reasonable, but that must be what made me think of my call to Ms. Pauley, and the letter. However, since Mr. Riley didn't say anything I guess there is no way you can help in that respect."

Chris tried to act as if he had not noticed the hard stare he was getting. If he was to make a move it had to be soon. "But I did notice the room looked like a terrific lay out, and you appeared to have a project underway. Perhaps I could be of help. I must have interrupted your work. Do you mind if I look at your set up?"

"It is in no condition to be checked right now, Mr. Braxton. Perhaps at some later date. But you are correct. The laboratory is adequate for the little work I do." Graig had a hunch something like this was going to happen, and had already decided that the man was not about to go in there. The papers were spread out in plain sight, inviting inspection. Even a quick glance at the material, especially Pat's meticulous dating of every damned day's entry, and especially for a—. But wait a minute! Braxton? Now he knew why the name sounded so familiar. Braxton was *Eagle 3's* boss. A surprise visit? On a night like this? At this time of night? This had to be more than coincidence. Damn! Why hadn't he taken the time to put those papers away? With those out of sight he could have gone along with this stupid pretense, whatever it was.

"Oh, I don't mind clutter," Chris said. "My first job with our corporation was in research, and I am familiar with a little confusion and mess. It adds to the fun of the game." He stood slowly, smiled, then turned as if assuming Graig did not really mean he could not go in, but was just apologizing for a messy laboratory.

As he started toward the hall Graig also stood, apparently losing his balance. He braced himself on the bottom of the opened drawer.

Chris acted as if Graig's stumble was amusing. "Honest," he said, continuing toward the hallway entrance, "I will never reveal you are like the rest of us, not recognized for your neatness."

"Mr. Braxton. I must insist. Do not enter my laboratory." Graig's voice had a cold, sharp, edge. The sound cut the air.

Chris was equally set to enter the hallway.

"Oh come now, Graig. You and I both know—."

"Look at me."

Chris laughed. Look at—?" A familiar metallic click caused him to glance over his shoulder. Oh shit. Nine millimeter. Eight rounds. Maximum expected accuracy at this range, one hundred percent. Where the statistics came from, Chris had no idea, but they were correct. He was looking at a truly unemotional manic psychopath, a cool professional killer with no emotion, and no wavering of intent. The gun pointed at his chest was as steady as if held in a vice.

"I insist you stay out of the laboratory," Graig said coldly. His voice had a guttural accent, previously missing.

The brief surge of fear in Chris's brain never reached his body. The inexplicable force from the jungle of NAM hit him like a hammer. There was no warning. No buildup. His nerves clicked onto the super-charged knife-edge tension of combat that he thought had gone. It was that stage where responses react before the brain knows the need. No parameters existed, only action. The dynamics of combat confidence filled his body. His muscles understood, but outwardly he was calm, deadly calm.

"When you explain it in that manner I understand what you're saying," Chris said. He turned and walked back toward his chair. "Of course, I think you are over-reacting. Your actions indicate a decided lack of stability. What possible reason could you have for the way you are acting? Unless, of course, you know more about the last few days than you are admitting." He turned toward his chair. "I can only surmise—." He came even with Graig.

Chris's right hand flashed upward. The sound of the exploding gun filled the room as Graig's hand also flew upward. The gun dropped behind him. Chris felt a sharp stab in his side. He pivoted left. If his body still worked, he would straighten and catch Graig in the groin as Graig completed his turn. It only partially worked. His leg swung out like a loose pole and caught Graig behind his knees.

Graig staggered backwards.

The gun hit a table then bounced to the floor, a welcome sound to Chris. Now it was man to man. He grabbed his leg, felt nothing, but it had come back under him. That was good

Graig tried to regain his balance. He grabbed a chair for support, lunged forward. "You lousy—."

Chris dropped into a crouch, clasped his hands and swung upward, concentrating on his good leg as he straightened. He had little strength left. Graig's chin looked like an anvil

Graig saw the swing coming and tried to turn. The crushing blow caught him in the rib cage and knocked him backwards in an explosion of air. He fell to the floor, stunned, breathless, but physically unhurt.

Chris grabbed a table lamp and hurled it.

Graig rolled to his right. The heavy base grazed his head, the lamp ricocheting off the floor, the bulb shattering against the wall. He scrambled up. Where was the damned gun? This guy was a maniac.

Chris felt a stab of pain. An excruciating cramp grabbed his right hip and upper leg, but released as he started to fold. He jerked back. The leg responded! He lunged.

Graig ducked to his right. His foot caught Chris's ankle.

Chris's bull like charge turned to a near miss. He sprawled flat, arms extended, helpless.

Graig caught his balance and straightened.

Chris saw the gun! It was under the edge of the chair. He grabbed as Graig leaped, jerking back his hand as Graig's heel grazed his wrist. The rug stretched under Graig's heel then jumped back into place. It was so clear when he was so close. Chris's wrist burned like fire, but he still had the gun. He glanced up. He had it, but by the damned barrel!

Graig, seeing Chris with the gun, toppled the overstuffed chair on Chris's head, kicked him in the side, and exploded toward the door.

Chris gasped. The warm cushion in his face was suffocating. He pulled in his arms, pushed upward and rolled before the chair could fall back. The kick had changed the side pain to a wrenching gut ache. He forced himself into a sitting position, gulped air. He was alone! He rolled, braced against the chair, forced himself up and ran to the door.

Graig leaped onto the dock, landing in a dead run for the gate. He was furious. He had a knife strapped to his leg! Why the hell hadn't he used it? He glanced back. Now he had the man coming after him. "And with my own damned gun."

Chris stumbled out the door, saw Graig running, and fired. The sharp sound brought him back to his senses. What was he doing? Kill the man and he could be tried for murder. May be worth it, but it was a stupid solution. He threw the gun toward the bushes along the bank and staggered toward the gate, his breathing easier, but his side a dull throb. Maybe he could no longer kill the man, but he could sure beat a confession out of him, if his strength held.

CHAPTER 44

Carl trotted along the dirt road next to the trees. The bow lights had made it more difficult to operate without being seen, but he was okay. The timers on the explosives had another three minutes before they activated. Should be quite a sight. When he reached the sidewalk he slowed to a walk. The sharp sound of a muffled shot came from the boat area as he opened the cab door. He glanced back, but continued getting in the pickup. Time would shortly resolve whatever differences those two men were having.

A car sped past, the driver apparently late for supper. Carl smiled. That man's supper was about to be delayed. He cranked down the window as he switched on the key. The closed cab had made the damp air stifling. A second shot sounded.

Carl senses reacted. That was outside the boat. In his rear view mirror he watched the taillights of the speeding car complete a swaying turn into the boat dock driveway. Now what?

Two cars had arrived while he was coming through the trees, but neither appeared to be responding to an emergency. He grabbed the M-16 carbine in the towel beside him and leaped out. Running back toward the trees, he unwrapped the carbine, flicking the towel around his neck. In less than a minute his problem would be resolved if they were still near the boat, but what was all the other associated activity? He darted in on the dirt access road, ran directly to the tennis court, braced himself against one of the metal poles, and glanced toward the parking area.

The car that sped past him had stopped within a few feet of the other two cars, its headlights outlining three people who must have been waiting. The driver jumped out and ran toward the others. Something was amiss. He quickly pulled a second short clip of shells from his pocket, happy he had the foresight. A rear house light flicked on. His muscles tensed. This was getting interesting. In another few second there would be plenty of light. Then everyone could see.

*   *   *

Jay Gilbert swung into the driveway leading to the carport and jammed on the brakes. That was a gun shot he heard, but his new agent, standing by the two officers did not seem perturbed. Atonement? That boy better have a damned good story.

"Wasn't that a gun shot?"

"Yes sir! The second one. It was out there in the dark," the young agent exclaimed.

Jay exploded. "Out there in the dark? Where the hell is out there in the—?"

The entire area lit up in a ball of light. In the garish red brilliance Jay saw a man at the far end of the field tumble across the ground like paper in the wind. A second man hung spread-eagle on a fence. Jay threw himself at the asphalt before him, hoping to beat the shock wave. The gritty sudden stop was almost a relief to the blast of heat that swept over him, but why did his face always find that one loose damned rock?

*   *   *

Chris had followed Graig up the ramp to the gate. The chase was rapidly becoming more physically challenging. He laced his fingers through the fence and leaned forward to catch his breath, his turned up collar pushing his face against the heavy mesh wire. One more breath and I can make it, he thought hopefully. His stomach felt like it had been torn open.

The earth erupted.

Chris felt himself pinned to the fence. The wire gouged his face. Searing scorching heat slammed against his back. Brilliant red filled his eyelids that had closed in reflex action. From deep inside an innate force closed his lungs when the air exploded outward. Crashing sounds engulfed him. The fence flexed forward as if hit by a bomb.

The blinding light dimmed to a flaming brilliance, the searing heat diminished to red hot, the rocking earth grew firm, the fence sprung back. Chris staggered wildly, clutching air for support, suffocating, but daring not to breath. He was in NAM. The bomb had missed. The jungle surrounded him, bushes, trees, but where did a fence come from? In the light of the flashing guns he could see the stinking gook who set the booby trap for Little John. The dirty sneaky creep had seen his last night on earth. Chris charged. The man staggered to his feet. The man was taller than the average gook. They fall harder.

*   *   *

Carl Eagleman glimpsed the two men by the boat-dock gate before dropping to the ground. When he jumped up, they were still moving! That changed everything. He dashed toward the trees, vaulted the split-rail fence and ducked behind a tree. There was no time for considerations. Mersick had compromised the mission. Braxton was a nonentity.

*   *   *

The explosion had knocked the cop flat on his back. He rolled over, staggered up, staring in disbelief. "Christ Almighty!" He turned to his partner still on the ground. "Get off your ass and radio the fire department. It's too damned late for the bomb squad." He saw Jay and the young CIA agent running forward. "And ask for back-up," he yelled, starting in pursuit.

*   *   *

Chris drove toward the object in his path as if he were a tank charging a nest of gooks. Flatten the whole stinking mess. Beat the man into the mud.

Graig Mersick had tumbled face down on the cinder path, his face like a piece of raw meat full of cinders. His left leg throbbed. Braxton must have hit his thigh. He stood and turned in time to see Braxton charge. Falling to his left, his good leg caught Chris at knee level, the force knocking them both the same direction. They landed in a low spot in the grass. A sheet of water flew up.

The wet grass and cold water brought Chris back to reality. Half blinded, he scrambled to get up, but Graig was too fast. He tried to duck. Graig's boot caught the side of his face. Warm blood and cold water mingled on his cheek as he saw Graig's leg buckle. He quickly caught Graig by the shoulder, spun him, sent a crashing blow into his face, saw him stagger, and sent a hammering right with both feet planted wide. Graig reeled backwards. Chris moved in. Now was the time. In his peripheral vision he caught the movement of Graig's knee aimed at his groin. He flinched, caught most of the blow on his leg. Its numbness dropped him to the ground. He gasped a breath, tried to roll. Graig's dark shape hung motionless above him, outlined in the red sky. He caught the flash of a slender knife blade in Graig's raised arm. He could not move. He was pinned. It was over.

*   *   *

Behind the tree, Carl braced the rifle against the trunk. From the far end of the field he saw three men rushing forward. He could squeeze off one shot. In the starlight scope the two men fighting were as clear as at high noon. *Eagle 2*, Graig Mersick, raised his arm, paused for the kill. Now! Carl's finger tightened. *Eagle 2* fell forward.

The three men running toward the scene seemingly were unaware. Good. Carl turned and ran toward the street. People came out their back doors, staring in disbelief. Carl stayed in the trees until he reached the street then walked toward his car, the towel around his rifle.

*   *   *

Jay Gilbert had not covered so much ground in as a short time since high school. The fact that his young assistant beat him by a good thirty yards was insignificant, only proof his track coach was right when he said, "stick with baseball."

"Don't touch them!" Jay yelled at his assistant. Shortness of breath prevented further explanation. Coming to an exhausted stop he saw Chris looking up, ruffled, but alive. The man atop him was staring glassy eyed into space, a bullet in his forehead, dead center as if placed with a micrometer. Blood ran over one frozen eye and down his cheek, the knife harmless in the grass.

Chris quietly watched the confusion. For some reason he felt safe. Until there was a change, he could not be harmed. He had faced certain death, somehow been spared, and was now secure in an epicenter of nothing. Everything was outward. There was peace in the thought. He watched Jay Gilbert gasp for air.

"Thanks," he said.

"Thanks?" Jay panted. "Thanks for what?" He sucked in a deep breath. "Looks to me like you solved your problem pretty well." He glanced at his young agent. "Get that body off him and help him up." He saw the blood soaked clothes around Chris's waist. "No. Wait, better leave him there until we get an ambulance."

The police sergeant was panting worse than Jay. "There will be one…in all those…sirens you hear." The area was filling with fire trucks and flashing lights and firemen in yellow coats with yellow helmets. Sweeping spot lights mixed with the eerie red glow of fire against low clouds.

Chris sat up carefully. "My wound must look worse than it is," he said touching his side. He saw the blood but had no trouble moving. The pain had vanished. Was he in shock?

"You keep your ass on the ground," Jay Gilbert ordered. He looked around. "Medic! Check this man out."

A team of two came running.

Jay turned back to Chris. "If you didn't, and I didn't, then who in the hell—?" His expression suddenly changed. "Oh shit. Did you notice which way Mersick was facing when he was shot?"

Chris was watching the medics unfasten his clothes around his waist. He glanced up. "I thought it was you, but you are right. He was facing those trees when he was hit."

Jay turned to the police sergeant. "Sergeant, could you get some men to scour that tree area? If they find anyone, hold him. If they find a weapon, don't touch it, or anything in the immediate area, call forensic. Look for a middle aged man, probably big. But look, goddamnit, look; and the faster the better. There is no way we can close off the entire area, but do what you can." He turned to his assistant. "And you, you get your ass in gear. Get out there in that muck. Find that guy. Bring me back *The Eagle*. Do that, and I will do my best to forget how you screwed up the rest of the evening."

The young agent looked at Jay in disbelief. He had heard of *The Eagle* for so long, he considered the man a legend. "*The Eagle*? Are you serious, sir?"

"Son. I am not running a damned question and answer period. Get out there and do something productive unless you want the local police to do your work for you."

The sergeant had already started setting up a search plan with his hand-held radio, three teams, one, to check the tree area, the other two to work their way though the two block area around the park.

"What are we looking for Sergeant?" The question came over his radio.

Incompetent sonofabitches! "Find a sonofabitch with a gun," he yelled into his radio. "Find a sonofabitch that looks suspicious. Find a sonofabitch that looks like a, a big sonofabitch."

"OK, Sarge."

Jay Gilbert stood quietly as the medics checked out Chris. This whole show was collapsing around him. He could not do a damned thing about it, but he was sure part of his problem had been solved. He would send a picture of Mersick to Munich, though he was certain who the man was: Doctor Helmut Von Becheimer, son of Standartenfuhrer Jurgen Von Becheimer, one of Hitler's top scientists. When verified, he would know the scientific brain was now missing from the project. The thought was gratifying, but where was that illusive, the word was catching, sonofabitch *The Eagle*?

"I'll check in with you at the hospital, Chris." Jay watched as the medics forced Chris to lay down on a stretcher. "There are things that need to be done. You may think I am full of crap, but I think *The Eagle* just saved your life, and if so, you are one in a thousand." Jay left Chris staring up into the cloud filled sky.

*   *   *

The small U-haul truck drove slowly along the street, the driver careful not to interfere with the emergency traffic. The cop monitoring traffic at the corner was doing a good job. He opened a lane to let the small truck leave the crowded area.

"Thank you officer." The driver stopped next to the officer to let another fire truck pass. "I would sure hate to have my furniture damaged by that heat. Got my daughter's stuff in the back."

"Glad I could help, sir," the cop answered, talking above the noise of the heavy equipment. "Be careful. Most of these people are watching the fire instead of where they're going."

"You are right, sir. I'll drive around the corner, and park while I wait for the traffic to die down."

"Now you are being smart. The farther you can get away from this mess, the better off you'll be."

"I could not agree more." Carl touched his forehead with his finger in a salute of thanks, and disappeared around the corner.

CHAPTER 45

"It's about time you woke up.'

Chris looked up, startled by his surroundings.

Jay Gilbert, seemingly at peace with the world, sat in a chair next to the bed.

"What the devil? Why am I in here? I thought we agreed I was okay."

"You'll be out as soon as the doctor has a chance to give you a quick check," Jay said. "He wanted to keep you overnight and his desires fit my desires exactly. We voted. You lost. Must have been the sedative that cute nurse gave you."

"Sedative? Overnight?" Chris glanced out the window. It was daylight. "You dirty dogs, it is the next day, isn't it? What do you mean, we voted?" He smiled. Hell, he knew when he was beaten. It probably had been a busy night, but now that he was rested it was time to go. "OK," he said grudgingly as he tossed back the standard hospital blanket, "you win. Where are my clot—." He winced. The wound had responded. He touched the bandage gingerly as the pain subsided. At least there was no pain when he was quiet. He tried moving his legs.

Jay chuckled. "You are OK, a resounding gash, but more of a flesh wound than anything else. Like the doc said, you will feel it for a few days, so you will have to treat it with respect. I think the main reason he wanted to keep you here was to make sure you remained quiet long enough to get yourself organized, and pay attention when he explains what you need to do. My reason is just as simple. You need to be briefed before the press gets on your case."

"Press?" Chris leaned back, his expression questioning. "It was quite a show though, wasn't it? Did you find who shot Graig Mersick? I would like to thank the man."

Jay gave another chuckle. "I did not miss it far. I bet myself it would be your first question."

"So?"

"No, I don't have a signed affidavit or a warm body to show you, but I know who it was. Who it was and how he did it. We found the empty cartridge. I probably even know why he did it, but finding him—?"

"I suppose you are referring to *The Eagle*. He seems to be your big hang up."

"You've got it. Has to be. Who else could be that professional?"

"Was he the guy in the U-haul truck?"

"U-haul truck? What are you talking about?"

Chris told about the truck in the shed after the taxi drove away, and how he first thought it was the same one he saw leaving the area. "Then I decided I was wrong. It was awfully dark."

"Son—of—a—bitch!" Jay shook his head in disgust. "Sure wish you had said something last night. The cop directing traffic said he let one through. Said the fellow was trying to protect his furniture from the heat. Damnation."

"I was busy with other things."

"I know. I will check it out later. At least it is a lead, but right now, we have to talk. The information we released to the press conforms to a pattern your story must follow, or the whole thing will fall apart."

Jay walked to the window. The press and TV trucks made the front entrance look like some motion picture queen was about to emerge. "The press are all over this thing," he said, "but we can keep it contained to the reasonable level if we handle it right. After all, we have nothing to substantiate our beliefs, so we are saying Pat Riley and Dahlia Pauley were killed by a mentally unbalanced Graig Mersick." He paused. "That could be partially true, you know; but to sell the unbalanced part, your story should sound something as follows: as a representative of your corporation, you went to see him because he was a good friend of Pat Riley's. When you questioned him, he pulled a gun on you. You have no idea why. Naturally, you were scared. As you turned to leave, he fired and wounded you, then he turned and fled. You must have been in shock, because without thinking you chased him up into the recreation area. The shot that grazed your side must have also hit a vital spot in a fuel or propane supply line. Of course, we'll never know, the explosion destroyed everything. During the fight in the recreational area his gun went off and, fortunately for you again, the bullet killed him."

Jay sat back down in his chair. "That is all you know. All. Wipe everything else out of your mind. And forget about the knife. The police agree it would only complicate a confusing story. We will take care of any loose details."

"You found the gun then?"

"Yes, and with your finger prints, backward and forward. Don't you know how to hold one of the damn things? It was on the river bank, down beside where the boat used to be."

"Am I in trouble?"

"By blind-assed luck, no. Not only are you lucky to be alive, you are as clean as the white driven snow; but if you let the notoriety go to your head, I will knock your halo askew. The press will twist the story around enough without embellishments on your part. Be careful."

"I had a friend in my platoon who would have called this fiasco a muddy mother fucking mess."

"G.I.'s really nail it down, don't they?"

CHAPTER 46

The man in the jogging suit was near the end of his workout and breathing hard. He had entered by the long entrance driveway, apparently not realizing the explosion had caused more than half the park to be closed. Seeing the large roped off area, he dropped down to a fast walk, staring at the damage in amazement as he passed behind the houses. At the end of the tennis court, he walked to the far corner. A rope from there to the tree line blocked further access.

"I'm afraid you can not go past here, sir," the guard said. "We are still combing the area, making certain we have not missed anything."

"From all the damage, I can understand. Can't be too careful," the jogger replied. "But I guess I am a poor one to talk. I lost a coin about two days ago, and haven't been able to find it. Last night, in all the excitement, what with the explosion and everything, I remembered I was out here watching my daughter play tennis about the same time I lost it. Thought maybe I dropped it then. It is a long shot, but I am quite attached to it, been in the family for years. I realized it may be an inconvenient time, but I decided to stop during my morning run and check anyway."

"That is a shame. Was it valuable?"

"Well, I suppose it would be, but the sentimental value outweighs any monetary consideration. It was a gold coin that belonged to my great-grandfather."

"No wonder you are concerned. Gold? Well, it should show up against the grass, if it is around here." The guard looked at the ground. "You sure this is where you were standing?"

"Yes, I remember leaning against that pole most of the time, just the other side of where you are standing. Even when it is your own daughter, two sets of amateur tennis can be tiresome."

The guard laughed. "You're telling me? You should try Little League with four boys. Supper and free weekends become nothing but fond memories. Hey, wait just one little cotton picking minute." He bent down and put his thumb and forefinger between the metal pole and the heavy mesh fencing. A big grin covered his face when he stood up. "Did it feel like a paperweight?"

The jogger suddenly displayed an interest that belied his previously casual attitude. His eyes were intense, his attention riveted on the coin.

"I was only kidding. It's not that heavy," the guard said with a laugh. He walked forward holding out the coin. "Is it yours?"

The jogger took a step forward, then stopped. "I must admit I am in a hurry," he said, "but I would like to prove the coin is mine before I take it, so I may leave if you are satisfied."

"Sounds fair," the guard exclaimed. "Try me."

"Is it slightly larger than a silver dollar, and a little thicker?"

"You passed phase one."

The jogger looked pleased. "Is there an eagle on one side with its wings open, different from…say, our coins?"

"So far so good."

"The writing look like it might be Russian?"

"Mister, I don't know Russian from African, but you have got yourself a coin." The guard held it out. "Here, take it. It has to be yours. There couldn't be another one like it around here. Might be one in Russia, but sure not here."

"You have no idea how much I appreciate your help," the man exclaimed. "If I had any money on me I would be happy to reward you. Tell you what. I live only a block away, over on First Street. Let me run home and get something."

"Oh no, that won't be necessary. Glad I could be of help."

The guard smiled as he watched the man disappear. He was impressed with the man's long easy strides. They were so effortless for a man so large, even when he seemed to be favoring his left leg. "Must be in damned good shape," the guard muttered as he turned back toward the roped off area.

*   *   *

Jay Gilbert drove his car to the front entrance of the hospital as Chris walked out.

"Well, how does it feel to be a celebrity?"

Chris shifted his weight slowly, gently leaning back in the seat. "Only one word fits, stupid."

Jay smiled. "I assume your remark refers to them, not yourself."

Chris chuckled, winced, and grabbed his side, all in one quick motion. Laughing hurt worse than bending. "Those people must only listen when you answer their one specific question. I answered the same question at least twenty times."

"Don't be upset," Jay answered. "It is all part of the game. Reporters believe the job justifies their obnoxious attitude and actions. Tomorrow they won't even recognize you, unless you decide to make a newsworthy statement." He glanced at Chris. "You would not do that, would you?"

"Me? You point this car toward the airport, and I will be gone before they can get your ridiculous story in print."

"I'm afraid you can't leave that fast." Jay said with a smile. "The locals still have to run through their established procedure. There are political rituals to be satisfied." He hesitated, then decided to finish his thought. "Let's face it, Chris. You are lucky you're not hanging by your thumbs in the local jail. What you did is not considered accepted procedure."

Chris stared out the windshield. Jay was right. But, damn it, he felt good, real good. There are things that are right, there are things that are wrong, there are times to do things, and times to sit on your butt and talk. Justice may work its wonders, but sometimes we wonder. Add it anyway you want, he was right: morally, ethically, politically, socially, and fundamentally flat-ass right. He looked at Jay. "What would you have done?"

Jay had stopped in front of the inn. The two looked at each other with mutual admiration. Jay's hard chiseled face cracked into one of his almost charming grins. "How would I know," he said slowly. "I was only a Master Sergeant."

CHAPTER 47

"Tell me that again." Jay Gilbert looked as if he did not want to believe what he was hearing.

The guard started over. Why was everyone questioning him? Naturally, his sergeant was not pleased with his report, but when did sergeants agree with anything that was not strictly by the manual? If he had turned the coin in, it would have been three months before the man got it back

Jay continued his questions. "The man said what?…And you helped him look?…It was a big gold coin?…Any precise kind?…An eagle with its wings spread out?…I am almost afraid to ask, anything else?…Russian lettering?…Of all the….No, You did what you thought was right. I am just tired, been up most of the night. You say he was big? How big?…You are very observant. Anything else?…Which leg?…Something else? Sure, go ahead…Lives in the next block? Fine. Thank you very much. You have been extremely helpful."

Jay walked back to his car. How many men look like a professional football player, have someone leave them a Russian gold coin larger than a silver dollar, and live in the next block? He shrugged. There was no need for a search party.

So that was why a check of the exits out of the Charleston area had been negative. How can you catch a character who will not run when he should? Jay picked up the microphone.

"Tom?" He gave two quick clicks on his mike button, paused, then gave four more. Screw all the people with their voice modulation detectors.

Tom Brennan sat at the console. The identification was as clear as if his mother were explaining it was time to go to bed.

"Speak, oh wise one."

"Changed my mind. I'll see you shortly."

The normal exits were already being watched. Extra men would not help. *The Eagle* would only be trapped through a well laid plan, or by blind-ass luck. If the people currently in place were lucky enough to apprehend him, fine, but how often did that happen? Jay headed toward the bridge. Wait until Tom heard how close he came this time.

But Jay was not disappointed. Good things had happened. He had additional facts that could be valuable, and even blind-ass luck, as Chris called it, worked sometimes.

CHAPTER 48

Chris drove along Wilshire Boulevard, the windows down, the music up. He leaned forward, increased the base. Kids today knew what they were doing. The rim of his dark glasses showed above the sun visor. He flipped them open, slipped them on, and rested his elbow on the door frame. Damn, but he felt good.

Los Angeles may be known for its fumes, eye irritants, and crowded freeways, but the basics still were around: mountains, lakes, ocean, low desert, high desert, rain, snow, surfers, skiers. It was all here, and if worst came to worst there was always Palm Springs, where a reasonable fee would let you pretend you were one of the rich and famous.

An afternoon rain had washed down the city. The streets were clean, windows sparkled, crystalline air filled the basin, and the sky was a solid radiant blue. The city was proving she still could be beautiful when given half a chance.

Chris entered the underground parking area and pulled into the parking space Ruth had reserved for him. He picked up the newspaper beside him. That the Charleston incident had made page 23A was a surprise, but since it did, he intended to use it. It would add credence to his story. The explanation of his fight with Graig Mersick was weighted a little too heavy on the heroic side, but as Jay had said this morning, "Lap it up, my friend. Your bread doesn't land jelly side up all the time." Jay had flown in to insure Dahlia's files had no references to her CIA activities, and had paid Chris a final visit before leaving.

"You do realize that you did a good job on this assignment, don't you?" Jay said. Now that the mission was terminated, he could be a little more open.

"You have to be kidding," Chris answered. "I did more damage than good: Clanton Darnel in a comma, Mrs. Strater in the hospital, Dahlia, Pat Riley, Graig Mersick, even his boat. That is some chain of events. Even I ended up in a hospital. Where is the good side?"

Don't be too sure about your conclusions." Jay gave a negative shake of his head. "And don't start thinking your actions led to anybody's death. That is being unfair to yourself. Too many other factors were in the equation."

Chris gave an unconvincing shrug. "You are probably right."

"Been there a few times," Jay said. "Sometimes a reminder from a friend can help."

Chris looked at Jay. There was a look in Jay's eyes he had not seen before, the cold shield of professional training set aside for the moment. The man was a friend.

"Thanks," Chris said.

"Don't thank me. I've got free advice by the ton. Also have a definite opinion of what might have happened if the outcome had been different. Some day I will give you my version, if you are still interested. But I did want you to know I have you on my list of people-to-call-in-time-of-need. The world is still turning, you know."

Chris laughed aloud. "I thought you were developing a sneaky look on that granite exterior. It will be a cold day in you-know-where when you talk me into another one of your schemes. And another thing," he looked around his office, "is this place still bugged?"

"Never was."

"I'll take your word for it. Just wanted to know how many people I am talking to. What is the final version of your theory on *The Eagle*? Was he here? Even Paul Kirkpatrick noted you never mentioned him in your presentation."

"He was here and he was involved." Jay shook his head in disgust. "We traced the U-haul truck to Huntington where the girl in the rental office remembered him. He used the same story with her as with that cop the night of the explosion. You know, about moving his daughter's furniture. Had to be the same man, and every little bit helps. We sent an artist to see her, to have a composite made up."

"He must be something."

"In some ways, I guess. We were surprised there was no mention of a scar on his face. Either our info is incorrect, or he has had corrective surgery, or maybe found a good makeup artist. The girl's description pretty well compliments the guard's by the tennis court. Incidentally, his story about the coin raises possibilities."

"You fellows read something into everything. A coin? Come on now."

"Not the coin itself, but the fact he came back to search for it. It is the first time I know of that he has responded to any outside stimulus. Perhaps we have found a vulnerable area, an Achilles heel?"

Jay stood to leave. He held out his hand. "Well, I do have to be going. I will leave a card for Betty to put in her file as I go out, just in case you ever need me. Incidentally, she is quite," he paused, "quite—."

"Get out of here," Chris said with a laugh. "As they say, it was fun, but don't hurry back."

The elevator stopped on the tenth floor. Chris walked down the hall. He knew he would never forget Dahlia, and he felt good with the thought. The relationship had been real, intense, and filled with honest feeling; but the deep full warm sensation filling his body now was also real. Everything he and Ruth did seemed to radiate a oneness, transcending description. There was a sense of completeness to the relationship. He pressed the buzzer.

"Come in stranger," she said, a broad Irish smile radiating from her face. "It's good to see our local hero in the flesh." He looked good, a little tired, perhaps a little thinner. Was that a self-conscious look in his eyes? He seemed genuinely happy to see her.

"God, but it's good to see you, Ruth. It is nice to be, home." The sunset reflecting off her auburn hair framed her face in a golden softness, the white silk dress reflecting the red and purple tinge in the sunset.

Ruth read his eyes. Regardless of the side issues involving that other woman in his obviously trying experience, she had passed her first serious test. The world was a wonderful place again

"I brought the wine," Chris said smiling. He wore a little-boy grin, holding out the plain brown sack that somehow had ended up with a big blue bow around its top.

"Well, bring it inside," Ruth said. It was time for some good conversation, or whatever.

CHAPTER 49

Jay Gilbert stood before his boss. "Well, that's it Chief, three dead, one missing, one defected, a lady hospitalized with a bump on her head, a houseboat up in smoke, the world loses valuable research on plastics, and I can not prove there is or was or ever will be a problem."

"Don't let it get to you, Jay. That is the type profession we are in." Bill Chason was sipping coffee from the mug his grandson had made to fit his large hands. His mass of gray hair was parted, but still held the look of a mane refusing to be tamed. He looked at Jay with a somewhat amused expression, admiring the delayed aging and rock-hard body. "Directive 10/2 covers your problem rather well. It says we are limited only by the requirement that the operation is so planned and conducted that government responsibility is not evident; and if anything is uncovered, the government can plausibly disclaim responsibility. Since you can't prove there was a problem, or any involvement by anyone; and your part in the exercise was not evident, I would say you fulfilled the requirements as outlined."

"The whole mess may amuse you, Chief," Jay said, recognizing his boss's expression for a smile, "but I am going to tabulate every damned item that occurred during this show. I still believe there is another man in Charleston who was involved, and if he is there, he better keep his ass covered. I have clued in Tom Brennan, and that man could find a fart in a wind storm. As for *The Eagle*, I'll also get him some day. I have some new data I intend to keep to myself for awhile, with your approval, of course. I am tired of having that man evade me at every turn."

Jay walked down the hall. He was not yet ready to mention his theory about a mole in the organization, but there was a leak somewhere. *The Eagle* was the toughest guy he ever ran up against, but the man was not a damned mind reader. Nobody is. The man had to have an inside contact. Maybe Tom Brennan could latch on to something. Rooting out a mole by going through an assistant was one of the oldest tricks in the business. Just had to be sure about the assistant.

*   *   *

Randy Blake sat at his desk, staring into space. The memo from Chris was short and to the point. He slipped it in his jacket pocket with the meditative look of thoughts adrift. What the CIA, the deaths, the boat explosion, or Chris's wounds had to do with their research project was beyond him, except they all erupted at the same time; but he had learned a lesson. "Tell the truth and you don't have to remember what you said" was not only good advice, it was an absolute fact. He died a thousand mental deaths before learning his actions would not be publicized.

He also understood Chris's comments about learning to "sublimate our personal needs and desires". He smiled. Chris was as good with words as he, himself, was with remembering faces, but, at least, now he knew.

*   *   *

Iraqi Airlines flight #126 had departed Istanbul two hours earlier. It was now making a wide turn around Baghdad, preparing to land at Saddam International Airport. Everything in Iraq seemed to have a "Saddam" tied to it in some fashion. Carl gazed out the window at the sprawling expanse of the rapidly expanding city, trying to remember it as it as it was before oil became a driving force in world events. Across the Tigris River the walled Ancient Round City, started in 762 A.D., was still in evidence and standing in marked contrast to the huge tracts of modern construction sprawling northward. The sun sparkled off the ancient turquoise tiled mosques sprinkled among the modern hotels and high-rises. The twenty-one story Ishtar Sheraton stood out as a centerpiece of modern construction, the beautiful terraced gardens clearly visible from low altitude. He smiled as he compared the accommodations he would enjoy tonight to his coming quarters with Azerki, hopefully in a yurt on the plains of the high plateau. The musty smell of dried skins and human energy gave the enclosures a sense of oneness with nature. It would be good to be home again. When he was with the Kurdahnka tribe he sensed that innate feeling of complete freedom he so wanted the rest of the world to experience.

That the Kesterson project did not produce the controllable substance he wanted, was unfortunate, but everything was not a loss. *Eagle 1* was in a position where his loyalty could prove invaluable, and the small vial of capsules of unknown reaction and strength that *Eagle 1* still had may also prove valuable someday.

He looked at the gold coin he idly turned between his fingers. Retrieving it may have been foolish, but he had no choice. The young guard by the tennis court undoubtedly recalled many details; but as his mother had said so long ago, "It must remain in the family, Karl. It proves who we are." Family? Perhaps he should start considering such things. Azerki always seemed to be content and happy

His thoughts turned to Jay Gilbert. Would the man ever considered getting another woman? The thought was amusing. Life would be so much simpler if the man had something to occupy his mind besides stalking every move of *The Eagle*. It was unfortunate the man was incorruptible. Jay Gilbert would be worth ten of the regular men he had to use.

Carl watched as the plane turned onto its final approach. He could almost hear Azerki's words, "Once again, *The Eagle* has returned."

—The End—

9 780595 184606